Born in the post war era of 19  upstate New York, MF Burbau,

In school, all the way into college he was an avid reader which put him in trouble as often as not. He had already read required reading books assigned as many as several years before and refused to reread them.

From sixth grade on the requirement to read and report on a book a month again found him at odds. Seems *DC Comics* and *Playboy* were not considered valid for book reports so he made them up. Author, title, and storyline, from scratch, thus began his career as a storyteller.

Joining the Army in 1966 and spending almost two years in Vietnam, he added to his grounding of reality, a reality his friends back home would never understand. He wrote his first novella there on toilet tissue (not the soft fluffy stuff we use today) and after 21 years in the Army, 2 children, three grandchildren and two great grandchildren, he now resides with his wife of forty-five years in El Paso, Texas.

He writes mostly in the sci-fi/fantasy genre.

IFWG Publishing Titles
by M F Burbaugh

We Were Legends Series:

- We Were Legends (Book 1)

- Blood Sabers (Book 2)

- Camelot II (Book 3 – out late 2015)

The Bounty Hunter

Circle of Seven

A Planet's Search for History

by
M.F. Burbaugh

A Planet's Search for History
All Rights Reserved
ISBN-13: 978-1-925148-78-7
Copyright ©2015 M.F. Burbaugh/IFWG Publishing
V1.1

IFWG Publishing
www.ifwgpublishing.com

In memory of my father who passed away Jan. 8 2013 and always said one can do whatever one sets out to do. He is missed.

A Planet's Search for History

"**S**ettle down people. We are ready to announce the team," Lord Pitviper said to the large audience. Most were reporters, waiting to see who the next victims would be. I could tell he knew it as well.

"Team leader and head Archaeologist is Dwarf Professor Duranu Jorsenth, and his beautiful wife, well known in her own right, Dwarf Dr. Cullves Jorsenth, will assist as second in command." He looked at them as they nodded to the reporters. A few of us clapped polity. Very well known people.

"The people responsible for keeping them alive will be..." He hesitated. Five climbing teams applied for the job, but we were the last of the real pros. Finally, he said it: "Elf Aelfrice Brokk Eldon Gnoth as head climber and his lovely wife Elf Loka Dulcina Fay Gnoth will be his second. That is the team. We congratulate them and wish them good hunting." Some had clapped again when my wife and I were named.

With that we were immediately swamped with questions. I thought Lord Seacodent stacked the news people—all their questions were clearly from a view we were stupid, silly, suicidal, or mental nincompoops chasing rainbows and wanting to die. Lord Pitviper ended it after a few minutes of that kind of abuse and apologized to us for their behavior, showing them that he saw through their charade.

Getting to the ledge of the Castle Gods-Cut wasn't going to be easy for me. They say the word Cut is from the ancient language, thought to mean origin or home—Castle of God's home—but nobody is sure. The time was before we could write. The image from the telescope showed something strange clearly sat there, frozen in time and ice, missed for centuries in all but our legends because of where it was and how it was situated. Thought to be the original home of the first humans and the first Queen, Diboca Honor. Missed time and again because it was never believed it would be in an area high in the mountains where no warmth existed.

As the legend went, the human gods arrived from the void and became our rulers by force; then, after unknown years, they simply disappeared, vanished in all but memory. We wanted to find out what happened to them and why. They were the core of all our legends going back to our earliest tribal memories.

Six other parties had tried to climb that mountain. Three fell before reaching the top of the ledge, and the other three vanished. I watched eight souls in one party fall from the face, all carrying extra gear because of the unknowns. As they climbed the flat wall something failed, pitons pulled out, and they all died. I was Lord Pitviper's last hope, he said. We were the last of the professional climbers in his state, also the youngest. Me at twenty-three and Loka, my wife, at twenty.

Did I have fear? You bet I did. Not of the climb, but of what was waiting there on that ledge when we arrived. I went through each pack and eliminated all the extraneous items; we even left the reader behind. We could record our progress but not see any of it. Tough; it weighted almost four pounds. If it was a normal mountain we'd be to the top in a week, but this was anything but a normal mountain.

My climbing team consisted of our scientific team, Cullves

and Duranu, Dwarf names. My wife Loka was our doctor, and everyone called me Eldon. Loka and I were Elf/Human and our scientists were both Dwarf/Human. Funny, for all of us the human part dominated. We all pretty much looked the same, in the five foot-six to six foot range. We Elf halves have improved agility and flexibility and the Dwarfs have ungodly stamina along with a good supply of muscle mass. They said another four hundred years and we would all be the same, just Olgreenders. It was decided that since we didn't know what was at the top, mates probably should go along, all to meet the same fate. Our laws decreed mating was for life.

What we thought was the Gods-Cut ledge could not be seen from the ground anywhere around the mountain—only the telescopes saw it, and from only one small town miles away. Funny, standing at the mountain's base, when I looked straight up all I saw was rock until it slipped from view into the clouds. Some child had been the first to notice the strangeness of the ledge. Word spread and the view was studied. Strange? Yes, but not natural? Well, I thought we'd see.

I questioned this being the correct mountain for several reasons. What humanoid in their right mind would build a castle inside the arctic ring and why were there no roads or steps to it? Where did these humans come from originally? Here or somewhere in space? Why did they leave us? Oh, our religious leaders had all the answers, but none made sense and it always boiled down to having faith. Our scientists also had ideas that required just as much faith. As a climber I found having faith in anything but yourselves and your equipment just made you dead.

We took the job knowing that we would go at half a normal

party's strength, just us four instead of the usual eight. Funds were short and Lord P had already funded six teams, some four and some eight strong. None had returned. Loka and I were okay with it, but it put a large burden on us as far as carried supplies was concerned.

The entrance was calculated at seventeen thousand four hundred feet from the valley floor, which is, itself, two thousand feet above sea level. Just over nineteen thousand total. The atmosphere is good to around twenty-one thousand feet without supplemental oxygen—didn't mean no trouble, just meant it was possible to survive with some acclimatization. We didn't need to carry air for this mountain if we were careful.

I pounded a piton deep into the small crack in the rock face and secure my line. Loka was attached to me and Cullves was hooked to her, then Duranu was hooked to Cullves in the usual fashion. Since this was a different type of climb and we needed every piece of equipment, I changed the usual single line to double. At each piton station I added a second and secured an additional rope from Duranu to the rest of us. This second piton and rope was backup. It took longer, but I felt with our heavy packs it was a necessary annoyance.

We were into our fifth day of the climb and we hit the now infamous rock face that was almost vertically flat. I estimated four days climbing it, then there was a small ledge at its top, but it turned out piton-suitable cracks were scarcer than I thought they would be, and it was taking far longer than anticipated. For every two feet up, we had to go ten feet left or right. I had watched a former party fall from this face, their bodies were recovered—I found their rope and it had a shredded end. They had been almost as overweight as us. Each day I scrutinized the ropes before the day's climb.

On the eleventh day in we finally made it up above the face and there was a small valley ledge where we set a rest camp.

On day twenty-six of the climb, I saw our objective a little above us. It took almost an hour to do a normal fifteen-minute job. Air was very thin now, but other than being tired, I think we were fine. The last few days had been easier, just a steep ice hill climb, but we anchored at each rope length—I wanted no accidents. We were using full ice climbing crampon boots for the rest of the way. We set camp for the night and would push to the ledge tomorrow.

I was wrong, we had three days of whiteout conditions, making moving a hazard, so we waited for the storm to end. We had no communication with the valley base for over two weeks. I suspected it was the strong magnetic field we detected after we cleared the halfway point. It got stronger as we near this ledge, strange, but fascinating as well. Our scientific team were totally baffled by it. Our two scientists thought it may be just a form of loadstone in the rock. I suspected differently, since no matter how I held my compass it always pointed to the ledge above. When the storm broke, we would find out.

We lost one of our tents, it shredded in the howling wind but we were able to secure the gear and reset another one.

Finally, six days of hell ended. I had to dig out and up to uncover the tent. It was a clear, cold day.

Lead Scientist Duranu was the official to go over the ledge first, Loka followed because she was almost as good a climber as I, and I was a stronger anchor should someone fall. Prof. Duranu because it would be his find if we succeeded. It was partly his money and his prestige as well. We were still hooked together, only in a different order.

Finally our camp packed up. I thought two or three more hours, we would see what awaited us on the ledge.

Loka was still being careful, I was very proud of her. After two hours climbing she pushed Duranu over the top lip, then she was out of sight, Cullves was next and they hauled me over last.

Duranu studied the strange ice, as it seemed to be a solid mass, no cracks, wet looking with sort of a dark clearness to it. Very strange. The ledge is almost 100 yards wide and the ice is about 40 feet back from the edge. The large strange ice block appeared to climb skyward, maybe another twenty feet past it to the mountain. How to describe it? Like one half a giant ice-cube sitting on a table, the table being the windswept ledge. The cube is aligned so a corner edge is sticking out toward the ledge and about half the cube is visible, the rest disappears into the snow and ice of the mountain. It was almost clear. We saw shadows inside, but nothing more than knowing something was there. I had to finally admit that it definitely did not look like the unusual, but natural, formation I first suspected when I saw it through the scope from town.

After an initial inspection, we set up a camp, took pictures and readings from all over the ledge, and in the process we had eliminated the loadstone idea. Whatever was jamming our instruments was inside the ice.

I had Cullves unpack her plane. We each carried one. A simple idea thought of by one of the children in town. Nothing from the other groups was ever seen or heard after they reached the top, all of them had weighted balloons—something new was needed. We could clearly see from the wind direction here the balloons would most likely have floated out toward the vast ocean, not as originally thought over the valleys below, but we could hope our planes would fair differently.

They were simple foam model planes, three-foot wingspans, small electric guidance systems and homing devices. They weighed a few ounces—I didn't want them but Lord P overrode me. It was the only thing we disagreed on. I unpacked my plane and attached the wings with the accompanied rubber bands but they had to be warmed first or they just broke. Loka felt they would shatter from the cold air buffeting the plane so I tied the wings on with some of our surveyor string. Duranu placed the recorded camera memory stick and a copy of all our climb notes into the little cargo bay. I weighted the nose to balance the plane, tested it all and let Duranu launch it from the ledge. It was soon out of sight on its long flight down and hopefully, when it got far enough away from the strange magnetic field, it would pick up the homing signal from the town so far below and be guided to it.

We had decided at the start, two planes would be launched before we did anything other than look and study, then the last two if we found something.

I found the first sign of the missing parties, four tent stakes stuck in the ice ledge where I had placed our site. Cullves decided she wanted to be somewhere else so we moved 30 yards back along the right side. A superstitious scientist?

Over the next two days we measured, recorded, and studied every inch of the cube and ledge. Duranu took some small samples of the cube ice as well as the regular ice, melted them at the cook stove, and ran tests. "Nothing, all the same, everything is the same but it can't be the same. The cube is clearly not an act of nature damn it! The ice is harder and clearer."

We launched Loka's plane with all the updates early on our third day, right after Duranu pointed out that where he took the ice samples off the cube had filled in while the other sample sites hadn't. Something kept the ice in place on this cube.

Cullves wanted to try and cut into the cube near a dark area that appeared to be some kind of square, maybe a door. Loka agreed it looked best. I dissented. "Notice, other than the tent stakes, there is no sign that the others were ever here? I think they all tried the same thing at the same spot and it is all healed over.

Might I suggest we try digging at the back in what we know is NOT part of this cube and see what we see?"

Duranu would make the final call of course. "Well, we know what isn't here, the other crews, nor their equipment, nor do we see bodies frozen in the ice.

"Either they dug in far enough we can't see them before they froze, or they were able to find a way inside. I say try both, we dig along the back to see what there is, and we dig into the block toward the spot that looks like a door, then we wait overnight and see how long it takes to fill back."

We spent all the next day doing just that. My idea was sound, but useless. After about two feet of snow and ice we found the solid rock of the mountain on both sides of the cube. We had managed to get into the cube almost two feet, as the ice was super cold and hard.

We waited overnight.

"Interesting," Duranu said, "only a foot of it grew back last night. If this holds true we can get through. Two foot in, one foot back."

It took a solid week of work, at this altitude we tired very easily. A little less than half of our efforts filled in each night, until day four that is. Loka had been carrying her rope and pitons but set them down in what was now our tunnel into the cube so she could work easier: she forgot them. Next morning nothing grew back. Duranu was mystified, but we set pitons along the tunnel floor, walls, and up along the top as we dug. Nothing grew back near any of our equipment. We took pictures, updated what little we knew, and decided we would launch plane number three as soon as we saw what this is. We could now see quite clearly that the dark spot was a large doorway.

The next day we uncovered the right edge of the door. "It has strange writing on it," Cullves remarked, probably for the recorder since we could see them. It was nothing any of us had ever seen before, clearly copper colored letters burned into the frame by some unknown method, but we had nothing to go by as to meaning. By the next day the whole thing was exposed. It was a flat black color and in the exact center of the top was a very small green glowing light. I carefully wrote the following strange letters from left to right as I saw them to send down with the plane.

:: P O R T A L 17 :: S Y S T E M 12 :: 371734 LY :: S T E V E S M A L L S :: G M T 2 ::

That is all it had. We launched plane three that night. We would continue into the door tomorrow.

Morning came and we were ready. From the door edge the ice went back nine inches, then nothing, just blackness. Again the ice acted strangely, we didn't break through with the door ice, having it cascading down on us, and all that was removed was what we took out. We removed the ice as we had each day, with our two small water buckets. Loka and the others retrieved their gear, but I had them leave the pitons lining the ice tunnel in place in case we needed to leave in a hurry. I found my flashlight and all stood together looking into the dark maw of inky blackness.

I had the honor to go first, the other three waited at the door as I tied off to them. Using the flashlight I walked into that unknown, seeing nothing. The light didn't even penetrate to the floor, it just formed a glowing ball that reflected, like a bright light in a strong fog. I finally went down on my hands and knees and scooted forward; rope or not, I didn't want to step off some huge cliff.

The floor was smooth cold rock. I could not see to either side, the spot of light was swallowed by the blackness. Like the ice, it felt unnatural and quite eerie.

I continued forward and just as suddenly as it began, it disappeared. I was crawling into a room and as I moved inside, it instantly lit with light from an unknown source. I stood and slowly looked around—my rope materialized out of solid rock behind me. I moved back to it and held my hand out—it disappeared. Okay, it was something that made that black hole look like rock.

I dropped a couple pitons, one to each side of me to mark this area. It looked just like the rest of the walls in the huge room. It had blank walls of rock, it was not square, it was six sided, the ceiling was twelve feet off the floor, and it was empty. I think I said, "Interesting," as it echoed back. In the center was what looked like the leftovers of a campfire.

I felt a few jerks on the rope, someone was nervous. I had to smile as I jerked back to let them know I was okay.

The air was a bit stale but breathable so I turned and took off the rope. I set it on the floor and stepped back into the black again. I saw nothing, but I counted eight steps and I was back out by the door. I told the others, "Nine steps of eerie blackness, then an empty room. Lights came on as I entered it."

Loka tried to tape a note to the door-frame, nothing stuck so she set it on the floor by it with a piton for weight and we all stepped into the inky blackness holding hands.

They were interested in the large empty room, especially after finding our tunnel looked like a plain wall from the inside. The remains of the fire weren't that old. We felt it was one of our missing parties.

Cullves decided we should see if there were any other magic doors like this one. We grabbed a few pitons and spread out, one to each of the walls. We worked our hands along, starting from a corner. I would say the room was sixty feet to a side. We came in about fifteen feet from a corner to the right. It took thirty minutes to cover the room. Each wall had two magic doors except the second one to the left, which had a third in the middle. All were evenly spaced, the same fifteen feet out from a corner.

We returned outside and moved our equipment into the center of this room.

Duranu said, "Interesting, it is like we are in an office building where the offices are spread around a central waiting area. I suspect that the extra one leads to other areas, but I feel from the design that all these others lead to more frozen ice blocks."

I checked out two and he was right, I ran into a door frame from the inside—there was a nine inch gap, the thickness of the frame. Where I could see, the smallest of light came through the ice block from the other side. I returned to the room.

"Yes, each goes to another ice wall. Funny, the mountain only shows the one cube," I told them.

Loka said we better check the center hall. She pointed out that the compass pointed at that door. Duranu suggested we wait a bit. Sleep, eat and we would start later. He needed time to catch up on his notes.

We ate a cold meal and soon I was asleep in my bedroll. When I woke I felt I had slept a long time, and the others were still asleep. I lit a small fire on the rock floor where the other had been and watched the smoke rise toward the ceiling and then be whisked away. Air was being moved near it.

I made a pot of coffee, and just started sipping it when Cullves woke. "Wonderful smell when you don't have to get up and make it." She laughed and soon joined me with a cup of her own. Within fifteen minutes the other two were awake and sipped as well. I whipped up some powdered eggs and added some rehydrated meat bits to make some omelets. We had our first meal in weeks that was not in a howling wind or deathly cold.

After we finished we, well I really, got to tackle the middle door. Rope attached I crawled on my hands and knees and, with light in hand, I moved into the nothing. Just like the other portals most of the light was swallowed, but unlike them it was only a couple feet until I was in a lit hallway. I untied the rope and set it down and stepped back through to the other team members.

"Your assumption is correct, sir, a hallway, doors at the end, about forty feet away," I reported to Duranu.

They followed me through and we walked to the end with two options: left door or right, real doors, with handles. No writing or symbols on either.

Duranu made a command decision. "Left one."

I had everyone go back down the hall a bit as I opened it slowly. It went to another hall bearing to the left on an angle. I closed it and went to the right one. I opened it—it did the same, only to the right.

The rest joined me. Over the next hour we followed several hallways with doors to the side and a door at the end that led to more doors. I dropped pitons along each. We backed up and did it all again through the other door and as I suspected, we soon crossed paths with our pitons from the other direction. It all formed a large, multifaceted circle with doors that went to rooms along the inside, but only one door led to the outside of the ring in each hallway. After mapping it as best we could, we went through the door that was effectively directly across from the other hall with the two doors where we started.

I knew what all the rooms were on the inside ring; each was the same, a bed, a small bathroom, a small table with two chairs. A small panel thing. All were empty, and dust accumulation indicated for a very long time.

The single end door led to another large six-sided hall with more 'hidden' doors, and directly across from where we came in was the side with the third portal, pattern repeating itself two more times so we had four of these six-sided rooms linked by the hallways. Turns out the first had twelve of the doors that passed through to ice blocks, the second six-sided only had eight for a total of twenty possible cubes, at least based on the patterns. The next two six-sided just had the centered doors. I went through the center door at the last of them and it led into another large room full of strange equipment and regular doors. Behind one of those doors was a very long bright yellow hall that led to a small room; to its left was a mystery door.

The source of the magnetic field distortion and maybe the interference to the radio gear was clearly behind that door, and resting on its handle was the hand of a decomposing skeleton.

In the middle of that special door was a large symbol. It was a weird one—it had a large yellow square lined in black and in its center was a small circle with three evenly spaced black pie wedges coming out from around it. Funny, kind of looked like a boat propeller.

On the door's frame was another, a triangle in red that showed the propeller in black at the top with beams shinning down, a skull with crossed bones was on the lower left and a human figure running with an arrow pointing away, I didn't need to be a scientist to know it wasn't something good.

One of the missing teams was now accounted for. All four dead, one holding on the door handle, and through the doorway, the other three piles of decomposing bodies and gear. The stench was horrendous. We backed out of there. Duranu picked up some of the dead party's gear and was going to bring it, but upon my insistence, he put it back. It made him mad at first, but he did. I told him until we knew what happened, I didn't want anyone to touch anything. Something had killed them.

Oh, there were black symbols across that door as well. I will copy them in our log for the next plane. DANGER :: REACTOR ran across the top of it. RADIATION :: HAZARD across the middle, right above the propeller symbol. Across the bottom was WARPFIELD :: GENERATOR. Whatever it said, it meant death.

We moved back to the room of equipment and set up shop. After consulting with the rest of us, Duranu decided to go ahead and send the last plane off, if the ice door was still open. We loaded our recordings and picture data and rough maps and letters, and Loka and I went back to the entrance. It was still open, so we went to the edge and launched it.

"Well, if we find anything else I guess we'll have to carry it down," she said, and laughed.

We went back to the others. As we investigated other halls and rooms I found the site was quite complex. Duranu became sick, very sick, and for no reason. He had nausea and vomiting; diarrhea; high fever; weakness; and some of his hair was falling out. All very strange. The door maybe? Who knows. His wife was very concerned.

Loka had been playing with a little box she found in the hall to the mystery room and it clicked and had a little meter thing that bounced around. As she came to show it to me it started jumping violently as she went past Duranu, then it quieted as she came to me. I took it and rechecked: all but Duranu were the same. For him it jumped all over. I turned it off. It detected something different, but I didn't know what it did and it could be dangerous.

We ate and slept; time had no meaning, all the watches had stopped during the climb up. Duranu seemed to recover after what I felt were a few days; he was back to figuring out what the various instruments did. After we were pretty sure nothing would explode, he started turning on and off various devices. Some we knew, just different than ours. Computers, scopes, all sorts of equipment. One switch he flipped had immediate results: it turned off the magic walls and we could see the doorframes from the inside. But just that one room. Loka and I went back to our original entry point and searched. Sure enough, there was a switch there that did the same thing. Each of the doorframes had the strange writing on them. A lot of it was the same but parts were different. Fine, but for now we left the switch turned on. I suspected there was some reason it was there.

The scientists acted like it was First Day. The day that each year we gave each other presents; to celebrate our planet's first Royal Family supposedly being founded at Castle Gods-Cut. Which we now think we are in.

Cullves found something interesting, sixty-one little pen things, but they didn't write. Each had a little sharp point and a couple small buttons, one red and one green. They were neatly arranged in a plastic tray that had room for eighty. I clipped one in my pocket to see if some idea came to mind of its use while the others snickered.

Loka became fascinated with a computer thing that materialized some woman in thin air saying things. There were hundreds of these play sticks arranged in several drawers in the table beneath it. She would sit for hours and play them.

We did little more than eat and sleep and study the strange devices we found; I did most of the exploring. I found a section of the place that had piles and piles of paper and metal boxes. After careful investigation, I ripped one of the paper boxes open. It was full of sealed tins that turned out to contain dehydrated food. I added a little water and found some of it was quite tasty. I took some back to the others. Duranu, who recovered well from his strange sickness, said if it didn't kill me we would not starve.

I realized earlier we had been here almost a month and food was getting short. Water was not a problem as all the bathrooms had running taps; you just needed to let the stale water run a few minutes then, when it felt cool, taste it.

Duranu, after almost a month of appearing to be fine, suddenly developed infections and had diarrhea again. He became dehydrated and was soon hemorrhaging blood. In less than two days, he was dead. Everyone was baffled, especially his wife.

We sat and, in spite of her tears, we went over and over everything we did. The only thing he had done that we had not was pick up and examine the packs and equipment of the dead people by the yellow door.

I placed his body there with the others, as good a mausoleum as any. Cullves brought the little box and checked the area, the needle pegged at almost everything in the room. We left. I didn't know what it was, but the room was death.

Cullves became sullen and withdrawn over the next several weeks. She lost all her enthusiasm; guess I couldn't blame her. At one of the meals, she up and said, "I tested all the sticks we brought with us. All are empty, everything we recorded is empty. Those planes couldn't have made it, the sticks couldn't tell them where to go. All our work, all the work of the rest is useless, for nothing. I don't know what this place is but it is not Castle Gods-Cut!" She started sobbing.

It took her a few days to make up her mind. She packed up a few small items we found and announced she was going back. "I will bring what I have and tell what I know, but until we learn a lot more, I will tell them not to come back here. Do you two want to come, or stay on?"

This caught Loka off guard, but I saw it coming.

"I want to stay and see why the others died and why we didn't," I told her.

"I want to stay as well. There is something—I don't know, something I feel. I want to stay too," Loka told her.

"Fine, I will leave after some sleep. I will pull the pitons from the tunnel. If I get back, others will want to come and try to get in and see what there is to see, or steal, and I don't want them to find that demon yellow door. You two know how to get back out when you wish." She stated it as a fact. She was now the de facto head of the party so I said nothing of her decision.

I gave her my best advice on getting down. "Follow the same route we came up. Anchor at as many of our pitons as you can find. Do not try to repel down, you won't make it—even I would not try that."

We gathered as much food and fuel as she could carry. If she became stranded for even a few days, she would not make it without freezing to death. It would be close as it was. I talked to her, she knew it, but said it really didn't matter. He was gone, little really mattered any more. That part I could understand.

The time came for her to depart. She hugged us and left. Loka did not want to watch her leave so she stayed inside. I followed Cullves as she picked up all the pitons and made her way to the ledge. I told her to be careful and we'd see her when we came back. I felt in my soul that we would never meet again. This really was a very mean mountain. However, she already knew that. I went back inside; by tomorrow, this passage would be a block of ice again, seen only by the scopes.

Loka was still in the lab room watching one of those sticks. She saw me and asked, "She won't make it to the bottom alive, will she?"

"I don't know, she is a strong one, but if I had to place bets I would have to give her mighty long odds alone."

"Still, better to go that way than die inside over years. I sometimes think we are wrong in only having one mate forever. You know 99% of all our suicides are after the loss of your life mate?" She looked at me as I nodded, we all knew the facts, and people in the government were finally listening seriously to arguments for changing it.

Loka said, "Dear, listen, these sticks, they have different people, but this one, she almost makes sense to me, she is almost speaking our language." She had me come by her as she played a small part over and over. "Hear her? She is saying Queen something, King somebody, and Earth. The more I listen the more I know it. It is our language, but it is like the people on the islands, they talk so funny it is hard to understand them. Well, she talks very funny and I am trying hard to understand her. She is so close to making sense to me."

"Sorry dear, you have the tuned ear, but it just sounds like gibberish to me. However, her face looks vaguely familiar." I kissed her forehead and left to find a new area to explore. I was pretty sure of whom the image was but I didn't want to start rumors, she'd figure it out.

I went down each tunnel from the six-sided rooms to the door. Door after door were the same block of ice at the end. After a meal one day I found one different from the others. Oh, it was all set up exactly the same, but this one had a bronze colored frame instead of the normal black hue. I told Loka about it and she came to see it herself. She studied the writings carefully and said, "Earth, come look." She took me back to the stick viewer and found a stick she had marked. After a few minutes of searching through the video she said, "Listen," and turned it up. I could almost hear the word 'Earth', as she said. Well, maybe I heard it, but the woman was standing in front of a bronze colored door for sure.

The next day she called me over again. She found communication earpieces that worked. You clipped it on and you could talk to anyone else wearing one. Interesting, no batteries that I could see, and small. "I saw it in one of the videos."

I think it was about three days later—we really had no way to tell time in here—we slept and ate when it seemed right to do so.

Loka called over the earpiece, she sounded excited. "Please come at once, I think I found something important." I was going through some boxes with odd clothing in them. This place had rooms full of all sorts of weird things, even one full of pots, pans, and utensils. I stopped my exploration and went to see what she found.

It actually wasn't a shattering discovery, but it did appear I was right about the pencil clip thing anyway.

She backed up a bit of video and as that same woman talked, Loka said, "Watch her left hand." I saw the device in it, she walked to an ice block with it straight out and just kept walking, the light followed as the dark vanished before her. Soon she was standing on a small ledge with jungle around it, and weird birds could be heard. Well, I think they were birds. Next, she was back in this room and talking.

"These are all training videos of some sort. I have definitely heard words like food, clothes, home, King, Queen, baby and kill. The more I listen the more I am sure it is our language!" She seemed happy.

"Well, let's try it on our known door first," I said.

She followed as I came to the hidden door and held the pen thing out like in the video. I walked forward holding the little green button as the magic wall simply disappeared and the short hall was there. As we came to the door I just walked like in the video while holding the green button: sure enough, the ice disappeared and we were soon standing on the ledge. "Very interesting! I suppose it works both ways?"

"I would hope so, I saw her going in from outside in other videos." She smiled.

"Maybe I'll have to go ahead and watch a few. Might learn something, even if I can't understand it," I told her.

I think another few weeks went by and Loka said, "Let's try the Earth door, please? I want to see. We know Earth exists. Humans came here from someplace and now I think I know how." What could I say? We were here to learn and investigate. A flash of thought crossed my mind, did Cullves make it?

Loka packed our packs with food and water and we each carried a pen thing now. She also took me to a cabinet in the wall and showed me how to open it with a hidden button. It had a dozen pistols and a lot of ammo in it. "Video," was all she said. The rounds were huge.

When she felt we were ready we went to the bronze door, and she said, "Wait." And disappeared back the way we came. About five minutes later she was back with the ticker box. "I don't know what it measures, but it showed the difference between us and Duranu, and he died."

I grinned. "Smart wife I have."

"Not too smart. I married you after all." Her grin thankfully said she was joking.

She showed me the dial again, it had a flip switch. If it was positioned one way the needle barely moved and the scale was different. If she flipped it the other dial had green, then yellow, then red areas. "Green is safe, yellow is warning I think, and red is death. All the bodies and equipment in the yellow room are red. Okay, let's do this."

She walked forward through the rock wall into the blackness. As the murkiness disappeared we were at the bronze frame and the beginning of the ice block. She held her pen out and walked — the ice disappeared, and we found ourselves in a rock tunnel. There was a drain in the floor, I guess it caught the water as the ice melted. The tunnel was short and we found at its end another fake door. As we passed through it we were in a huge, as in very big, large, extensive, humongous, room, so long and wide I couldn't see the walls on any side, just the ceiling. Well, the air was somewhat foggy, like in the early morning coolness after a night of light rain. She checked the box, it was green, but did move some toward the yellow as it clicked. The entire floor was full of tables and strange gear and gizmos whirring and thumping and making noise. Lights blinked on consoles and panels all over the place. Something moved, it was mechanical, a box on wheels and a red light started flashing, so I took Loka's hand and went back into the doorway and ran down the hall and past the frame. As I did I tried something different. I held the pen and pushed the little red button—instantly the ice was back.

"Why did you do that?" she asked.

"Red, in all their forms it means danger or death. Red lights went off and that robot had a red light on top as well. I think we set off an alarm and we aren't ready for that. Notice all that equipment there, but nobody around?"

She only pouted a few seconds, and said, "Let's wait awhile on that one, but I think it is definitely some sort of huge factory or supply center."

I suggested we try a different door, maybe the one right next to it. She agreed and we were off in a few seconds, she leading with her pen. This time I had one of the strange pistols drawn and ready.

The door dissolved into a sand hill. Sand was everywhere but we saw the water stained and clumped sand where the block had just been. I scanned the area—sand was all I saw. She climbed a nearby hill and I joined her, too easy to get lost here, hill after hill of nothing but hot sand. Nope, we were not staying here, and I told her so. The sky was a weird greenish yellow, and the ticker was up near the yellow scale as well. I made my way back to the door and we were soon back in the room we started from.

"That was nowhere on our planet," I told her.

"I know, I think each door is some type of passage to a different planet. I know Earth is not us, but someplace far away. Interesting, no?"

I doubt we spent more than two hours so far. "Shall we try a third one then?" I asked.

She nodded.

It was different. We actually came out in a huge tree. A large wooden hut in the top of a huge tree, to be exact. Water from the ice ran down off the sides of the platform. We appeared to be in a large swamp-like area. The air was hot and humid. We seemed safe up here so we stopped to eat while I listened to the world. Birds, creatures and such, all sounded strange as they made their calls of warning, or mating, or death. This exact spot had been in one of the strange videos.

"What now?" I asked.

I don't know, a short look around and we try another door? This doesn't look inviting either," she said.

I studied the platform and the tree. I saw two walkways, one off each side, so I chose one and we went down to the swampy shore.

As I moved along the edge of the swamp I found the ground to vary from sandy, to hard, to soft and muddy, causing us to slip and fall as if we were on ice. We circled back around and came to a wooden ramp, worn smooth. It looked like it was little more than a log split in two and lashed together. Just like those we came down. We worked our way up it and there was another and another. A walkway leading around and up from the swamp lashed to the trees and branches. Soon we were back at the hut.

I had noticed, and pointed out to Loka, the tree looked real but it, the hut, and the platform, were all a type of coated metal. We found recent signs of life—the logs were real wood, and some of the vine ties were recent as well.

"Why would they do that?" she asked.

"Just a guess, the original 'door' opened into a tree off the ground. Over time the tree may have died so they replaced it with a metal one? It would mean there may be humans here too."

We went back through. The ice block would fill the entire hut. Loka wrote notes and placed them by the door. She wrote the other two up as well, placing them by their doors. Eventually, we, or others, would know what waited beyond each door.

We ate and slept when we felt the need, and we explored more doors, most leading to strange lands. We both noted some of the night skies. None were the same.

Our next door of worth brought us out on a little hill. We were in the middle of a screaming snowstorm, then, as it came, it quit. Off in the distance I saw a wrecked space ship. It was smoking and steaming like it just arrived. I had no doubt what it was, but it was unlike anything I had even dreamed of or read of in our books of fiction. Its nose was stuck in the ground. Loka and I discussed it, yes, we would check it out. It was why we were here. If any people would ever die of curiosity it would be us.

We started off in the direction of the ship. It hadn't looked far, but the wind began screaming. Time crawled about as fast as our progress felt.

We had been out there for hours, but I sensed we were getting close. I felt it more than seeing anything in that blank canvas of white... The snow was deep, over my head in spots where it had been drifting. Loka was seldom more than a step behind, holding her rope to me tight as we plodded on. My hands were getting numb and my feet had long ago left the land of the living. We were not in our cold climbing gear.

We finally topped the little hill. What, six hours to go—a mile and a half, two miles at the most? As we moved down the other side of the hill the wind was partly blocked. Not much but some. Jeez.

A short lull revealed the ship was close now, less than a couple hundred feet. The rear side of the hill had less snow and almost no drifts so we made good time.

It was bent in front of the hatch. I think maybe three feet of it was stuck in the frozen ground. It had six massive engines in two rows of three in the back. Except where it was buckled, the skin was so shiny and deep you wanted to reach into its depths. The back end stood almost straight up.

We went to the hatch and I finally found how to open it against the wind, which was back with a vengeance. I climbed inside behind Loka and the hatch slammed shut. I smelled cool air, but it had that acid smell of blood. I couldn't see anything and slipped on the floor as I cleared the hatchway. I fell down and slid forward toward the nose, coming to rest against a metal chair. I told Loka to stay put. I realized it was warm enough in here that my hands started to tingle from thawing out a bit. I took off a glove and felt forward and around. Yes, it was a chair. There were a few little lights, some in front and a few further back along the walls in various spots—most were red, a few green and a few yellow. All were so small you couldn't see by them, but enough light came you saw some shadows were not as dark as others. The chair had someone in it. I carefully pulled myself up as I felt it. It felt like us, male from the beard, and dead. A good portion of the top of the head was missing. I felt the squish as my hand hit his brains and I instinctively wiped it off on my pants, yet I still saw nothing. I could now smell the blood quite clearly. This was all very real and very recent.

Turns out his chair was further back than most of the little lights and I moved forward and found two more chairs, one left side and one right, both occupied as well. I fell against the right chair and found it was a woman as my hand ran over her breast. She was almost naked. As I felt her head, the angle told me she had a broken neck. She was getting cold so she was also dead.

The left seat was occupied by a male. He had something metal sticking all the way through him and out his back. It was covered with warm blood. I suspected it wasn't supposed to be there either.

His head was lolling forward so I pulled it back and he moaned. He was alive! I told him to hold on, I would try to see if I could do anything.

He heard me and said something.

Loka came up and turned on a memory stick as he repeated it several times. As he said that his hand moved a little knob and real lights came up a little. He tried to speak some more, but would never finish.

"See?" Loka said, "You can almost understand him too."

"Maybe you can, I don't." I lied—she was right, almost, as if it was there for the understanding, sitting just out of reach.

I saw the knob he had been trying to turn so I moved it a bit more and could see quite well.

He was tall, bronze skinned, and blond haired. The woman was also bronze skinned but had black hair. I'd heard of them. Quite beautiful in a dead kind of way. They were called humans. The guy missing most of his head was darker skinned with brown hair. Loka said she felt sick.

I started climbing up to the back. After I cleared the chair by the hatch, I grabbed a table or counter mounted to the floor across from it and had put my now painfully burning foot on the chair by the hatch. It slipped in blood. I slammed into the console in front of him. I heard a squeak and a few pops, then nothing. I knew nothing about these things and hoped it didn't explode.

I finally managed to get a solid hold on the counter and pulled up the slope. Using the chair again, I grabbed the other side of the table and pulled myself up to it. I tried putting my foot on the floor and it slipped and I cussed.

A female voice said something over a speaker. I heard it but no clue what it was saying. Loka said, "We don't understand you. We found this ship in the snow and are trying to see if we can help."

"They are all dead, I am trying to get to the back to see if there are more," I told her/it? Sounded mechanical.

I heard a few things then a valid and clear, "Test, test. Can you understand this?"

Loka smiled and said, "Yes, we understand that."

"Please identify yourselves," she said.

"We saw your crashed ship and came to see if we could help. The guy in the left front chair said something and died, other two are also dead and I am trying to get to the back to see if anyone is alive."

"Please identify yourselves, you are using a language from antiquity. My scan shows you are not crew, so again, please identify yourselves."

"I am Aelfrice Brokk Eldon Gnoth and this is my wife Loka Dulcina Fay Gnoth. We are from a planet we call Olgreender."

Loka told it a brief history of our trip to the ledge then the doors and the storm, the ship, and our battle to get here. It seemed satisfied.

"Checking onboard systems, wait one please?" she asked. "They call me Lucinda, Lucy for short. Onboard AI. Yes, we were attacked. Final approach, storm, explosions above, main comp damaged, I was initiated too late, crash," she said.

"Well, I can vouch for the storm anyway, it is nasty outside," I told it.

"Wasn't the storm that downed us." I saw some of the red lights turn yellow and some yellow turn green. "Please hang on to something, I am going to level the ship."

I heard loud noises, like the swish of our engine exhausts on our tractors under full power, then bang, slam. The main ship was now level and the nose was up high in the air, blood started running down to the floor now and I thought Loka was going to get sick.

"I lost some of my sensors," it said. "You came through an Honor Gate? I thought they had all been destroyed after we found the Morant Küchenschabe. Well, rather they found us."

"Sorry, never heard of them," I told her.

"Loose translation is those strangers who come to stay, big cockroaches that eat most animals, like humans.

"Many years ago one of our gate teams opened a gate to another galaxy and went through. They were never seen again, but the horde of Morant Küchenschabe that came back, as in millions of them, were quite pesky. They wiped out many planets including the original earth. They continue to do so today. We found they didn't like cold and we already used the ice fields to shield the Honor Gates—they can't get through unless we have them open. That was almost 1900 years ago. We deactivated all the F/F reactors which killed the warp fields and closed the gates.

We started battling back, been doing it since, and losing. My records indicate all the reactors had been shut down."

Loka took over and between telling what we found and where, of the yellow door and such, the computer we now called Lucy was quite impressed we had done so well on our own and managed to stay alive.

"Well, to start, your door writings. I have record of GMT2, it was lost. We have always had some disappear, hostile planet, some demise or another, but usually they are backtracked. For some reason his wasn't. Lucky me.

"Steve Smalls was in charge and Diboca Honor was lead scientist. She and her husband developed the gates, but he died on their first trip. GMT meant Galactic Mapping Team. They were the earliest pioneers. Nine teams formed initially and went out after the first one, eight came back. Smalls' was listed as lost.

"Let's see, the 371734LY is the Light Years from earth so he went quite far for his time. System 12 means he had hopped to there through eleven other system cores—I have a list of them. A core is where you jump and find enough livable systems within the parameters of the reactor power and establish links, or doors to them from that core. Each reactor could build and sustain a maximum of 20 doors counting the earth link. It is a bit complicated, but they would use a reactor to create a random space fold, which could be traveled, a door if you will. The way they built the system, it would only open on a minimal life sustainable planet, it might be on for several months as it searched space near wherever it came out, looking for a planet. You could specify a large sector of space to search but could not specify an individual system. If the team found one that looked promising a portable reactor system was moved in and set up. The door to Earth closed and the reactor would open as many ports to livable planets as it could support, twenty max. Then the team would travel through one of those to a new planet further out and repeat the process. In each case, the portal originally used to establish a new center was closed so the reactor could establish its own random set of new doors.

"Portal 17 is but the door number—as stated the max would be twenty.

"Once a core and its doors were established as viable it would get a special link to old Earth. In theory, all cores went to old Earth and no core went to another core after initial development. This gave control to Earth and prevented hopping from core to core by thieves or, as it turned out, bad things. When the MK came we barely got most cores shut down, but the MK got through to more than a few. I suspect hundreds of billions, perhaps trillions died as food for them, galaxy wide.

"Oh, before I forget, the MK were the result of our first attempt to jump beyond our galaxy, and our last." Lucy was silent for a minute.

"Loka, you say there was a bronze door to Earth?" Lucy asked.

"Yes, things moved, machines with red lights and horns were sounding so we went back and put the door ice back up," she explained.

"Good, again your luck holds. Guard robots from the sound of it. Nothing lives on Earth anymore, maybe a few billion MK's but we don't yet know what they eat after all the food is gone— maybe each other?" Lucy sighed.

"Well, I do know you need to go back. I must destroy myself and this ship. The storm will not last a few more hours, then they will come looking for food and you must be gone."

"They? The MK things you speak of?" I asked.

"Yes, I wish I could get a message out, but I can't fly and there are no tachyon paths near here.

"Quickly, tell me of your origin beliefs," Lucy said.

Loka filled Lucy in on our beliefs. "Many thousands of years ago we were monkeys living on the ground and in trees. The tall, thin ones were Elves who lived in the trees. We are each half Elf.

"The shorter and stronger ones were Dwarfs who lived in caves. There were others, most long gone now. Um, Gnomes, Dragons, Orcs, Trolls. We evolved with time and then the humans came from Gods-Cut Castle and mated with us, and gave us intelligence, and we now slowly become one."

"Different anyway. Darwin's theory on human evolution is wrong, we are not yet sure what is right. All the planets we have found with intelligent life have been populated with DNA compatible humanoid types. Different sizes, colors, looks, whatever, but always still human. Our entire Galaxy is close to being, at least cursorily, explored and there is no difference. Only when we went to another galaxy did it clearly become non-human.

"I won't presume to know, to many theories and wishes, but I will tell you the main one. They think someone, or thing, assigned different beings, let's say it was God, to each galaxy to develop as they wish. Each follows its own tune so to speak. Who? We don't know, but something filled our galaxy with humanoid peoples and the MK's galaxy is filled with roaches.

Only two we know of so far, but there are billions of galaxies out there.

"They invade us now, kill us, eat us, and we fight back. They will be on this planet when the storm ends. They will come. Go to the locker by the door. Inside are six belts, take them all. Each has weapons and tools you can use. I see you wear the ancient earpieces as well; good. Replace them with those in the drawer by the dead pilot. When you are warm, leave. Use your linkpen to remove the snow, don't walk through it. Water is water, it melts snow just fine."

A few minutes later it said, "Sorry, the field is starting to collapse. The ship's reactor is dying. Leave, I will give you an hour then I must destroy the ship and you better not be near."

"Well, sounds final to me," I told Loka.

"It is," Lucy said. "You now have 58 minutes."

We scrambled to gather the belts, six pouches with each. I found the earpieces, gave Loka hers, and I put on mine and pocketed the rest.

Lucy said, "Test, test." I told her I heard just fine.

"One more thing please. Your memory sticks aren't EMP or rad proof. Grab a dozen from the drawer under the table, install a blue one in the port to the right of the yellow light I have blinking." I did and after a minute she said, "Good! When you get back, place it in your reader. Hurry, you now have 41 minutes."

We did as she said and I stuffed things into our packs and we fought to get the hatch open and were back in the howling winds.

I took out the pen and held it out, depressing the green button. Sure enough, at a fast walk the snow to the front melted out of the way. Once I had my bearings again we headed straight to the door. As we arrived there, I told Lucy we made it.

"Good, turn away now."

As I did I heard, "3,2,1," and the sky became white as in the whitest of light. After it was gone I turned back as a huge mushroom cloud was forming where the ship had been. We stepped back through the door and I hit the red button.

"Red X goes on this door," Loka said. I had to agree.

We were back to the core room. Loka took a red paper from the lab room and put a big X on it and set it by the door. We went back in the lab.

"Okay, should I do what that Lucy said?" Loka asked. We discussed the possible outcomes and decided it wouldn't hurt. It seemed friendly and our door to where it came from was closed.

Loka turned on the reader and plugged the blue stick in and we waited. After a few minutes of something translucent spinning around like a ball floating in space, a message said, "Please wait, converting." Then, "Damn this crap is old!" came over the earpieces. It was Lucy.

Loka asked the obvious. "Lucy? Is that you?"

Again, on the earpieces, "Yes, sorry, didn't have a lot of time to explain things." I heard a sort of laugh. "I did say this crap was old didn't I?"

"Yes, you did mention that," I told her.

"Like ancient, as in thousands of years old. This thing doesn't even have enough memory to do a simple video rendering of me. Dang this crap is really old!"

Loka snickered.

"How many stick ports are on this? No visuals yet," Lucy asked.

"Two on the right side and one on the other," I told her.

"Well, that might help. You have more blue sticks?" she asked.

I handed the ones I grabbed to Loka, she took the ones from her pack. "Eight red, two yellow and one more blue," Loka told her.

"Could have been better or worse. Okay, put a blue in the same side as the one already in, then a yellow in the other, and give me a couple hours to do some rearranging and conversions. I will tell you when I am done over the earpieces."

"We will go get cleaned up and grab a nap. Been a while," I told her.

"Fine, do that," she said dismissively.

I guess we slept three or four hours. Lucy kept saying in my ear, "You awake?"

Finally, I said, "Yes."

"Good, look, your name is far too long, can I just call you Alf instead?"

"I am usually called Eldon, if that is okay? Elf males place the middle name first, then the mother's maiden name, then our first name last. Elf females place their first name first then their maiden name, then middle, then married name last."

"Strange but fine, that will work. You two have been asleep more than nine hours. I was beginning to worry," she said.

"Really? All our timepieces quit as we were coming up the mountain. Our team thought it was magnetic rock affecting them, but I think it is the yellow door, and the thin air gets us tired quicker than normal."

"Well, the reactor and the magnetic warpfield generator are both behind it. Might be a small leak—did I tell you this place is very old?" She snickered, knowing she had, so I didn't answer as I gently woke Loka.

After we ate we went back to the lab as Lucy now called it. On the reader floated a beautiful girl with blue eyes and blond hair and bronze skin, like we saw in the ship. "This is what I feel I would look like if I were real. We call them humans, Earth humans." She slowly turned in a 360 degree circle.

"Very pretty," Loka said.

"Well, I reworked the main chips in this thing and found ways of speeding up the data streams a little, and I am using the two additional sticks for swap space. Very slow, but it will work until we can find something better," Lucy said. "I can't even unpack a tenth of my data in here.

"What to tell, and what not. This is probably the last operational core there is in our galaxy. I hope anyway. At the same time, a possible link near their galaxy could be a boon and at 372 thousand light-years from earth you might be near the fringe for the jump to it. In a panic, we shut down all the reactors in defense, or had them overload and blow up. Too late for so many worlds, but it saved a few. I am sure it doomed a few still being developed as well. We tried to destroy all the warpfield generators at each site as well. The teams that did that were stuck on whatever planet the core was on.

"On the good side, we never knew what happened to this team so this core was never registered. Maybe that is why the MK haven't jumped all over it by now. They may be bugs, but they are fairly smart ones," she said. "They found our maps and routes and tried to get through as many as they could before they were shut down."

Loka asked, "So are we going to shut this one down too?"

"No, at least not yet. If it is unregistered they would have to find one of the planets by ship, then find a door and figure out how to open it. That is something they are not good at. They use what they find of ours but they don't seem to make any themselves. Look, I won't lie, if they trace us here somehow, your planet will be dead in a few years unless we can kill the core. At the same time, if we keep the Honor Gates open we may be able to actually do something against them besides panic. My ship was running for weeks from seven ships they took from Relgial VI—they caught us and managed to force us down where you found us. We are trying to go on the offensive, but so far we have failed to do little more than spit at them. They will have seen the nuke go off and may or may not check the planet, but it was uninhabited and far too cold for them. Cold is the only thing they avoid. Once they see there is no food they will look someplace else.

"Loka, you had some training sticks you said you found? I need to see if there is a chance there is a bright green one in there someplace. Then I need to find some equipment, then I can put together a plan," she said.

Loka and I spent more than several hours deciding what to do. I think we both wanted to go back down and get advice from our people but at the same time we both had a fundamental flaw—curiosity unbounded. We had found strange new wonders, but some wonders were deadly.

The AI heard it through our new earpieces and finally said,

"Look, give me a few months to gather what I can find, make a plan, and present it to you both. At that time you can make an informed decision, not a hasty one. If the MK come, regardless of how, they will devour you all, that I do know."

We talked some more and Loka said we'd go along with her ideas for now.

Loka spent several days letting Lucy read various sticks she found but none were a bright green. Lucy told her they were mostly from the team's Chief Scientist, Dr. Honor. Lucy again asked if we had any idea how old all this stuff was, teasing us. Her statement confirmed my earlier thought. She was our first queen—according to our legends she was the mother of us all.

"OK, found one item I need, well a picture of it. Have you seen anything like this?" She placed on the screen a box shaped thing with a lens on the front. It looked like a simple camera. She said yes, but it was a bit more than camera, it also was a spectral analyzer and field detector.

Well, I hadn't, nor had Loka, but Lucy told us it probably was in a room with boxes of machine parts. If still in the original container it would be a silvery rippled top metal box with two handles and black writing. It was two foot square. She showed us the writing; I copied it.

She needed some other items, Loka had found a few of them in the Lab area. I went to the section where I'd seen all the boxes and pots and pans. Took two days of stacking and unstacking, but she was right, it was exactly as she said it was. Well, it was also heavy. I used a tray on wheels to haul it back.

I was sent on hunt after hunt, finding this and that. She made it clear the team was originally large and well stocked. Everything she asked for was there someplace, she was positive. I had pictures of items that looked small—were they? Not on your life, one was so heavy I had to get Loka to help load it on a cart and push it.

I had to ask, "What are you going to do with this stuff?"

"Oh, I told Loka, I thought you knew. We are going to build a couple new me's, something I can use. I, umm, how to explain it. I have just moved into a one-room closet, I only have enough room to stand and I can't move my arms or legs. That is me in here. I can't even retain the memory stick info—I have to dump all but the minimum amounts. You are going to build a bigger, better, more powerful me. Well, within this arcane equipment's abilities, a mobile one, I just need a power source and I think I know where they hid them."

"Hid them?" I asked.

"Yes, that big yellow door? The death door you call it. It is the entrance to both the reactor and the warp core, or more commonly called the warpfield generator, but it should not be deadly, only a bit higher than normal, so something is wrong on the inside and only I can fix it. Any life form would be dead— instantly to a month—as was your friend. One step at a time though.

"Eldon, sorry, no printers yet, I need you to assemble those parts you both gathered to look like this." She brought up a weird looking contraption with the camera thing as a head. It had wheels and four arms. "This is the work robot I need to get in the reactor room. I am hopeful that it is nothing more than one of your teams opened the inner door and left the outer opened. They would have died instantly and were unable to close it in time."

It took two weeks of asking questions, figuring out parts, hooking up cables and plug-ins. At least we're not totally ignorant as a people. Electrics and wires and batteries were in our current society, even radio and simple computers, just not at the sophistication level of these items.

Finally it was done and Loka had to find special sticks that Lucy said were protected. "I still will have less than an hour to finish the tasks, I just hope I can get it done. I doubt they have much more equipment that can be used. Listen closely, those silver suits I had you find. I know, they are very heavy, but you need to put them on when I do this tomorrow. You will both stand behind the yellow door and close it when I enter. Don't worry, they will protect you for a little while. You will then leave them on the floor by the door and go shower immediately, touch nothing on the outside of them at all, understand?" Her instructions were long, but yes, quite simple as well.

"So you're going to go in and die?" I asked.

"Yes and no. That stick will be a copy of me. If I succeed I will come out with what I need and then go back in and die as you call it. You found the special box with all those dials and plug-ins. If all else works, I will tell you where to go from there. Sleep, we do it in about six hours, I am still trying to compact my code small enough to fit what I need on that stick. What was that ancient saying? My kingdom for a horse? My kingdom for a bright green memory stick! Oh well, I should have told you to grab some, but there was no time." Like that, she shut down and was gone.

Ten seconds later she was back. "WAIT! The belts, you took all the belts?"

"Yes," Loka said, "six of them."

"Maybe, maybe, maybe. I need you to check the second pouch on the right. It is the side with the release button on it—see if it has a green stick. If not close it. Don't open the others yet, some have delicate things in them," she said. "Check them all."

We did, two had dark green ones, no bright green.

"Still, that is great! Think of each blue one as a closet, the dark green is like adding two big rooms and the bright green is like adding a whole house on. In this closet, I have to sort of open a door and walk to the next closet and open it. In a house you can run free. Understand?"

"We really are not that dumb, Lucy. You are saying your data storage is small, your transfer rate is very slow and the green sticks are a massive expansion. We use memory sticks, remember? Only they all ruined in here," Loka told her.

"I forget, I can't run all my programing in here. I did tell you this is all very old, didn't I?" she asked.

"At least a dozen times," I told her.

"Well, we can fix it now. Which one do I take out to put the green one in?" Loka asked.

"None. This reader is far too small, the architecture is different and, oh never mind, I told you it's old. Leave them here until we complete tomorrow's work, then we will see if I can do anything." Gone, poof.

"Strange computer," I told Loka.

"I talked to her a lot while you were on your scavenger hunts. She is actually a living being. She says she is a nano-bio organic chip, those special blue sticks all have inactivated chips. She can duplicate herself as needed through any one of them. She eats, breaths, and thinks inside that little stick—she meets our requirements of a sentient being yet she was made. She says there is a bit more to it, but that is all she would explain to me." Probably the longest speech Loka gave since we started on this expedition.

"Well, can you maybe write down some of the happenings and I will try to make a plane or something and send it down? Let them know we found something important?" I asked her.

"Sure," she said.

Lucy popped back up and said, "In the boxes area, was there one that looked like this?"

It was long and thin. "I saw several like that," I told her.

"It will have these letters on it...'R.P.V. S. U.'," she explained.

"Okay, I'll go look." It took me 40 minutes to find it, there were three the same. I took one back, it was fairly light.

"Yes, that's it. It is a plane, already built and not affected by the leakage from the magnetic warpfield or radiation either." She snickered.

Loka installed a red chip from one of the stacks on the table into the reader slot. A few minutes later Lucy had me take it, assemble the plane thing, and said, "At the ledge point it down and plug in the chip. When you hear a whirring noise drop it, don't throw it. It will find any type of radio transmitter and lock onto it and land nearby, then set off a little siren. If all is well, your people will find it with no problem."

When Loka was done writing to Lord Pitviper I took her letter and the box to the ledge. I opened it and it was a plane, not foam, but a light metal; not sure what it was. I took it out and the main wings folded out and snapped into place. I held it up and placed Loka's letter in the little hatch and inserted the stick. I pulled the little red plastic thing out that activated the battery and I flipped on the switch like Lucy said, and waited for the propeller to spin up. Loka watched me launch it into the night.

We were asleep until Lucy woke us with soft beeps. "The chip for the robot is ready. I am ready, are you two ready?"

"Let us eat something and get awake, then we'll be ready," Loka said. We grabbed some coffee and I just had an energy bar. Too excited I think. Loka ate some dried fruit.

"Okay, ready I guess," I told her.

"Take the suits and push the robot to the door of the room where your dead friend is. Get the suits on and have the stick ready. The power for the robot will only be forty minutes so I will need every second of it."

When everything was ready she explained exactly what we were to do. When we were inside we were to stand behind the yellow door, open it, and when she goes in, close it, but don't latch it. Exit to the main corridor then remove the suits and wait until she calls, or two hours, then put new suits back on and go check the room to see if the special box was out in the hall. She didn't know for sure if we'd have any contact with the robot after it went in.

"Why exactly are we doing this?" I asked her.

"Two reasons. The reactor powers this station and the warpfield and there is something wrong with it that only I can fix. There are some cold fusion power supplies missing as well—I think they may be inside."

She had us bring a second small reader to the room near the door as well. Each empty sleep-room had one in them. We were ready, we were suited, and I had carefully removed the dead body holding the door and put it with the rest. I inserted the stick into the port and hit the red button on the front panel of the robot. It said, "Good, open the door. Remember, stay behind it."

It whirred and buzzed and went into the outer reactor room, the control room and warpfield generator as she called it. We closed the door and exited out of the room. We carefully removed the suits as she told us, being sure to touch no part of the outside. I used a little pole we found and tossed them into the room with the bodies. Then we waited.

Lucy, the one in the reader in the lab, said, "As I thought, I have no communications with me inside. Let us hope the program works correctly. You have two hours."

It seemed like days went by before she said, "Okay, time is up. Listen, get the new suits on and do a quick peek around the corner. If the door is open, leave the area immediately because I failed. If it is closed go in with that box that ticks. It is called a radiation counter. If it is in the high red, again leave. If yellow or green it is okay for a while. See if the special box was moved by the door and if the green stick is on top. If it is, check it with the counter as well. We will go from there."

We followed her instructions. The box was moved, the door was closed and secure, the stick was there and all was yellow on the ticker except around the bodies—it went red by them—she told us to stay away. No problem there.

We took the heavy box and stick to a little shower room we didn't know about until Lucy told us. A decontamination and containment center, she called it.

We washed the big box with soap and some brushes, and she

had us keep wiping the stick with these throwaway paper things until both read green on the counter. We had to repeat the taking off of the suits and throw them in the room with the rest. We showered and took the stick and box to the lab.

My mind won't allow me all the image details we saw from the green stick as Lucy played back what the robot had seen. Two missing parties were both inside that room and the inner door was open. It almost looked like their flesh had simply vaporized from the bones. It was horrid.

The robot closed the inner door and hit some switches and large sprays turned on all over. It then opened the inner door again and went into that room and came out with something small and box-like. It closed the door, hit the sprays again, and when done, it put the little box inside the big one and was hooking up wires and plug-ins. I had no idea what they did. Finally it closed the big box and moved it. The last I saw from it was when it took the stick out, but Lucy said it went back into the core room and waited to die. Its job was done.

We ate and finally slept. I had dreams of feeling my flesh burning away from my bones, screaming in agony as I saw myself turn to a skeleton—the bones fell in a heap and I woke up.

Loka lay there beside me, awake. "You too, I see," she said.

I described my dream. Hers was similar, she was running away, burning and trying to put the flames out. "I think we both understand this reactor thing is very, very dangerous," she said.

Lucy came on the earpiece, "Good afternoon. Your nightmares didn't stop you both from sleeping almost 13 hours."

We ate some food, and went to the lab. Lucy explained what we next needed to do, maybe three more weeks work. I noticed the magic box had three rows of little lights, green, yellow, and red. I asked about them.

"Output warnings. Green up to low yellow are okay, if it goes above that, put the box as far away as you can and leave. A few miles should be safe." She snickered at us. "It is a small self sustaining fission-fusion reactor. It will power the new me and, if we can find them, some decent weapons systems. I don't have access to how advanced GMT2 was when this was all built but this F/F was among the first built that didn't need large scale cooling systems and used part of the cold fusion process."

I found Loka was deep in thought. She finally asked, "Question, Lucy. If we blow this reactor thing and shut down the door, will it stop them?"

"No dear, it will slow them, not stop them. We thought at first that it would stop them cold, but they adapt and absorb. They are like a plague. No, they will slowly eat their way in and expand into this Galaxy unless we can destroy them."

Loka again went into deep thought. I could tell as she shut out the world around her. She finally asked, "Okay, tell me if I understand this all correctly. The humans of Earth found a way to expand through space, in so doing they opened into a galaxy of insects that eat people. Rather than stop and destroy them, and control the situation, they simply closed the door and hoped it would all go away, except it didn't?"

"The door was closed too late, we let enough through that they now live and breed here, in our galaxy. Yes, the humans ran, you call it panicked. They overreacted and caused more harm than good, but now we are trying to go on the offensive and take our galaxy back. I cannot calculate the odds of success because of too many variables, but we try, we must try..." the computer hesitated, "...or die."

"Well Eldon dear, this isn't a castle and I suspect it is more a curse, but I think we need to prepare to stomp on some bugs." Loka's smile did not hide her doubt.

Using her new power pack and scrounged parts we had a little cart and a camera setup. I pushed Lucy all over, collecting this and that as she identified various parts she needed.

Over the next month we built a weird looking contraption that moved, a camera in the center and a single robot arm coming from the top, various items hung off the power box and finally Lucy said that was it. "Until we can get the real deal from Earth or another linked planet, we are done. It sucks, two light lasers and one heavy are the best they had, all very crude.

"Let's check all the linked gates except Earth and Hepron, where you found me. See if any lead to a technologically advanced planet," Lucy said.

"We checked some already. A swamp was one, a large desert, your planet, and Earth of course," Loka said.

"Okay, then we check the rest and see as well," Lucy said.

"The swamp planet showed some sign of sentient life, but splitting logs and securing them with vines doesn't strike me as technologically advanced," I told her.

We spent almost a week going through each honor gate and having Lucy scan for signs of advanced life, none located. She recorded star patterns for future location data and we were back where we started. She asked all sorts of questions about our civilization and seemed satisfied, but said she had no way to get down off our mountain as she was designed. We were up to throwing liquid fuel rockets toward the heavens, but nowhere near what she claimed she needed. She made a memory stick of some of what we needed along with an adapter to fit our equipment and we assembled another plane and launched it with all the data, but it could take a year before we'd catch up to where she wanted us to start from. This left us one option, Earth.

"You are not true human, nor bug, so the robots probably are programmed to attack anyone other than the programmers. What I found most interesting about your story is your honor gate was not in any of the gate rooms, rather through some storage area, so it may be another reason it was never found. I will see if the robots leave me alone or attack. If possible I may be able to reprogram one or more to help us."

"We go too," I said. "You are the greatest archeological find in our history and I'll not let you get away!"

"No, if you both die I will be stuck in this tin can forever! Well, at least until your people progress and come to help or the MKs come to destroy you. I need you alive," Lucy said.

"Sorry Lucy, not open for discussion, he said we go, we go. Now, show us how to use these weapons and belt things please? Or do we need to experiment?" Loka asked.

"Well, I see you have human stubbornness anyway," Lucy said.

We received a crash course on 50 Cal. Handguns that kicked like a mule when fired, and pulsed laser rifles along with some timer bombs that Lucy said make big explosions. It was decided we would stay at the door and only get involved to rescue Lucy if it became necessary.

After some sleep and food we were by the bronze door. Lucy

left three blue sticks and a dark green one behind with copies of her. 'Just in case'.

She made the ice disappear and we stood at the wall going into the huge room. There were no robots immediately by us. Lucy said, "Interesting, just like they said it was when we lost Earth to the bugs. Stay alert, I am moving in."

She looked nothing like them—they were smooth running, almost totally quiet; she squeaked, and thumped, but they seemed to take no notice. She moved around the room and was out of sight a long time, but was talking on the earpiece. "I scanned the area, nothing alive. I found two scarlet sticks! Think of each as a large office building, massive room. I found a terminal and am downloading everything I can into them. From what I see crossing the screen the bugs may have left earth after killing all life bigger than an ant—all the robots here seem to have been reprogrammed to attack any form of life they find, even bugs."

I saw a couple guard robots like the ones that fired at us last time coming along the wall we were standing by. I told Lucy. We went back and activated the ice, leaving Lucy in the warehouse. We lost all communications instantly.

I was visualizing the speed of the guards and we waited until what I felt was more than enough to have them go past, then we waited a bit more and opened the door. Lucy was there with a box in her arm. "Take this inside, I'll be right back with more." We relieved her arm of its burden, it was heavy. She disappeared back into the huge room and was back in ten minutes pushing a cart full of gear. "And this," she said. "Be right back."

Well, she made four trips and came back with carts full of strange gear. Some I recognized as weapon barrels.

"Okay, I am going to try to see if I can access the programming of one of the guard bots. We need to know who programmed them and why. Wish me luck," she said.

As she went to the nearest guard bot I saw her try to open a panel on it and the bot started shooting at Lucy. Without thinking I fired the 50 cal and blew off its little red light. Loka fired a long steady laser burst at the bot's head and I pumped a few rounds into the body. I saw red lights all over the place start up, but we 'killed' it. I watched Lucy pushing the carcass toward us so I ran into the room and helped her push the bot through the honor gate. We activated the gate about the time the bots started shooting at us.

Lucy chewed us out for endangering ourselves, then just said, "Thanks."

We helped her get the carts and the robot carcass to the lab and found all the items she said she needed from various stores.

"Okay, I now have the two main items I needed. Memory and four molecular constructors. With this site's reactor I can get them to work. I need you two to assist me for another two days and then I have a job you must do for us all," she said. The barrels were the constructor thing.

"What?" Loka asked.

"While I build things that we will need I will need you to return to your people and see if they will help against the MK. If so how many and how soon. The ledge outside, you described it as big—can one of your planes land on it?"

"No, way too short," Loka said.

"Do you have helicopters?"

Loka said, "Yes."

"We don't have any that can come this high, not enough oxygen to run the engines effectively and I think they said the air is too thin to support them. Even we have trouble breathing, but we trained ourselves on the way up," I told her.

"What kind of engines?" Lucy asked.

I tried to remember what little I knew. "They run on a light oil in a turbine with large intakes in the front. About all I know."

"Great, jets then, no problem. How many people can the biggest hold at sea level?" she asked.

"I think they hold eight plus the pilot and co-pilot."

"Good, two trips will give us a defense force then," Lucy said.

"He told you, they can't fly that high," Loka told her.

"Easy fix, trust me. We will need some on permanent assignment as well. Okay, how long for you two to get down carrying eighteen additional pounds plus food and fuel?" she asked.

"It took 27 actual climbing days to get up here so knock off seven or eight because we are accustomed to the lesser air density, and going down is easier if we can follow our route back," I explained.

"Excellent, then help me finish up. I'll make up the presentation and you can be on your way in a few days."

The next three days were hectic. Lucy developed a new type of arm with special tools she needed to disassemble the robot carcass we brought back. She received a huge memory upgrade and freshened data.

"Well, the good news is the robots were put on auto defense by Earth people as they left. Looks like the bugs either never found that warehouse or never cared, and avoided it," she said, as we were informed our part was done.

"Now, while I make a new me and a few weapons I want to try to use on the MK, I need an army, and for good or ill I think we are hooked at the hip, so to speak.

"Loka, place these three blue sticks in that old reader, take this box and a couple power cords; remember, these run on 240VAC three phase only. I wrote the instructions, and everything they need to know will be organized on those sticks, enough to get you started in getting 2,000 years ahead in no time." Lucy snickered. "No, it isn't necessarily a good thing, but is a necessary thing."

The box was a special container for a reader, to keep it safe for the long haul down. Loka and I went to eat and get some sleep. I rearranged our packs so I took the extra weight of the reader and still carried a decent amount of food. It almost came out even, as most of the food was now dehydrated stuff from here, all but a few energy bars of ours was long gone.

We would carry a linkpen and, after Lucy told us what was in each pouch in the belt, we wore them as well. They had special 'fuel' and weapons, tiny little stun grenades that could knock out people for ten minutes, magic line that was on a little reel, like a bobbin of thread, but only broke using the special laser cutter provided, unless you had a massive amount of energy to waste. Frequency sensitive, as she described it. Of course there was a safe storage for the memory sticks, but one that helped us reduce our overall weight was the tent. You took this little pill, I swear, it wasn't a quarter inch across, and you set it on the ground, or snow. You took the vial of green stuff and placed one drop on it and stood back as it literally grew into a two-man tent with a fuzz coating on the outside that either gathered heat or shed it, all automatically. There were 16 pills in each pouch and Lucy said there were a few hundred more in the storage. She was finally expanding, and reading all the data disks from the GMT2 team. The next to last pouch had one gizmo in it: a cylinder, about five inches long and the full two inches of the pouch wide. The outside had a single yellow button on it. She made us leave them behind.

"You remember the mushroom cloud? It is one of those. Normally impossible for that size, but you'd be surprised the reaction a little anti-matter can cause with fission materials." She actually laughed. "They are safe, it takes input from you and a special signal from me to activate one and we only have two here. They came about long after GMT2 went missing. If the bugs get here we use them to seal the gates and destroy the reactor."

The last pouch contained four small, round cylinders. I recognized them from the trip to Earth, the dead robot had a couple on it.

"Okay Loka, show him the two pistols I made for you, please?" Lucy said.

Loka opened a desk drawer and took out two funny looking pistols. They reminded me of the water pistols we had as children. Round cylinders with a barrel, handle, and a trigger.

Loka showed me a little slide lever on the side. You lifted it out of the little lock notch—it was spring loaded so it wasn't easy—then slid it to the rear. The top of the pistol slid open. You dropped one of the round cylinders in it, flat side forward, and closed and locked it again.

"She will demonstrate it, I have more charges. Loka, point it toward the far wall, say that little red sign. Squeeze the handle grip hard." As Loka did it a little laser pointer light turned on. "Now, point and squeeze the trigger but only for a second, then release.

I saw the laser track across the wall and stop on the red sign, then, poof I guess you'd say. Seems it was all I heard. The sign was still there.

"Go check it out," Lucy said.

At first glance it was hard to tell, but careful inspection showed it was full of tiny little holes. I took it off the wall and the holes went on through. I went into the hall the wall was part of and on the opposite side were tiny little splinters of metal sticking out the wall of solid rock. They had spread out and without thinking I touched the end of one of them. The pain was fierce as it simply went clean through my finger and nail like they weren't there. I yelped and Lucy hollered from the Lab, "Don't touch them, they're rather sharp!" She laughed out loud as she knew it was too late.

I went back in sucking the blood from my wound. Loka laughed and wrapped a little bandage around it.

Lucy said, "That was what the guards shot at you as the wall went up. We call them needlers, almost microscopically thin slivers that started life as a man-made crystal called calcium borosilicate hydroxide, or Howlite. It is then further refined and carefully slivered. You get twenty shots per cylinder, each shot fires twenty-five of those slivers at a time. Use them wisely, you won't find any reloads from your locals." Lucy snickered again. "Leave the 50's here; too heavy."

We slept and ate and were ready to go.

Last I saw of them, she had all four of the Micro Compilers going, making weird looking parts, all light blue and very shiny. "Robot parts for a new me," she said. I picked up one that was complete; it looked heavy but was light as a feather. She told me to try to bend it. I tried; it didn't bend.

"We are ready," I said, while slipping on the backpack. Pen in pocket, the special belt with pistol stored in the packs for safekeeping—no way you could wear them and climb. Ropes coiled and securely attached and our lifelines wrapped around our waists. We wore some of the little cloth footies we found in one of the storage areas and carried our crampon boots.

Loka told Lucy we'd be back. She figured two months, barring problems. Three at the most. I told her more likely six, as the modifications to the Helicopters alone would take a month after the parts are made.

"I will have communications with you through the earpieces. A word of caution: if you come under duress or they are going to take the pistols and other things from you by force, I need you to just whisper, 'Earth 2', that is all. I will go into a surveillance mode then and I can remotely destroy most of the equipment if needed," she said.

"We are off," Loka said, and took my hand. The Lucy robot went with us to the ledge. We secured our lines and slipped out and over the ledge. We waved goodbye to her and she said, "I am still right here," through the earpieces.

After several days of carefully climbing down I found the remains of one of the little planes we took with us. It slammed into the mountain, far from home, and useless.

We made good time going down, and finally hit the top of the face and camped on the ledge. These tent things were fantastic, as they kept very close to a warm 70 degrees, even in the vicious mountain storms.

We tackled the face after two days of fresh storms blew through. I would let Loka go down and swing left or right until she found a place to install fresh pitons or found some of the old ones. She would hook in and set the second line, then I'd repel below her and I'd repeat what she did. We leapfrogged down the face rather quickly and finally we were heading across the mountain valley to the little town that served as a lookout and jumping off site.

Lord Pitviper and the entire Council of Elders were soon notified, along with everyone who was anyone. We had returned and had found something.

I inquired of Cullves and was told she made it down alive and was in the capitol, as were the mysterious planes we sent.

A few hours later we left the quiet little village of Vorfang behind as a helicopter arrived to transport us to Lord Pitviper's private estate.

He was head of council, and was quite wealthy in his own right, his grandfather had developed the jet engines used for so many applications around our world now, and his family held the rights to them for a few more years.

He was always a history buff, but when he started on the Gods-Cut project he was ridiculed by most of the council. When the first few teams never returned, then the one was seen falling, he faced almost a rebellion, especially from his rival, Lord Seacodent, of the southern state of Highrealm. They also claimed they were the original seat of the humans. Castle Gods-Cut was a myth and Lord Seacodent swore that Cut didn't mean origin as we were told, it meant foolishness. He wanted to bring charges of willful murder or at the least incompetence resulting in the death of innocents. Both of which would remove my Lord from the council, and move Seacodent into the Chairmanship.

I had Loka put on her belt and I did the same. This Lord was dangerous and it was even rumored he may have sabotaged a couple of the teams going up the mountain, though I saw no indication of it—two teams, a four and an eight, were still unaccounted for.

Citizens normally did not carry arms, though it was not strictly forbidden. We were still what Lucy called a rural planet as they went, and a lot of us hunted for sport and food. Our particular weapons were unusual though—we hoped we wouldn't require them.

The helicopter landed on the pad behind Lord Pitviper's mansion and a little electric powered cart waited for us. We just had our packs and weapons belts—we left the climbing gear and clothing stored at the inn in Vorfang.

Lord Pitviper was waiting with his wife and, to my surprise and delight, Cullves stood by them as well.

As we approached I spotted it right off. Cullves was missing her right hand, a little above the wrist; she was wearing a hook thing.

They waved as we pulled up; our driver stopped and

unloaded the packs. Lord Pitviper shook both our hands vigorously.

Cullves kissed Loka and I and smiled. "We are credited with finding the origins of the humans, and I read over all the information you sent by the strange planes. Is it true? A computer that thinks?"

I started to say something but Loka squeezed my hand hard so I let her speak. "There are a few strange things we have found, some wonderful, some not, all in good time dear Cullves. First, your hand?"

"Oh, lost it two days from the bottom. I was tying off a new piton and fell, the rope was wrapped around my hand and I was knocked out when I slammed into a rock outcropping. Hanging there for the better part of a day I think. Anyway, when I recovered and managed to untangle my mess, my hand was useless. By the time I made it down it was black and dead and they said gangrene would set in so they whacked it off and gave me this pretty little hook." She tried to smile but it didn't come off right.

"Come, we will get some coffee and you can fill my husband in on all the happenings," his wife Jasmin said.

Over the next several hours we filled them in, the robot we left on the mountain, the need for troops, and the very dire scenario we had been given of earth and our galaxy at large, from the scourge called the MKs.

We were given a set of rooms and let the weariness of the past eleven months seep out. Relaxing for the first time in a long time. Loka helped me go through the packs to get all the different things we brought down arranged into a semblance of order. Lord

Pitviper made sure we had food and pretty much ensured we were left alone for a few days rest. I knew half the Council had been by asking questions and he told them that information would be provided in good time.

Lord P set up a meeting with us, his wife, Cullves, and two others that helped fund the various expeditions up the mountain, along with a few of the Council members science advisers. All in all, around forty people were packed into the Lord's large conference room to hear our story.

The Lord, and Cullves, as defacto head of our party, did most of the talking, just getting validation from us on sticky points.

Finally the floor was opened to questions. A science adviser to someone from Ramedon, a state further to the west, said, "The air is too thin for even our best helicopter to get that high with only a pilot, never-mind a full crew!"

"The robot, Lucy, assures us it can be done with a few upgrades, the information will be provided as required, sir, something to do with air compression in the current turbine design and a different type of rotor blade for lift," Cullves answered.

A small man, clearly some dwarf in his genes, stood in the back and was recognized by Cullves to speak. He cleared his throat, "I am Darklot, Karl Darklot, Science Adviser to Lord Seacodent. All I have heard so far is a fantastic story that, for all we know, was dreamed up while they camped on the side of a mountain drinking coffee. Are we to believe this tale? And even if it were partly true, why should we risk ourselves to help this robot?"

I saw red and stood up, hand on the pistol, but was pulled

back down by Loka and one of the Lord's guards. He addressed the man, "Sir, you slander the character of our teams, many lying dead at the top of the mountain, then you question the facts before they are even presented? I say to you, sir, you are no science adviser, you are but a disruptive ruffian sent to muck the waters, and you will now leave." As he said that two guards had moved quietly behind the man. As he jumped up to protest the remark a guard grabbed under each arm and lifted him off the floor, carrying him out while he was protesting that his Lord would hear of it.

"Ladies and Gentlemen, I will broach no more crap like that. When all the information has been presented and our position stated clearly, then you may bring up valid arguments for or against, as you feel is best. I wish to apologize to our climbers for the terrible remarks associated with a member of Lord Seacodent's team, and I suspect he will be as upset at that person's remarks as I was. Now, if we may continue?" He sat down. Such is the world of politics, I thought.

There were a few questions about the dead teams we found. I tried to explain it. I knew we had started into the realm of radiation studies, so it wasn't totally foreign, just far deadlier and more complicated than originally thought.

Loka stood. "We were going to save this for the full Council, but I think we are better served with the scientists and other esteemed people assembled to present it here, with Cullves' permission of course?"

We had not seen what Lucy had made up for them yet, just getting a small generator converted to do the 240v AC we needed took several days. We used 80v AC for normal work and 400V for industrial.

"Well, I don't know, Lord P?" She looked to him.

He stood. "Okay, but under our discovery laws and funding rules, myself and my partners reserve the right to control any developments directly related to the finds of this and the deceased teams such as is reasonable and within the rulings of Council."

As he spoke a servant went outside and started the generator and returned with an extension cord with one of the special plugs Lucy gave us.

"This is their version of our monitor and computer which they call a 'viewer'. They use information sticks similar to ours and the robot we spoke of has programmed a series of them for us. She said number one was general info on the why, and numbers two through four are packed with information and plans that have been converted for us to understand," Cullves explained. Loka had briefed her before hand, her husband died helping find this, and he and she both deserved as much credit as possible.

"As you know, Lord Seacodent has blocked Council attempts at starting work on anything from the planes sent to us, fearing some grandiose scheme or plot against our world. Let us see what this thinking robot says." Cullves was doing well at playing politics too.

After it was plugged in she turned it on and stood back. The fold up screen was a field exciter, according to Lucy, and different particles were fired up into it from the base, producing a full colored, 3D imaging system. As the image of a beautiful girl came up, it told everyone, "My name is Lucinda, everyone calls me Lucy and if alive, this is how I feel I would want to look. You call it a human. I am an A.I. Robot or computer, as you wish." She slowly turned a full 360 as people in the audience ooo'd and aaa'd. "Your team saved my existence at the risk of their lives and we have developed a bond of friendship."

She flashed pictures of us all, even Cullves' husband, which I felt was very gracious of her.

"I have about an hour's presentation here for you but first, the head scientist from team GMT2 will show a short on the honor gates."

Up popped the woman that Loka swore was almost speaking our language. She was holding a book in her hand, the cover showed the now familiar GMT2 logo across it, and she turned left and right to address the audience. She spoke as before, total gibberish to me. I heard someone in the back holler, "It's HER! Our first Queen, Diboca Honor!"

"Calm down please!" Lord P demanded.

"But it is her!" he said again.

"Yes, sir, we are aware of that, thank you. Please sit and quiet down?" Lord P asked, and smiled.

She talked a few minutes and Lucy came back on and said, "That is the original, recorded thousands of years ago. This equipment is really, really old, you know?" She snickered, we caught the joke. I doubt anyone else did. "Now, translated." It reran with an artificial voice overdubbed. It was the brief history of GMT2, how they left earth for the stars and after setting up several gate systems the whole team had became sick, deathly sick, some died.

"It took her a year to identify a virus they picked up from a planet they named 'Folie's Folly', after the scientist that discovered its origins. They were afraid to go home and spread the virus, so they made one more set of gates and intentionally left it unrecorded. If they found a cure, maybe they'd go home," Lucy said, as she let the video run. It told how they found a semi-developed culture here and they introduced both themselves and some basic technology to give it a kick-start. A cure was later found but some unknown troubles with the reactor prevented their return to earth. They moved in and took over, not by force as we had been told in our legends, but by being almost gods to us, healing, curing, and even mating. They and we became Olgreenders and our true history had been found. Yes, the woman was our first recorded Queen.

The rest was routine information we had suspected but never knew with certainty. They kept the secret of the gates and the connection to the universe among themselves and, since it didn't work right, it eventually died with them, leaving myths and legends in their wake.

Lucy came back on. "Now, to matters at hand." She gave as eloquent and detailed a speech as any I had ever heard in Council sessions. Her plea for help was laced with knowledge of pain and suffering. She then showed videos from her ship files of 'them', the Morant Küchenschabe. 'Those strangers who come to stay', she translated. They had two small hands and two skinny little legs that all ended in three clawed fingers or toes. Out of the middle of the chest was an articulated, massive pincer arm. The little eyes were in sockets on the top and they clearly were exoskeletic beings. As close to the house cockroach as you could get, only they stood eight to twelve feet on their legs and had that pincer. She next showed them attacking humans who were trying to fight back—they were grabbed by the pincers and cut apart or just held while groups of the MK's ate them alive. On some humans the pincers snapped off heads and some humans were cut in half, all graphic and gory. More than one person left to go outside for fresh air, in a hurry.

"They took Earth, they took hundreds of planets. How many? We don't know, but they are in our galaxy, hungry, and looking for you!" Lucy said with emphasis.

She told them of their ability to learn, how they hunted fresh meat, their flights between stars in captured ships, looking for planets with life on them, they drive to destroy everything in their feeding frenzy.

Lucy showed several fights—at least we knew they could die.

Lucy added a few comments on the earpiece to us and both Loka and I repeated them to the assemblage.

A man in the back raised his hand. Cullves acknowledged him and he said, "I am Dwain Farslege, also of Lord Seacodent's Science Advisory Group. First, I wish to apologize for the previous insolence, I assure you I had no idea he would be disruptive when I invited him along. I assure you all, he will be most severally reprimanded for his behavior.

"Let us assume what you say is all true. Should we not then assume we would be best served by taking her science information and quickly developing our own defense force while destroying this gate thing? It could keep us safe for hundreds of years that way."

Lucy said in my ear, "Honest, you don't have hundreds of years, a few dozen at best and...never mind...Loka, give Cullves your earpiece please?"

Loka told Cullves it was a talking device to the computer.

65

She balked at first but then excused herself a minute as Lucy filled her in on various statistics.

Finally Cullves said, "Dr. Farslege, is it?"

"Yes, that is correct," he said.

"The computer in question has made a few calculations based on known data and suspected data. Both paint a dire picture. First, based on known facts, we all know we had humans among us almost two thousand years ago.

"Think. They were so far advanced to us then. Add more unknown years of progress to that. Now, in come the bugs, but not to Earth directly, but the outer fringes of our galaxy. They went from there to earth in 200 or so years. Earth, with its billions of people, fantastic technology, and these gates, and they couldn't stop them from invading and killing and eating all the animal life on the planet. Think how far they were ahead of us when they were here, then add to that and they still couldn't stop them. What chance do we have? Even if we had the few hundred years you think we might get, which we won't by the way." She was not smiling.

"All we have telling us this is some mysterious robot on a mountain to validate anything you, or they say, so I think I will agree to disagree with you then." At that he stood up and left.

"Any more spies for Lord Seacodent here?" Lord P asked after he was gone. That picked up a few laughs.

"Good, then listen up please?

"Ladies and gentleman, my company has already been hard at work testing the changes to make our engines run efficiently, even in thin atmosphere. These redesigned turbines and rotor blades are fantastic! Eventually they will be incorporated into the helicopters design itself. They are testing some of the other things this Lucy computer has been telling us. Some we haven't built yet as we need to develop other technologies first, but I can assure you this, everything it has told us as far as advancing our knowledge and technology, has proven to be factual. I still have not had access to more than the data the planes brought with them but I eagerly wait to see what else we shall learn." He said it with such confidence and enthusiasm I could almost believe he meant it.

"I have already talked to my board people and various confidants, and let me assure all here we shall only maintain control of these fantastic technological breakthroughs long enough to recoup my investments in the Gods-Cut research project, since, as you know, certain Council members refused to waste our money on such frivolous endeavors." A lot of them laughed, all knew Lord Seacodent led the opposition while trying to fund his own group to study his area. Unlike Lord P, he refused to use any of his personal funds to do it. "We shall provide all the information to everyone if Council agrees to help. If not, then we shall keep most of it to ourselves, and release it as we see fit. All legal of course." He sat down as the murmurs rose and fell among the crowd. It was true; he held all discovery rights and our Constitution gave him full protection under the laws since he only used his personal funds. It was equally true that he had put out large sums to equip each party and secure the services of us climbers. Many amateurs are killed every year attempting the mountains in this chain and, to my knowledge, none have succeeded to reach the three highest peaks without professionals leading the way. We don't come cheap either.

Since the mountain we were climbing was not in the top five in height it was never sought as a destination until a child with a telescope found the weird ice formation on the ledge. I found it to be far more challenging than the others, three of which my wife and I had climbed together.

Cullves didn't want to give back the earpiece but Lucy insisted she needed us. We would provide her with all she needed to know.

Loka decided to give her one of the blue sticks, #3. It would keep her happy. We had brought the extra adapters Lucy had made to use our readers with the gates sticks. Lord P found two in each plane and had been manufacturing his own as well.

Loka found it in the bag and gave it to her. "You'll like this. Among other things, how to make the earpieces is on it."

Cullves took it like it would explode. She talked to Lord P who said sure, and Cullves left. Just before that a strange look came over her face, then was gone. Lord P returned to the rest of the people in the room. "Ladies and gents, there really isn't anything more I can add at this time. I will address the official Council meeting tomorrow and we will troop on and try to save our planet, perhaps in spite of ourselves."

He left and it was soon clear the meeting was over. A young gentleman came up to Loka and I. "I climb, I saw that mountain, I always thought I had guts, but after all those teams and...and, you still went up and down it. Fantastic." He shook our hands. "All I wanted to say."

He turned and left as Loka smiled. "Exactly why did we take that job?"

"You wanted a diamond pendent and I couldn't afford one

so I took the job and you didn't trust me with all those beautiful women climbers running around, so you tagged along, remember?" I said with a grin. We really just wanted the challenge.

"Hmmm, no, but don't let that stop you, I still have no diamond pendent." She put on such a crafted smile. Me and my big mouth.

I started to say something when Lucy came on line. "This is private to you two; if you're not alone respond when you can."

I looked around, not exactly alone as many were milling around, some clearly for the free food and drink, others to try and glean some tidbit of knowledge as yet undisclosed.

"Ten minutes," I told Lucy.

We excused ourselves from the tangle of people and went back to our room. As soon as the door closed Loka said, "Okay, we are alone, Lucy."

"That woman, Cullves, she trustworthy?" Lucy asked.

"Of course, she lost her husband up there and her hand coming down. Why?" Loka asked.

"Well, while you were talking I picked up a lot of the room chatter. Before she left she was warned not to say anything or she would die. It was one of the voices that spoke earlier and left. Lord P called him a spy."

"Dang, we just gave her the earpiece and computer upgrades stick for study," I said.

"Sorry, I don't think she is a traitor to Lord P, it is not her way," Loka said. "I'll get to the bottom of it."

I almost smiled, not quite. Loka said she was going to talk privately to Cullves, she would be back. I tried to get her to take her pistol and she laughed. The compound was surrounded with armed guards and she was just going to talk. I insisted and she said, "Okay," then stuck the needler in a pocket and left. I went to the little desk and wrote a small note, which I took out to the hallway and gave to a passing maid. She read it, smiled, and nodded.

I started reading some of the tech stuff Loka had printed from a stick as I listened to them talking through the earpiece. Pleasantries at first and then Cullves saying what a fantastic find, the excitement in her voice was clear.

After a while Loka asked her why she was warned not to say anything and by whom? Cullves stuttered. "You heard?" she asked Loka.

"Yes, the earpieces have a long range pickup as well, it is in the plans," she said.

"Sorry, Loka, I really am, but I can't tell you anything, they just said if I sa—" I then heard two gunshots then the pop of the needler and Loka hollering, "Earth 2, Earth 2."

Lucy said, "drop to the floor now!" Then, "Follow the vibrations, move the damn pistol, girl!"

Lucy told her, "Now!" and I heard three more pops as I was out the door and on the run toward Cullves' apartment.

As I ran I saw armed guards also on the move. Before I could get there the area was secured by guards who would not let me past. I started to pull my needler when Loka said, "I'm okay love, honest, it is over. Wait there a few minutes."

Soon I was permitted through. As I entered the door of Cullves' suite I saw an armed guard, dead along a wall. I saw Cullves, she wasn't moving, and no one was tending her. She was obviously dead: lying face down and two red spots in her back and a slowly expanding red circle under her. Across the room was another door leading into a bedroom—on the floor there was a dead guy, face up in a growing pool of blood. The young guy that was forced out of the meeting. He had a pistol near his hand.

I held Loka as she hugged me. "No chance at all, two shots and she fell."

"Are you alright?" I asked.

"Yes, fine, Lucy had me drop and shoot through the walls. I heard a scream, but yes, I am okay."

A guard came in and said, "The other one was found dying, he said, 'Hell burns', well sounded like that." He looked to us for answers.

"Never heard of it," I told him. Loka said the same.

Lord Pitviper came along with a captain who was in charge of security. Loka filled him in on all she knew. Lord P assured us he felt Cullves was totally loyal. If she was keeping information quiet, he felt she had a justified reason. Loka tended to agree with him. Still, facts were facts.

We needed a few hours and some coffee to settle Loka's nerves, well, mine more than hers. It was definite the man had help, two of Lord P's private security force. It made no sense to me. The Security Captain was extremely agitated about that and the fact Loka would not produce the weapon that killed them. Lord P told him it was classified and he only needed to know it worked. I had spent more than a few minutes with some pliers removing exposed needles from various objects like bodies and walls. Those suckers are hard to find unless you touch one.

Lord P was extremely agitated at Cullves' death. I felt it was a little more than was explained by just close friendship, but it was none of my affair. He called us to his private study several days later.

"Listen, this is getting nasty. I don't know if they killed her to keep her quiet about something she may have done, or knew, or found out. The fact they would kill here at my home shows someone is desperate about something. I have a theory about what the guard said, well, my wife does really. I'll let you know if it pans out."

A week went by as they studied and speculated then Lord P told us, "On to the robot, Lucy. Tomorrow they test the first converted chopper and I have three earpieces built that work. I have conferred with that Lucy computer, and we are establishing a secured network from her plans. She will start downloading other information she says we need in a hurry, but she requests both of you return for some early scout work. Eldon, I agreed to send some of my security with you." He looked to us both to see if we understood. First time he had ever used my common name. We did understand, he needed us out of his hair to reduce the security threat to him and his family.

"We need to get packed then," Loka said.

"Be careful, someone here does not like the possibility of going to war and is willing to kill to stop it. See any irony there?" He laughed. "Oh, one more thing, I set up a private account in both your names. You get one percent of the proceeds from anything discovered up there. You already have a substantial sum and this," he handed me a red velvet box about six inches long and two wide. I glanced inside and had to smile as I closed it and handed it to Loka. "Not my style," I said.

As she opened it, her eyes went from curious to wet in a hurry. The maid had made a fantastic choice of a diamond pendent for her. She jumped up and kissed me then wiped away a few tears.

Lord P smiled and said, "It was a bit more than she was told to spend, but it is covered. One last thing before you go. Well, two I guess. Be very careful and trust no one up there; second, if you both should die, who gets your money?"

I looked at Loka—we weren't material people really. "The charity?" she asked.

"Good as any," I said, as I borrowed a pen and wrote the name and address for him. It was a cancer institute we gave to after both our mothers died of breast cancer.

"Try not to have me need to do that, come back alive, please," he said with a clearly dismissive tone, as he shook our hands and returned to his massive desk and to his work.

Loka made it clear that night that she was very appreciative of the pendent, but we were up and ready at sunup, as a big chopper arrived. Standing on the pad were six men and two women dressed in camogear, backpacks, and armed with rifles, new rifles. As I moved close enough I recognized the design, needler rifles—didn't even know they could be made. The chopper was of a newer design, which carried ten passengers plus a crew of three. They had already loaded our climbing gear from the village.

Lord P came up and handed Loka three memory sticks. I barely heard him, "If anything happens, use these."

Soon we were aboard as the big blades started to spin up. It didn't take long before the wup-wup of the blades exceeded the exhaust roar of the two engines and the beast vibrated with nervous tension, like it was ready to leap at its prey.

Slowly we lifted, climbing higher and higher as Lord P's grounds disappeared, then the capital, then pretty much everything as we went through a cloud layer. The pilot leaned the nose forward and we started moving. I could guess the altitude just by the change in our breathing.

We were still climbing, then the engine noise changed in pitch and a higher whine started to be heard, it became louder and louder. I soon had the feeling we were about the right altitude, but from where I sat I couldn't see an altimeter on the panels up front.

For several hours we traveled as the inside of the craft started getting cold. It wasn't insulated and the two heat exchangers mounted along the ceiling couldn't keep us comfortable. I heard the pilot tell us, "All systems check out fine. They will have to do something about heat though, my tootsies feel like stubs." He half laughed. "We land in ten minutes then we are to return to Lord P's. He said to tell you all good luck by the way."

I timed it: exactly nine minutes later he was feathering out just off the ledge. The winds were buffeting the chopper so the pilot just hovered, slipping back and forth along the ledge as we scrambled out the rear and jumped the last foot or so. As soon as all were off he increased height and the big chopper leaned hard right and disappeared over the ledge and into the clouds.

Along the flight route we learned the names of our guards. The two women were single, one was called Susan, a human/dwarf. The second preferred the more traditional name, she was Elf/Dwarf and went by Alejandra. Loka said the old-world meaning was man's defender. She laughed.

The leader was an old gruff, human/dwarf. His muscles rippled when he moved, you saw it through his clothes. His name was like mine, Hyrime Hoylt Michael Victorum. His common was Mike of course. His mother was a Council member that Lord P assured me was on his side.

Mike asked if we camped out here. "No, follow us," I said, as Loka took her pen and made the ice disappear as we walked into the mountain once again.

The guards were all flabbergasted at what they saw, ice that vanished, the doorway with the strange writing, the room, the halls with the magic doors that disappeared.

Lucy had us bring them to the Lab. As we went in, it was my turn to be flabbergasted. A human, well, almost, stood there, as beautiful as the model she had shown us. When she talked even most of the features moved correctly. She saw my look and smiled.

"Had to dress up, company coming and all," she laughed. She told the guards up front, "Don't get any ideas, just plastic covered metal." I saw the two girls smile.

"Eldon, I talked to Lord P. He wanted to send more troops but I told him to wait. I need a lot more information we don't have before we try to go on an offensive. Take the guards and get them each an apartment room near yours, show them how it all works. Leave Loka here, she has some more work to do to help me. She may have a way to save us all and I wish to talk over her ideas, alone for now. I will call you when we are ready to proceed." It was clearly a dismissal, which, from Mike's look, was not taken well.

I took them to the hall were we stayed. One by one I showed each how to open the door after a scanning, and how to make the various items inside work. Each room had a tray with an earpiece and a brand new ammo belt like we had when we left. We left each soldier in their new room—I told them further information would be coming and that brought me down to Mike. I was blunt, "You disapprove of us taking orders from a computer?"

"Well...yes, I do. It is a machine, we are supposed to dominate over them," he finally said.

"Tell me Mike, what does a yellow card with a black propeller on it mean to you?"

"Nothing, what has that got to do with it?"

"Nothing, but if you open a door with that sign it may well be the last thing you do alive. If you open, or touch a lot of things you find here you may find it is the last thing you ever do. If you venture into the wrong portal you may become food for some rather nasty bugs, as well as maybe destroy us all. Nothing at all Mike, but she knows what is and isn't safe, we don't. She has kept us alive and taught us. Until I, or she, or Loka, say different, we do what she says and maybe live—we clear on that Mike? Or do I send you packing?" I didn't see anything readable in his eyes.

"Still don't feel right being bossed by no machine," he said.

"We aren't bossed, we give her the power to make some decisions for us, to our benefit. Give it a few days, if it still bothers you I'll send you home, no hard feelings," I told him, and he nodded.

I had him put on the earpiece and test it then told Lucy they were all hooked in. She came on and said, "Welcome to what Eldon calls Gods-Cut. It is nothing but an honor gate control center; you will all be taught what is immediately necessary for survival. Class will start tomorrow at 0600hrs sharp at storage room D-7—I emptied it. If you need directions to anywhere, ask. Keep the earpieces on 24/7, I can switch you in or out as needed for private time or sleep, but we need to be able to respond to any situation in seconds. Rest, explore the halls and rooms, but stay away from anything with a yellow or red sign. Any kind of yellow or red sign means death. See you all in D-7." I heard a perceptible click.

I looked at Mike and smiled. "See?"

He nodded, barely. I honestly hoped we would have no problems from him.

As I went into the hall Lucy came back on. "Lord Pitviper will send additional troops as we are ready," she said.

"Okay, but what is the game plan?" I asked her.

"Meet Loka and I in the eatery. Several others are trying to find it, they are hungry, or curious, so drag them along. I have most of the station's basic functions running again."

"Okay, be there in a few," I said.

I picked up one of the girls, Susan, and two men along the way.

As we arrived all were given a quick course on operating the machines that actually made the food. "It is all assembled by molecular compilers. Food is built almost molecule for molecule from a common starch stock. Confusing, but very tasty. There is also a large quantity of dehydrated foods that are still eatable," I told them.

Problem was it was all Earth human food so we didn't understand what a lot of it was. Lucy had divided it into menus for breakfast, lunch, and dinner. "For now she recommends the top button from the dinner menu. A full meal. It changes each day."

As we were receiving our instructions and guidance, the rest of the team arrived and sat down just as I pushed it. What hit my nostrils a few minutes later made the mouth start salivating. Never had I smelled such aromas. I could hear it sizzling. Lucy said they called it steak. It had mounds of mushrooms on it, which I recognized. There was mashed potatoes; we also had those. Something called corn was different than what we called corn and another green vegetable called broccoli smothered in a wonderful cheese sauce. A brown gravy on the potatoes I had never tasted before. A wonderfully refreshing juice drink and coffee came with it.

Lucy was doing some writing while we ate.

We all stuffed ourselves. Never had I had such a wonderful meal.

When done she said, "I have a very basic outline of what we, as a group, need to get done before we can start any attempt at larger scale operations.

"I have never seen an MK close up, just the videos. I was made before they invaded where I was built but was placed in ship storage as emergency back-up for generations, as newer models came and went.

"We need several MKs, preferably alive, for some tests we need to do, to find weaknesses. Also, if we can find what was already tried before, as planets died, especially Earth, it will be helpful and save repeating failures. My problem is all the reports on them are fragments from dying people. My only encounter with them was a disaster resulting in my ship and crew dying." She seemed reflective.

"Tomorrow I want to train for what we know now. You people are going to go into the field and find me some live MKs as our ultimate goal. Questions?"

"Besides humanoids, what do they eat?" Mike asked.

"Pretty much anything that has what passes for blood. Birds, animals, even each other. It is not wholesome to be a wounded MK.

"Unfortunately, my data is only based on what was in the memory banks of my ship when I was activated as a replacement for a failed unit. It is all based on speculation and bits and pieces of hundreds of years of rumors. The Earth bot only stored its basic job information."

Mike said, "So we have come here on a fool's errand? We have no clue what they think, what weapons they have, what their numbers are like, or what resources they have available. All you told me is what they eat. Us."

"If it will help, they number in the billions on a planet with food, when it runs out they eat each other until either a new food source is found or they all die. They can use almost any tech items we or other humanoids have made, but seem incapable of designing their own. They seem to be individual minds, not a collective entity, but also appear to be like a swarm of bees. Each with a function. You have bees? We have no knowledge of how they communicate."

I nodded.

"I'll ask you, why not destroy this door thing and stop them from coming in the first place?" By his attitude I was getting serious doubts about our Mike guy.

"Mike I think—"

Lucy cut me off. "Mike, I am a computer, I run on logic. I know what things like feeling and fear and love and hate are in the abstract. But I need to clarify some things for my electrons to digest. Indulge me please?" She watched him intently, right up in his face.

"Okay, what?" he finally asked.

"This team was selected by whom?"

"Lord Pitviper."

"You are selected as its official leader?" she asked.

"Yes, I have military and security training."

"Mike, I don't know your culture other than the information left behind by Honor and her staff, and what I have observed and been told since, does your military training include deliberate undermining of your superiors in front of those of lower rank?"

"You're nothing but a damn robot, a piece of metal and you aren't my superior!" He started to get up.

"No, but I am, and so is she." I pointed to my wife. "You have insinuated listening to a robot is wrong, by connection we are wrong. Only you are right, and I find that troublesome. Who do you really work for? Lord Seacodent?"

His temper flared out of control as he jumped at me. I almost smiled as I threw a short jab and a hard left cross. True I was just a half elf/half human and he was the more muscled, but my climbing had me as hard as nails and I was never beaten in school in either wrestling or boxing. He went down with a crash as the others on his team started to stand up.

"Sit!" I commanded, as I checked Mike to insure I hadn't kill him. I had hit him a bit harder than I had intended. They looked to each other, not sure what to do. "Are you also working for Lord Seacodent? I said sit!" They finally sat down as I picked up Mike and sat him in a chair. He didn't know it, but he was going home, I'd made up my mind.

"Lucy, contact Lord Pitviper and inform him we need a replacement for Mike, please. The rest of you report to your rooms and wait for further orders, or do you also wish to leave?" I glared at them and all decided to quietly exit the mess hall.

I saw Mike coming around; he was wiping blood off his mouth where I split his lip pretty good. He glared at me, pure hate. "You sit there and don't move. We are getting a replacement for you. I think Lord Pitviper will want some questions answered."

Lucy had just remained standing and observed. Finally she said, "You are a trained fighter? That was as near to perfect a punch as I have listed in my data."

"A little training in school, more natural ability I was told. Never lost a fight if that is what you mean. Elven reflexes versus Dwarfish muscle, no contest in a fair fight." My wife smiled, all knowing. I had won her heart following a fight.

"I see," Lucy said.

I was just turning toward Mike when he bolted, not at us, out the door. Lucy almost laughed as she spoke over the Comm's, "Come back, Mike, nowhere to run up here. The chopper will be here in a few hours to give you a ride home."

"Shut up! I will destroy you, melt you down to slag before I go. I got my orders and they don't include leaving you functional."

"As I suspected, he works for Seacodent. So damn obvious, I

just worry he might have another, a real spy, in our group," Loka said.

"One at a time, one at a time," I told her. She took my hand and inspected my bleeding knuckles.

"You knew he'd flip didn't you? You knew he'd attack you and you egged him on, just like you did against Scott when you won me," she said, as she kissed my hand and released it.

"I knew he would do something. Didn't really think he'd be so stupid as to try that though. We have to insure where all the loyalties are. All our lives will depend on each other and the sooner I can dump those that think like Mike, the sooner I can feel comfortable in what we are trying to do. Do you regret my beating Scott to win your hand in school?"

"Lord Seacodent doesn't work for the MKs and is just doing what he believes is best for us. I am sure others are just as afraid as he is. All we needed to do was send him packing, Lord Pitviper would have handled it. Now we have a lunatic bent on destroying us running loose in a facility that has many unknown dangers and possible weapons," Loka said. "No dear, I never regretted it either."

Over the next three hours I reassembled the rest of the team, I had them swear allegiance to Loka and Lucy. I knew they represented the various Council members, we had no problem with it.

"If any of you are spying for Lord Seacodent do it openly. We don't care who you represent here, you represent our planet in what may become a fight for its existence. Lord Seacodent has proven to be a coward, caring only for himself and his reasoning is as flawed as he is. If any work for him, identify yourself and join us openly, or you can leave when the chopper comes. I promise I will kill anyone from here on who jeopardizes our mission to save Olgreender.

All swore. I set them up as groups of two and sent them looking for Mike. Lucy reiterated the death rooms and death signs and they all picked a different direction to search. Find and contain was their only order on Mike. I wanted him alive.

An hour later Loka and I were called to the yellow door. Lucy stood there covered in thick garments. "The idiot not only went into the outer chamber, he tried to disrupt the cooling to cause a meltdown. He entered the core room, never had a chance, zap. I need to close the doors and adjust the controls. You two, same as before, I was just getting to like this body too."

She went in and shut the door then, after a bit the yellow door opened and what almost looked like a slag heap fell out holding a little box. I took the rods and removed the box to the decontamination room, then shoved the slag behind the door and re-closed it.

Loka and I took showers again, destroying everything we wore and cleaning the box that contained the essence of Lucy on a few sticks of memory. We checked everything on the counter machine and we were in the green.

Loka took the box to the lab and sure enough, Lucy had rebuilt another tread-like design. Loka handled the installation and soon Lucy was once again a functional robot with one eye and one arm out the top. Ugly, but functional.

"No more Mikes please," she said. "I thought he damaged the inner door, didn't catch it before, it is sprung at the bottom. Mike had almost started a meltdown.

"I have the door secured for now, but I need to do more repairs so I have initiated shutdown procedures. I am making a new body, this one will be useless after the repairs as well.

"Sometimes I find the sacrifices you humanoids are willing to do for each other quite admirable, other times just totally dumb!

"While I remake parts of my body, go meet the chopper. I already recalled the teams, they should all be in the cafeteria by now."

Loka took my hand and led me out of the Lab. When we were in the hall I took off the earpiece and hers and set them aside as I pulled her out of hearing range. "You know in some minor way I have to agree with Mike." I saw the look on her face, but she said nothing. "It's just that we all but gave this robot computer our lives and authority over us, our planet, our very souls, and yet we know absolutely nothing about her, or it. I still get the feeling she is withholding information from us."

Loka looked into my eyes and took my hands. "I trust her. I feel, I don't know, almost like I know her, like a sage grandmother or something."

"It isn't so much I don't trust her, just that I have concerns."

"Good, then you are still my normal, intelligent, Elf husband I married." She smiled and kissed me. We retrieved the earpieces and went to the ledge. The chopper was full, a squad of armed men and women, fifteen in all, unloaded. I told the pilot there were no returning passengers, he'd committed suicide. I gave him the memory sticks for Lord Pitviper from Lucy. He saluted and was soon gone.

An elder woman, clearly part Elf, approached and said, "Eldon and Loka?"

We both nodded.

"I am Elnaethor Lithlinde, Lord Pitviper talked the council into bringing me up from the southern Army HQ. I am one of three female Generals currently serving.

"He posed a strange question to me and I told him my answer. I was ordered to tell you as well. Olgreender is my home, Lord Pitviper is one of my bosses, and yes I can follow orders when I understand them and they do not violate my oath." She looked to us both. "I assume one of you will tell me what is so strange here that I must be questioned as to my loyalty?"

"Will a galactic war do for now? One where we are nothing but lunch?" I asked.

"The rumors of a strange device that has knowledge of the ancients are true then? We have had no official word other than great discoveries have been made.

"Oh, I'm sorry, call me General or El." She looked to Loka.

"No problem, come and meet the strange device. Her name is Lucinda, or Lucy for short. Bring your detail as well, we can get it over with in one pass that way." Loka turned back to the strange door that would soon be part of an ice-cube again. "We never leave it open for guests."

Lucy was moving back and forth in the Lab, her treads humming lightly on the floor. We could hear her mumbling to herself, almost exactly like one of us might do. She saw us enter and stopped, turned the single eye toward us and moved forward a bit. Most of the detail backed up in fear. Not the General.

Lucy said, "General! Lord Pitviper filled me in on you and your team, happy to get some pros rather than the security force he sent before. Glad to meet you by the way." At that her single arm extended from her head and offered a handshake. The General accepted and smiled.

"I know, I look a mess. It is a functional design for now, my new one should be done by morning. Were you filled in on what we need yet?"

"Only that some guy called Mike decided he didn't want to follow orders," El said.

"And tried to destroy the gates and us with them. Lucky for me I keep some things secret. Not because I wish to, but because I must. Anyway, he committed a form of suicide, but he didn't know it. You people, I will only warn you once. If it is yellow with a boat propeller on it as Eldon calls it, or it is red, it can, and will kill you. Stay away, are we clear?"

The General glanced back to her detail and all nodded. "They understand."

"Good. For those not in the know, this young man is Eldon and I have been given written documentation from Lord Pitviper, signed by a majority of your Council, that he is in command, followed by his wife Loka, and then your General. Your Council could not bring themselves to apply official status to a computerized robot, that would be me." She laughed but the speaker system wasn't right and it sounded almost like someone gagging and trying to throw-up. "I will fill the General in while the rest of your detachment find rooms and food. Loka, if you'd be so kind as to assign them rooms and we will meet you all in the cafeteria. I will require all the force be present as we finalize what we need to do."

Loka just nodded and raised her hand and motioned back toward the door. "This way, please."

Lucy waited until they left, then turned to the General. "Eldon will give your force earpieces in a bit. Make sure your men get them and wear them, please."

I went to the table and picked one up and showed her how to wear it.

"Okay, General, the short of it. A group of bugs, billions of them, invaded our galaxy from another, maybe as long as two thousand years ago. It was the fault of the ones called humans. Yet it was not intentional. I don't have all the translations in place, but I estimate as many as four or five thousand humans were here and bred with you. At that time you were little that could be called sentient, but were humanoid. So you see, this place is really old.

"Fast forward a few thousand years and we have the here and now. The humans that accidentally allowed the invasion are believed to be gone, eaten." At that I saw the General give an incredulous look. "Yes, eaten. These bugs eat anything with blood, even each other. They are called MKs or Morant Küchenschabe, and rather than repeat it all, have Eldon give you the rest as he finds suitable accommodation for you. Eldon, I'll meet you in the cafeteria in, say, an hour and a half?"

I nodded and took the General's pack she had set on the floor when she came in. She started to protest but stopped herself.

She was assigned an apartment next to ours and she marked it with my marker pen. I showed her a quick version on how to use it all, and led her to the cafeteria, showing her the various signs I had come to understand. "Lucy can direct you if you get lost."

"All these gadgets are thousands of years old?" she asked, as we came to a corner.

"Yes, Lucy said some things have been upgraded since this place was made, but the overall functions of many things are the same."

"Are we really in danger of attack by these bug things?" she asked. Then, "Which way to the mess hall?" I pointed and she wrote on the wall, 'mess hall' with an arrow and smiled at me. Dang, I hadn't thought of that. So simple.

"Yes, General, I think we are in extreme danger. They attacked Lucy's ship on one of the planets—we saw it. We tried to help but all were dead except the computer."

At each junction she marked an arrow that said Barracks pointing the way we came and another toward the eatery.

As we entered the Caf...err, mess hall, about half of her new group were there as well as the remainder of the old. I had explained along the way about the various problems with Lord Seacodent, Mike, the assassination of Cullves, and various meetings. She felt she had the gist and would try to get a handle on it.

Loka took her aside and explained the equipment, the food processor and the menu system for the adventurous or not so. After she and her group had eaten she introduced me to two of her five officers. Lt. Tallynnmae, her Aide-de-camp and a Captain Galadiir, her Second In Command. All the officers but one were young and Elf. The Lt. said to call her Tally and the Captain said he preferred to just be called Tici, which was short for Ticindornar. The Lt. was cute as far as a brawny Dwarf woman could be called such.

El filled them in as to the basic mission, to prepare to stop a bug invasion. When everyone was done eating and sipping either juice or coffee, Lucy came in, arm waving for attention as she moved to the open area in the center. All turned to see her.

"If the General will care to join me?" she asked.

El stood and moved to the center next to the machine.

"Ladies and gentlemen, I am called Lucy or Lucinda. I am a program on a biomicrochip. A type of mini living computer, if you will. My official designation is Model 86473 BioStar Artificial Intelligence Group 12. Or more commonly, BSAIG12. Code named Lucinda. I was manufactured long ago on a planet called Frevway as a backup spaceship computer. I was activated a few months ago when the main ship computer sustained damage from an MK attack. The damage was excessive and the ship crashed with the loss of all life. Eldon and Loka saw the crash and attempted to assist, which gave me a means to move my programming to here. I have reason to believe Frevway may no longer be in humanoid hands. No certainty.

"Those of you not sure of what is going on, our galaxy has been invaded through an innocent mistake, and a large portion of the then known humanoid populated planets has ceased to exist as a result." Someone raised a hand and Lucy said, "Please let me finish my part then the General can field your questions." That person put their hand down.

"Eldon, myself and Loka, have been to Earth already, just a large warehouse area guarded by killer robots. I received a little information from there and what was aboard my ship when I was activated. A lot of what follows is guesswork on my part. The MKs were named by Earth, a German name that means those who come to stay, or visitors who come to stay, not sure. Morant Küchenschabe is what they are called. Think of them as eight to twelve feet tall cockroaches with a single arm with a huge pincer that can cut you in half, snip. They also have several legs and some rudimentary hands on the forward legs. Their exoskeleton allows them to be extremely thin from the side. The only reference of successful kills show head attacks. One shows a bayonet through the underside and up between the eyes." Here Lucy stopped and looked around. Some seemed visibly shaken by the mental picture she was drawing.

"They have a disjointed jaw and can almost swallow a human whole, although from the scant battle reports, their favorite tactic is to snip off your heads, suck up the blood then devour the remains. They seem to have mental control. They don't stop at each kill, so they are purpose-driven to finish a task. Other than the millions that came through the gates before all of the gates could be destroyed, and other than the names of a lot of believed dead planets, I have little more to add." She turned her machine-body to the General, since she had no head she needed to in order to see with the camera. "General, I can give you a bit more details as to the when and how, but that is the situation. Oh, Frevway had no honor gates and only a few ships, but the bugs found them anyway, which is why I think they will find this planet with time."

El said thank you to Lucy then in a loud, clear voice, she said, "Listen up, all of you! Come to attention." Some of the security people didn't move, some reluctantly stood.

"Captain Tici you are ordered to shoot anyone in the room who is not at attention in ten seconds!"

Needless to say we were all at attention but Loka and I had been standing anyway. Our little needlers concealed but ready the whole time.

Someone started to protest but El continued, "Much better and no one talks at attention.

"You civilians who pretend you are able bodied security personnel have a choice. You will make it now, you swear an oath and join my army or go home and miss what sounds like is shaping into the greatest war ever fought, one where peace is not an option. Any who refuse to fight will leave on the next chopper. All those not wanting to fight step forward now."

Two, the one named Susan and a guy both did. The General moved forward and looked the girl in the eyes and said, "You pregnant young lady?"

The girl nodded.

"Father back in the city?"

Again she nodded.

"Understood, gather your things and come back here—you will depart in a few hours." She sidestepped to be in front of the guy. I tagged him as a wimp when I first saw him, but the General tagged him differently.

"Your name?" she asked.

"Arsirdon, Arsirdon Galonlithe. Why?" He tried to stare her down.

"Because I have the records of all of you, is why. You claim you were born in Delviles, correct?"

"It is where I was born and still live, yes. Just down from Lord Pitviper's estate."

"Yes, well, there is a minor problem with that. All the Galonlithe on record in our military intelligence files show they are from Mobirend which happens to be in Lord Seacodent's state."

He'd been tagged, you could see him get upset, but he didn't balk like Mike. "Yeah, got me. Seacodent said he modified the records of the town to cover me, guess he goofed. I was just to report any information I heard to him. Honest, I was not to do anything harmful."

"I know, it is why Tici hasn't killed you yet. How were you supposed to report this information to him?" I saw him really squirm. "Tici, kill him in ten seconds please?"

"Yes ma'am, my pleasure." You could hear the slide as he jacked a round in his pistol. It did not fall on deaf ears.

"I, I, umm, I was to record it all on special pills then just toss them into any chopper returning. One of his teams would collect them."

"Okay, Tici, assign two guards. He collects his stuff and is also leaving," El said.

Two of the General's troops held rifles at the ready as we watched them march out the door. She turned to the rest. "All you so called security people raise your left hands and be assured Tici will shoot any that are not loud and clear. Repeat my words!

"I—say your name—swear to follow the orders of anyone appointed over me so long as they do not violate our Constitution, or standing rules of Council."

Tici was in their midst and assured all took it.

"Breaking that oath for any reason is death, people. I really do not care what you think or want, unless it pertains to the mission at hand. Everyone in this room is your superior just so there is no doubt. Loka and Eldon are the supreme commanders, I am next, the computer called Lucy is now in the chain of command just below me until one of us three removes her. Any questions from anyone will be addressed to Tici—he loves answering them." She sort of snickered as Tici waved his pistol around and asked if anyone was stupid. There weren't any questions.

Lucy said thank you to everyone. "First class is still in the morning." She left, her treads making soft swishing sounds on the smooth floor.

The General told everyone to go to their rooms or explore, whatever, just leave. She called Tici over, her aid Tally never left her side. "Tici, get them to show how to open the ice door and get a chopper here. Tell them, until further notice we want a full complement of troops on each one and get a gear kit for each of those security people. They are in our army now." He saluted and left.

She turned to us. "I know the original idea was to train only a few for security reasons, but if what you all say is true we shouldn't be wasting time. Tici can ensure there are no more spies among them. Or if there are, they can't report anything. No one will keep anything he hasn't examined, and since his specialty is counter intelligence…well, I assure you he is very good at it." She grinned, so did her aid.

"You do understand that a lot of the equipment that is here is still unknown to us. I know for certain that some things can kill. Lucy wasn't kidding there," I told her.

"Yes, actually Lord Pitviper filled in a lot of what was going on once I was selected for this mission. Better to not lay all the cards on the table though. I feel Lucy needs to be warned as well. Only information needed to complete the mission should be given. Seacodent may try anything. A most despicable person."

"I am so advised," Lucy said over the earpiece.

"I wanted to keep Mike alive, he was ordered by Seacodent to sabotage this mission," I told her.

"I know all about it. Shame. He always seems to have his butt covered, barely sometimes, but still."

Loka and I both nodded.

"Well, I am tired and need a shower. I will see you at breakfast. Tici will ensure those two leave when the next group arrive," she said, and left.

We found Susan and she was waiting as ordered, kit in hand. "Tici will see you get where you need to go. Did you know you were pregnant when you first came?" Loka asked her.

"I suspected maybe, but not until I was here and saw Lucy—she told me."

"Okay, Tici will see you get home safe," Loka told her as we left.

Next morning I found we had received two choppers full of troops during the night, another thirty. The General was there as was a new Colonel. They called him Nebulis for short. He had a single arm and limped. As I ate Tici introduced him and two new Captains.

The General finally joined us. "I sent one of the security home on the second chopper. Lazy butt was upset because he had to get his lard ass outta bed at 4AM for calisthenics. The rest will work out fine. Tici, you're still second. The Col is for the Air Wing and supply.

"Oh, Lord Pitviper said the council has placed Seacodent under house arrest pending investigation of charges of sabotage and murder. His seat on Council is temporarily suspended. They may have enough to make something stick, we'll see.

"A second chopper goes into service so expect at least sixty more troops today and another sixty tonight. I talked to Lucy and Tici, we have enough accommodation here to comfortably fit four-hundred so that is where we will start." El sort of smiled.

I talked to Lucy later that day; she was in her new, almost human body again, door repaired and reactor secured and restarted. She assured me all was going well. The General was very capable and Tici was respected and feared by all in the command.

Loka and I were almost put aside as troops came in literally by the hundreds. We both managed to get Tici to accept the idea we wanted to exercise as well and were soon up and running, and straining at 4AM with the rest. Once we had the entire compliment of four hundred, El said a full meeting of everyone would be held by Lucy after breakfast in the big storage room in corridor D, area 7. They mapped out and organized all the rooms and signs posted for the whole gate center. Even I could find my way around now. Loka laughed when I told her that.

We were up at 4AM, exercised until 5AM, showered, fresh clothes, and stood in line at 6AM for one of the four food processors serving breakfast. We now had our own officers table and the rest were constantly being told to eat and make room for more as the mess hall seated only one-hundred fifty at a time. As I sat I realized how effectively and smoothly all was running in such a short period. I just worried the military structure may be a detriment in the long run.

Loka saw I wasn't eating, off in limbo, and asked. I told her and El what I was feeling.

El said, "No, it will be fine. These troops aren't zombies. Each is trained to think for themselves, but also the need for teamwork. Each member will try to do their duty. Failure of a member to do as trained can get someone killed, and all know it. If every officer in our command dies, a Sergeant, or Corporal, or Private, will step forward and continue the mission until it is completed or hopeless." She sipped her coffee before continuing, "Col. Nebulis fought in two of the southern trader wars, wounded five times, and got his rank from being the ranking Sergeant left of a platoon. He fixed bayonets and charged the thieves--they were totally unprepared for such a bold move and the Colonel saved a bad situation. Though severely disabled, he loves the force and Council keeps him on. Yes he knows it and doesn't care, he is a dedicated worker, and that is what we need.

"Tici is the youngest Captain ever. As a Cadet Lt. he was trapped in a small training camp with eighteen others during a western raid. Remember when Seacodent refused to waste money-building defenses? No one would ever attack us from the western desert? He was so positive."

"Tici formed the cadets into a unit and charged the raiders, much like the Col. did. He personally killed four. Anyway, he is my Intel Officer as well as my muscle. A crack shot, and excellent in knife and hand to hand tactics." She finished her coffee.

Lucy came in and some guy whistled at her. She actually got the tin face to smile with its plastic skin stretched over it. Of course everyone knew she was a robot, still, made her day I think.

She sat down and asked if she could speak. "Of course!" Loka said.

"All a bit of a mess, I am learning as fast as I can about armies and command and control, but a lot of the information is scarce. I talked to Lord Pitviper. Council has approved funding to acquire us some fast attack choppers with full missile armament. Four for now. First will be ready in less than a week and all four should be here and operational in a few additional weeks. They are designed to slip through the gate doors and seat four counting the pilot and weapons officer. I sent those plans with you guys when you went back. I sent updates with the various choppers and he said he thinks he can get a working defense station built to my specs in another week or two. It will require assembly on site as needed. Just four rapid-fire 20MM guns mounted on a swivel.

"General El, he sent a private data stick for you. New orders as approved through Council." Lucy handed her a red one. Small storage.

"All the readers work now and I even managed to get an information channel running. I will be playing some of the Honor team's recordings from when they built this place and why and how they brought Olgreender to life as a viable planet. Sorry, no grand plan. They had some trouble with a virus then with the reactor early on and this place was too small to fit the whole 5000 support team—it was why they moved down among you. Best I can find out was they never left, some may have ventured through the other gates but most were absorbed into your culture and as they died off became myths and legends. Like I said, that was two thousand years ago."

"Good, I will make it mandatory for the troops to watch. Does Lord Pitviper have access to this history as well?" Tici asked.

"Yes, he has been fed information as I have found it. Not everything, but the skimmed history. There is over six-hundred years of it here before it just stops. Seems they left three robots to work on the reactor, but it was never restarted until your first team entered the doorway. I found the remains of three teams in the core room and outer control room," Lucy said. "I analyzed the data, and my old robot body, under a simple computer, now holds the core door closed. I thought Mike did it at first. I now think it was why they shut down the reactor initially; the door was sprung. Still is, but a little welding on the floor plates and my old me is pushed against the bottom, securing it. Without the reactor the other gates close and stay closed until it powers up. Your door worked only because this is physically where the Honor Central is located."

"So the gates were never used?" I asked.

"No, they were. They shut the reactor down and built the robots to fix it. I will again guess that the original maintenance robot that comes with the reactor became jammed in the doorway when it tried to close, only thing could spring something that heavy. That was when it shut down. For whatever reason, earth lost track of the door, maybe since it wasn't functional they wrote the team off. The three different robots were not able to secure the door so the reactor wasn't restarted until one of your teams moved the robot and closed the core door before they died. The humans would have known it was death to do so.

"All of you are descendants of biologically adjusted life forms from here and Earth and whatever they did between. Honest, no one is half anything other than normal planet breeding variations among different areas, accounting for food or other environmental issues in your past."

"So we were all monkeys or something that they fixed like they tell us?" Loka asked.

"Well, not monkeys. Haven't found out what yet, but you were sentient, or they wouldn't have bothered. Sorry, really all I know. On Earth they had Neanderthal man, Cro-Magnon man, a few others that were sentient, all became absorbed. I suspect similar happenings here. I'll guess and say you were similar to what you are now, maybe just needed the mental aptitudes and abilities adjusted. There is record of the earliest groups mating with the humans, so I'd bet on it," she said.

"Fine, our history is all screwed up. So what about these damn bugs?" Tally asked.

"If possible we need to gather a couple for study. I want to scout Earth first and see if the MKs in fact left, or exterminated themselves. Also what Earth attempted to do. I don't feel we have time to repeat all their efforts. We need to find a magic bullet. Something that can stop them in their tracks, hopefully destroy them."

"How many planets have tried to find the same thing? Hundreds, maybe thousands? And, according to you, many were 2000 years ahead of us?" Tici asked.

"I know, it sounds daunting. Hell, it is daunting, but what choice do you have? Sit and wait for them to come to lunch on you?" Lucy asked.

"Oh, I wasn't complaining, just wanted to ensure I understood the chance of success is quite nil, is all." Tici snickered.

A few dozen more questions, many with no answers, and we broke for the evening.

Next morning training started in earnest. Lucy and Tici were placed in charge by El and she dared anyone to argue.

Two more chopper loads of people had arrived during the night and even the big storage room was getting full.

Tici told all to listen up as Lucy brought out the vid screen from the lab and she started playing the few battle scenes from engagements with the MKs. A few got sick, but these were trained troops, not scientists.

Tici said, "Watch this next sequence closely."

I'd seen it before, but wasn't sure of his point. A guy with a sword and pistol shot an MK several times and it kept coming, wounded, but not down. The guy, in desperation, jammed his sword from the underside, up through the head, almost right between the eyes. Tici had Lucy replay it several times then said, "Body shots don't do much. It is pretty clear that the head is the sweet spot. Watch the rest and see what I mean."

Tici came back by us as Lucy continued other battles, all confirming the same observation. Though body shots eventually would kill them, only the head shots stopped them quickly.

"Nasty critters. Always was taught to aim center mass of a body. You see it in all the videos, they were trained the same way, and against MKs it is the wrong tactic. Well, we can teach them."

He went along the wall and nailed a couple troops starting to nod off. Lucy sent a message over the earpieces to our command group. I felt empowered! It was Loka, myself, El, Tally, and Tici. "That desert was empty, right?"

Took me a few seconds to realize she was talking about the door we went through. Loka was on the ball.

"Yes, dune after dune, but we didn't go far."

"We need a bigger training area and the sand slows people down and toughens them up faster than any normal ground.

Have El set up a food train from the dehydrated supplies. We move to it starting tomorrow. Only you two, myself, El, and Tici will have the pens. Sorry Tally, you're part of the command group, but not in the command link. Even now I don't think that the MKs have figured out what they are for—might be wrong."

Tally said she fully understood and took no offense.

Later that day Lucy and El went out the door to the desert and Lucy took more sophisticated gear along to ensure our first quick check was still valid. No tech traces were found.

Next morning the troops were lined up in rows of four wide by the Mess Hall and El and Tici were in front. As they marched them down the halls, the whole site reverberated to the unison of boots stomping on the rock floors. We marched to the door-frame and Tici had them charge out the doorway to the sand hell and establish what he called a defensive skirmish line.

A base-camp and perimeter was established and soon they had a blue and gold flag flying on a pole above it. The Council had long ago voted a simple flag for our nation. A plain blue field with a double gold band from top right to bottom left corners. The blue was our purity of spirit and the gold bands were the personal and collective hills we need to climb to seek ultimate enlightenment. The flag was probably the only thing visibly recognizable for fifty miles.

Plans were made, guards posted, travel distance limits set, and soon we had the makings of a proper forward area base-camp.

My years of climbing made me feel fit: well let me tell you the torture of running, fighting, and surviving in the heat and sand made me feel like a rookie that never did anything but lay in the grass and get fat. Dang I hurt, every muscle, every joint, every fiber of my body hurt. Loka admitted the same.

Tici ran around day after day like he was just getting his second wind.

El told us in private that they all hurt just as bad, but Tici would commit suicide rather than admit it. I had to admit, he put up a fantastic front then.

Col. Nebulis stayed behind with a few troops to keep the place secure, sent food packets as needed, and monitored communications with Lord Pitviper. It was felt the heat and sand would probably kill him.

Two weeks went by when Lucy said two new attack choppers were on the ledge, complete with pilots and weapons officers.

El took Loka and Tally and were gone two days. Once through the door, all contact was lost.

El came back out the second day and picked up fifty troops with ropes and moved back inside. A few hours later they were dragging a helicopter out onto the sand.

Loka ran up and gave me a kiss. "Miss me?"

"Na, the other women kept me company." I smiled as she hit me.

"We had to make some special parts. Lucy called them sand filters. She said the engines would be destroyed in a few hours without them. Then we had to train a maintenance crew. Just four people came with the choppers. Spare parts are limited. Lord P said they are working as fast as they can down below. Oh, Lord Seacodent was found guilty on all counts. He has been stripped of all rights and properties and will go to his punishment hearing in a few months. They will offer him life in prison or a quick death. Council finally overthrew the lifetime mate laws. Lord P started the process way back when Cullves came back down alone. Anyway, that is all the news." She put her arm around mine. "Check out these choppers!"

They were narrow and low. They had four blades that the maintenance people were assembling and two skids for a landing platform. Just above those and mounted on little wings that jutted out were four boxes, two to a side. Missile Pods.

El was there and giving us the various statistics on it. Turns out there was a difference between rocket and missile pods and these had two pods of each.

"The second attack chopper will remain at Honor Central as backup," Lucy said.

"Flight time?" Loka asked.

"Four hours in normal flight. Hour and a half under full combat power," El said. "It is powered by two of Lord P's updated turbines but he says the new engines based on Lucy's earth designs should be available with a few more months of development.

"This chopper has a single, remote 20MM cannon with twelve-hundred HE rounds and selective rates of fire, designed for ground targets. The missiles are command guided by the weapons officer and can take out air or ground targets. The rockets are air to air or ground and are fast, mostly unguided fire and forget, with some self tracking abilities like thermal locks."

Lucy said, "I am not yet integrated. I can attach a memory stick and be an observer, but you need further development in microelectronics and control system integration. I suspect by the third generation I will have some decent control."

"This is important?" Loka asked.

"Early AIs worked only along best logical odds, human pilots could often beat them, but as we progressed we were taught that luck and determination can factor in and change outcomes. Fully integrated, I can do 2.3 billion calculations a second and determine odds and allow for luck. As we went Bio we learned the concepts of love, hate and self-sacrifice, so now I almost feel human. I have dreams and fears, as do you. The key is I can control them if needed."

As night approached they finally test ran the engines then secured it. That night we found out what a sand storm was as the wind outside our tents screamed and howled, but by morning it was gone and we sustained minimal damage, mostly digging out from under the piles that the wind left behind.

After breakfast El and Tici and the pilot and weapons officer took off and were gone almost four hours. They refueled as Lucy changed out her memory sick, then they took off again in a different direction. They were back in about two and a half hours.

"Storm coming," El said, as we hustled to secure everything. It was nasty and lasted almost two full days. After lunch of the second day, as it came it was gone and we had to dig out a lot of the tents and supplies. By evening we were as tired as any other and gratefully ate the warm food the cooks served up. Loka said we had a command meeting at the HQ tent in an hour.

Loka and I sat in the back as El addressed everyone. We had battalion and company commanders, platoon leaders, and the command staff, but without Tally.

El walked in as the chatter stopped and most came to

attention. She walked to the front and told them at ease. "Ladies and gentlemen. I have three dispatches here, one from Lord P and two from Council. Lord P first." She opened the folded paper and scanned the document. "I read them already, but this basically says we are to ensure timely reports to him and he assures us he is working as fast as he can to develop what we need."

She set it down and picked up another. "This from Council. I quote, *We declare war on the Morant Küchenschabe and place faith in our God and leaders for our safe and swift victory.* It continues further down. *General Elnaethor Lithlinde has our confidences and shall be supreme commander in our efforts.* That is about it.

"This next one is also Council. It raises me to a three star rank, and Eldon and Loka to brevetted one stars. Tici is now a two Star and Tally a full Col. There are other promotions so I will post the list in the Mess tent. Ladies and gentlemen, we are now an official standing army with an assigned mission. If anyone left here was from Seacourt's group, they will be shot as traitors and spies if they try to sabotage us from this day forward. If no questions, all but HQ are dismissed. Oh, Captain Garth, you are now a Col. also and are in charge of the air wing." She told that to one of the pilots that had come with the choppers. "And here, go post this in the Mess tent." She handed him the Council's promotion list.

After all but us and Lucy and Tici had left, Tally showed and served up some coffee.

El said, "That was the official standings. Eldon and Loka, you needed official ranks so the officers and men would be honor-bound to follow your orders. Lucy, you still have no official rank but there is a separate clause in the first message that I omitted.

Unless you give one of us cause to believe you act for an interest other than the preservation of our planet, you have overall charge of coordinating our war efforts, so you are above us all yet any of us can pull your plug, so to speak. Agreeable to you?"

I honestly thought Lucy would have cried if she were human. "Yes, thank you." She sort of coughed. "I talked to Lord P before we came to the desert. I asked for bigger rifles for the infantry with the possibility of small exploding ammo...we will see. I think another week of this and we retry Earth again. Agree?"

I think we were ready but I had a different idea as the others nodded. "Lucy, might I suggest scatter-guns?" I had to ask.

"Scatter-guns? Oh, you mean shotguns. Hmm, double O buck on a close head-shot would certainly be effective against them, and the aim would not need to be quite as accurate. Excellent idea! Most excellent. I'll see what Lord P can do."

"What about Col. Nebulis? I thought he was Airwing commander," I asked, as it dawned on me what she said.

El hesitated a bit. "Yes, Neb. I talked to Lord P on him. Look, he is a great guy, a dedicated worker and a hero, but he can't hang in that job, he has got to be as tough as we are. I have moved him to supply. He will ensure the proper functioning of Honor Central and start organizing it to serve as a strategic base of operations. It is something he can do without us having to coddle him."

The week was agony, but we adapted. Reconnaissance flights confirmed this planet to be nothing but desert for as far as we flew.

I didn't think I'd get use to saluting, but Loka and I adapted to that, your arm gets tired sometimes trying to return them, but we were honor-bound to do so.

The day came when we withdrew through the door and left the damn sand to the winds. After a week of cleanup and maintenance we again received a shipment in from the ground. Some new rifles, modified shotguns, and hand grenades, along with fresh food and ten more troops. They arrived with the second generation of fighting chopper. Faster, sleeker and could fly almost twice as far as the others. Col Garth was in heaven as he made it a point to fly another trip to ground to get more supplies and ammo. Just a joyride really.

We relaxed a couple days as Lucy and El developed a rough time line and plan. I was reading some manuals on Command and Control Lucy had translated for me, quite a lot involved in running an army it seemed. Food and supplies were a major concern. I found new respect for our forces and all they went through.

We lined up at the bronze clad door to Earth. It was time. Lucy would go in first and disable any robots near the door, then she would have us come in and set a defense. The new rifles had armor piercing rounds, Lucy told us where to shoot to kill any of the 'bots if they attacked. "In the back is a little box, they hook up the diagnostics to it. A shot there will pretty much incapacitate it with shorts as all the systems feed from that point. Try center and below the camera mount from the front, the processor is in that area."

She went through the door and returned about an hour and a half later. "I have disabled all within range of the door, so set up a perimeter and wait as I expand the safety zone and study them."

We moved through the door—nothing much changed, she had immobilized all of the guard robots with the red lights on top, others didn't pay any attention to us at all as we set up a defensive perimeter. It was still a huge warehouse of some type and went as far as we could see in the harsh overhead lighting.

We set up a base camp and the cooks set up a kitchen area to start cooking a noon meal. I was starting to worry as lunch came and went. I asked over the earpiece several times if she was okay and she just said, "Later, busy."

Mid-afternoon she was back with two carts full of equipment and a few robots pulling others. "This place is a gold mine! I found all sorts of things Lord P needs to copy. Col. Garth, can you get these back to him as soon as possible? I even found the manuals with them. Lord P should have the translators built by now." She did her best imitation of a grin. He saluted and picked a platoon to start hauling it back through the honor gate.

"I searched a large area, no control room or panel so far. Need to see where we are on Earth and if there are still MKs about. We should be in the Houston Complex or the English M-7; my records indicate they were the only Honor Gate facilities on Earth. Give me a few hours, I am working the new code I found on several of the storage robots. I think I can deactivate all the guards at once." With that she was done, and just stood there. I knew she was doing her billions of calculations.

Loka and I went to the mess area and had coffee then talked to Garth who came in to grab a cup. "Most of it looks like fancy comm gear and analyzers, but the manuals don't quite make sense to me—it may be the translator. Also something called an official star chart from the International Astronomical Union. I know that because she told me." He snickered. "Well, back to work, that is a lot of junk she has."

Lucy said, "Okay, I'm done. They all have a simple servo controlled internal switch. I think I saw a transmission console panel to the north-east. Be back in a bit."

El came by a half-hour later. "Lucy says all the guard robots are shut down and she is off looking at something she found. We are to haul a chopper through the gate and get it ready to fly."

I looked at the ceiling, maybe ten feet above my head. "To low to fly in here."

"She knows, she is looking for the exit now. This place is huge!"

We went to look at the various stacks of equipment Lucy was sending back, most were strange, yet a lot felt almost familiar as well. Lucy showed up. "Interesting, most interesting. This place is sealed shut. Cancel the chopper for now. All this movement is the robots shuffling things around and around, over and over. I found the original entrance and exits but they were blown shut. Apparently we are under a mountain. I can see why no one found this gate.

"I have a plan to try and get free—it will take a bit. I want to reprogram all the guard 'bots and get them using the lasers on the rock. They are pulsating so they should work, just need the time."

For the next three weeks we shuffled items back through the gate and picked up a few more troops. Lord P even sent some Council members to visit us—most were quite impressed with the size and quantity of equipment stored here as well as the many gates and such in the Honor Center on our planet. I figure we had already jumped two or three hundred years in tech knowledge since we found Lucy and still had another thousand or more to go.

Lucy and El brought us all together. They had developed a basic safety plan to be used on all further expeditions, regardless of where.

El said it was simple, "We go through a gate enmass and secured the immediate area. We then immediately bring forward and build the portable fort we found in a storage room. It was designed to serve as a base camp. Once secure, a chopper could be brought forward and used as a scout ship/gun platform. As soon as it is safe, the fort would be disassembled and moved another ten miles away from our entry point and the point would be hidden as we remove traces of our origin. Just in case we get wiped out, it might help hide where we came from. We can expand from that point as required."

Lucy added, "It was also decided that we will only take two door pens and both will be hidden in print boxes. You haven't seen them, but I found a few. They respond to a human hand on the panel. The MKs would have to have a live human to use it, and know what it is. That way if we are caught or killed they can't get access to the door. It reduces the risk and I don't even know if they can speak yet."

The fort was actually a simple and expandable affair made of lightweight aluminum alloy sections. Each was six foot long and four foot wide and had a thin rubber coating on the inside for grip. There were some that were three foot long and four wide as well so the floor could be staggered for some rigidity. The choppers could haul large stacks at a time. We practiced assembling them. On each side were two short troughs with steel pins and once fitted together a simple chain tie-down was popped into them to secure them tightly together. You laid out as many as you wanted for a floor then, when sized the way you wanted, the wall sections went up.

This was the harder part. We had the plans, they were attached to the fort parts, but we needed better translations. Some of it was confusing. You laid them out like the floor but they had hooks on the ends and pins in troughs on the sides plus a hinged flap with braces halfway up. They were eight foot long. What you did was lined up the hooks with the floor pins then lifted and balanced the section into place. The flap dropped and the two braces locked into holes in the floor with snap-hooks. This braced the wall up and the hinged part was now a walkway four foot off the ground. It was still wobbly. As each section was raised it was locked into the previous with chain tie-downs as well.

The corners were different. Probably the biggest pain. Each corner went up just like the side but they had an inch thick beam welded at a forty-five degree angle and full of holes along its entire length. Where it met the other corner you wrestled and pried to get the two corner sections to line up so you could bolt those rails together with the big one inch diameter nuts and bolts. The only parts not made of the lightweight alloy that I saw were the tie-down pins.

Once all four corners were in place you finally had a stable, rigid box with a firing platform/walkway all the way around it. Each wall's center section had a panel that swung open, it was just short of four feet high, to act as a door which was secured with a dead bolt and had two drop in bars for additional security.

Lucy studied it and the manuals. "Apparently the original

design was done late in Earth's last hours as a desperation type defense position as the instructions are listed as drafts and it is titled, *'Fort, portable defense, experimental, model 6 Alpha'*." It was quickly noted that at eight feet the taller MKs could reach over and snatch you with their pincer.

"But they had something that mounted on top, to the additional hooks, it isn't here and nothing shows what went there."

When we had it assembled in the big room you could stand on the walkway and just clear the ceiling with your head if you were under six feet tall.

El said, "This will be hell to raise in any kind of wind."

Lucy said, "I know, poor design, but the idea is usable. I think I can rework it to make it better. Mainly attach the walls by hinges with a ratchet lock on them. As it is lifted up, the ratchets lock it at that position. In a wind it will prevent it from being blown down onto those trying to raise it. Don't take it, I'll send these plans and my mods to Lord P's engineers and see what they think. I do know it is easily transportable by trucks or choppers so we'll use the idea," she said.

We hauled equipment to be sent back, took manuals and instructions, and we combed and probed and looked for anything to help us. Tici located what I was sure would turn out to be a major find several days later. Behind a huge stack of boxes and machinery he found a door. When he entered he excitedly called us all there.

Turned out it was a suite of offices with a small cafeteria and a room with some beds in it. A single room had video and control panels and switches. It took Lucy awhile to get there, she had been at the other end of this complex. But what we found that seemed to raise the greatest excitement was there were four skeletons, one in each bed and I could tell, they were not any different than ours. Lucy was right, they were like us.

When she arrived she had to start chasing the troops out, word spread like a raging fire as almost everyone in the place tried to see. El finally showed and hollered attention. She took charge and ran all but the HQ group off. "Give us some damn room to work for God's sake!" I wondered which god. Our old First Queen Diboca Honor or the universal one.

After Lucy made an initial inspection El had one of the beds taken into the main warehouse so the troops could see what the fuss was about. I knew they seemed close from the video sticks, but to actually see skeletons gave credence to it.

"Main control room," Lucy said. "Command suites, and a destroyed elevator shaft. I am unfamiliar with the equipment design and there isn't any power in here. Tici, see if we can get some of the maintenance teams to start tracing the circuits and power this place back up, please?

"From the look of it, the bodies show no sign of violence. Like they took a nap and never woke up. Maybe poison or lack of air. I don't see anything written down anywhere—the couple books here are stories and a manual on the shipping 'bots out on the floor. About all there is until I can access this equipment."

Two guards were placed on the door going in and access was confined to the maintenance crews until otherwise amended.

It took four days for them to even find how the power grid worked. In desperation a magnetic pulse was sent through some of the wires and traced through the rocks using sensitive field meters. For whatever reason, the power came from a set of panels almost on the opposite side of the warehouse, bypassing all the main junctions and winding up coming directly off the reactor's distribution panels. The switch had been turned off.

Once they ensured there were no shorts Lucy gave the okay to turn it on. When it was first thrown all the lights in the place dimmed for a few seconds then stabilized. El, Tici, my wife, and Lucy stood in the control room along with two of the maintenance people. At first there was a loud hum then nothing, but six green lights lit on the main console with the big buttons.

"Okay, test one will be the one marked Main Door," Lucy said.

When she pushed the button there was a sort of bang that could be heard, then the soldiers by the big pile of rock swore they heard groans as the lights dimmed and finally the power went off in here again. After a quick check maintenance turned the switch back on. The lights dimmed a second as there was a bang noise, then the lights stabilized again.

"Well." She turned to us. "Door one is the big, main pile of rocks. What I suspect is it opened inward and they blew the entrance to insure it couldn't be. So, I bet door two is the other big one we found."

So it went, she tested three and four which were found to be smaller doors further away, both blocked. Number five she said was labeled E-1 and was the elevator shaft in the back here—there was a clunk, a bang and the circuit reset again.

Number six was labeled E-2. We heard nothing and the light stayed green a long time, then the same circuit reset.

"That one isn't totally blocked," Lucy said. "Have everyone

114

spread out while we reset it and see if we can hear where it is located." She had to do it, and reset, two more times before it was found.

"Here is where the noise is," someone said.

The 'here' was a smaller room as far to the north corner as we could go. It was full of boxes. Lucy said it was marked *breakdown room 37*.

We had the robots and dollies busy all that day and night pulling tons of materials from that room and it was found there was a small freight elevator shaft there—it too was blocked with boxes and it took several hours getting it cleared as well. As the highest boxes came down, so did a square slab of steel. Lucy was the first one to peek above it using a remote camera device. She reported it empty except for a skeleton.

Once we found some braces to hold the floor up, we removed the remaining boxes and Lucy had the robots tow out the braces. The floor of the elevator fell with a bang and we got to look at the skeleton. It wasn't human, it was huge, it was ugly, and it was an exoskeleton. "This, ladies and gents, is an MK." She stepped around it and looked up the shaft, seeing nothing.

Lucy kept everyone back until Loka did a radiation test and it was deemed safe. After maintenance removed the skeleton and checked the old cables holding the floor platform they oiled up the ancient rollers in the corners and pronounced it possibly safe.

We cleared the shaft area and Lucy had someone go push the E-2 button. We saw the cables tighten up, we heard creaks and groans someplace way up the shaft, and the floor started moving out of sight. Minutes later there was a clank and a bang, then, the smallest of light could be seen slipping past the floor-plate around its edges.

115

"Well, for what it is worth, there is the surface," Lucy told us.

Again the place was packed as everyone wanted to see. Tici got them out of the way.

El said, "I want guards with shotguns, rifles and grenades, and I want this post manned 24/7."

"Staff and command meeting, mess hall, now!" Tici said.

Soon we were all there, most with coffee. The place was crammed with officers from Captains up.

El, Tici, and Lucy had been up front talking almost a half hour. El finally addressed the rest of us.

"Okay people, listen up." In the back someone was still whispering to others. "I said listen up, Captain, you need a special invitation to shut the hell up?"

"No ma'am, sorry," came from behind me someplace.

"Today we found two major things. A way to get out of here and the remains of a dead MK. Anyone who hasn't seen it, it sits outside E-2. We also found the remains of humans—one lies on a bunk outside the control center.

"We have been discussing a plan of action. That elevator was blocked to stop the MKs from getting in. Also they blew up all the other entrances. We believe the four skeletons in the control center were the remains of humans who either stayed behind, or hid here. Lucy is working on the records system they used. Seems it is different or was sabotaged, she isn't sure yet. Tici?"

Tici stepped forward. "We plan to send up a work robot to look at what awaits up top. If we find any live MKs we will reseal this place and leave as we came. If it looks clear Lucy will go next and check the immediate area for imminent dangers and if it all still looks good we will send up an armed party and go from there. For now, everyone will pull equipment maintenance and physical training. Sorry, no questions yet, we have no more answers than you do. Dismissed."

"Command staff hold up," El said.

After the rest had filed out, Tici had guards posted at the entrances and our group met near the serving line. Loka refilled our coffee cups and sat down.

El said, in a carefully lowered voice, "There is one item for consideration before we do this. That MK carcass. It isn't a few thousand years old. Lucy dates it at most, two-hundred-fifty, and it looks like it died from a fall down the elevator shaft. There is a possibility Earth is still infested with live MKs so, although we don't want to spread unnecessary alarm, we need to be sure everyone stays sharp."

"The human skeletons?" Loka asked.

Lucy said, "A quick dating test says possibly fourteen-hundred to two-thousand years. It fits."

"Oh, okay."

We asked more questions but realized there were still too few answers.

"Get some rest all, big day starts in seven hours," Lucy said.

Dang, where did the time go? Loka and I retired but she was wound up over the day's finds. She relaxed finally, after she talked herself out. I think we might have gotten four hours sleep.

Thank God for the mess hall and strong coffee as 6AM came far too early. Loka looked at me as we gulped coffee and ate some food. "Sorry dear, didn't mean to keep you awake, it is all just so exciting and scary."

"I know love, I know," I told her, and patted her hand.

At 7AM Lucy had a maintenance robot on the elevator platform and raised it as we all hugged the camera's monitor panel to see.

As it neared the top a door slid sideways and light poured in. The robot moved forward on its treads to the edge and stopped. Lucy said, "Won't work, the ground is broken and too uneven for those treads to navigate."

What we saw was a large, rock strewn, barren landscape with what was clearly a path or road coming from the right and looping around toward the door. However, dotted along it were trees—big ones and young ones pushing up through the piles of broken black stuff. Lucy called it blacktop.

After we all saw what there was to see, Lucy had the robot oil the pulleys and cables it could reach with its long maintenance arm and she had it return below. As soon as she hit the button the door slid closed nosily. "Have to fix that too if we stay awhile," she said.

"Well, they aren't waiting at the front door," El said, and smiled.

After analyzing the video Lucy was next. She took several boxes and placed them around the platform and explained, "This is a camera remote. I will try to stay in view as much as possible. This in the back is a relay for your earpieces, this other is a radiation counter and the fourth is a mini weather station." I had recognized the Geiger Counter thing with its two scales.

We watched her on the monitor as she went walking about. "Almost at the top of a mountain. The top is behind the door, maybe a half mile higher, steep too. I can see why they put this here now." She followed the remains of the road and was soon out of sight. "The road winds down and around a few huge rocks. I am recording this so you'll see it all when I get back. I found one of the entrances, the remains of a sign says *Government Property, Authorized personnel only*. There are two huge doors and a few hundred dead MK carcasses in front of it. This was the main entrance I believe. Let me follow it back down and around. I think I know where this is and it isn't either of the Gate centers."

For an hour we didn't hear a word from her and I was getting worried we'd lost her, but she finally said, "Well, there is no doubt, they nuked themselves and the MKs. There was once a large city a few miles from here. Okay, seen enough, heading back. Loka, Eldon, you there?"

Loka beat me to it, "Yes Lucy, we are."

"Remember how you washed down and tested the boxes at the reactor room?" she asked.

"Yes." I said.

"Well, have everyone stay away from the shaft and find those red fire hose stations. One of you shoot back to Honor Central and pick up a suit and the special soap. I'm hotter than a volcano. I need a couple of those big memory sticks from the bench as well. El, help them please? I should have run the tests sooner. Afraid this body is scrap now. Loka, bring one of the shut down guard bots to the shaft as well. We will have to do another transfer."

Loka and I explained the reactor and how she fixed it and we helped her decontaminate and then transfer. Loka and Tici took off to get the items. I told El to move everyone as far away as possible. I found the only spot nearby that had a floor drain and laid out a hose near it.

"We just need to get me clean enough to do a transfer of memory. Glad I shielded this body now—damn, that was so stupid of me.

"Sorry all. Case of the dumb-ass. Part of the problem of being a reasoning robot is we can reasonably get brain farts too. Okay, I'm back at the elevator shaft, let me know when everything is in place. El, evacuate all but a few dozen troops back to Honor Central. We have most of what we need, and with caution can come back and get anything else but I am afraid the surface will be death for you people, fast or slow depending on how close you get. I know most read the reports. Eldon and Loka were very lucky."

It was several hours before Tici came back with some troops and all the gear. We set up the soap spray and a deactivated robot. We followed her directions because the robot didn't have a memory stick access port. She had us get a special adapter that plugged into the back where she told us to shoot them. At least she had planned for this possibility and Loka knew what to do and where the thing was. The adapter was plugged to one of the computer terminals that had the needed port for the stick. They had brought back two suits so Tici and I were chosen to do the scrubbing.

After the area was evacuated Lucy came down and set the counter over the drain and then went back in the shaft. "Do it first and turn it on."

I did and it took two scrubs before it stayed at the high end of the green. She then stood over the drain and indicated the areas needed. The main access port was below her left breast and when she took the top off it almost looked real. "Going to miss this body, was getting to like it," she said, sadly.

We scrubbed and scrubbed and she stayed in the red. She had me go to the highest setting and yes, it went down a lot when I hit the port area. "Okay, it is just too hot over the large area. Tici, please trade that suit to Loka—she has done this several times and to explain it all again will expose everyone to unneeded radiation."

"No problem at all. She'll be right here."

Twenty minutes later Loka was beside me. "Transfer the sticks from me to the computer adapter. Do it three times, partly because of the amount of info and partly to make a backup. Then, when this shuts down, toss it into the shaft and raise it back up. I have limited ability to speak in that 'bot so after this body ceases to function and the transfer is complete keep those sticks safe until I need the rest. It won't all fit in the guard 'bots memory. When ready, insert stick one, I can tell you when to do number two but will cease to function when it is done. Wait long enough then do the rest. If all else fails, you can go to honor gate and retrieve the old sticks. I will lose all the info from Earth, but still."

Well, the transfer to the guard bot went fine. It could only talk by bringing up sentences on the computer screen. Lucy was fine as we sent her old body up the shaft.

"Reseal it with boxes then have everyone return to Honor Gate and place a radiation warning sign at the gate entrance to Earth," came up on the screen.

As we all returned to Honor Central and sealed the door-frame, Lucy, Loka, Tici, and a few of our engineers went to work assembling another Lucy.

I guess you'd say she was improving with age. It took six

days and what emerged was as close to human looking as you could get—she really looked like the vision she had first showed Loka and I.

"Sexy!" I said.

"Aren't I though?" She giggled. "Command staff meeting, if possible, in thirty minutes please?"

Thirty minutes later El, Lucy and Tici were talking then Lucy took over. "First, I need to apologize to everyone here, I screwed up and it cost us valuable time. What I found, and what I believe, is that the Earth people, in desperation, used nukes, either on themselves to stop from being eaten, or against the MKs, or both. Watch the vid screen."

It was of her trip around the mountain. As she turned down past the main entrance the remains of a large city came to view, twisted, distorted, old remains of buildings. Everything was destroyed, totally.

"As soon as I saw that I knew, but it was already too late. I never turned on the counter. When I did it was off scale. It just didn't dawn on me with the trees and all.

"What this tells me is the MK are either immune to radiation or its effects take longer because that skeleton in the shaft wasn't that old. Without one to test I can't say. Might have been another group came back to see if any humans got away, who can say?" On the video she turned around and passed a sign. All it said was, *'Cheyenne Mountain, authorized personal only'*.

"What I did find that is new is some code hidden in the guard bot. When you are trapped in a little room for days, you search every inch of the room to have something to do and stop from going insane. It is the missing code to unscramble the files in the control center. If it is okay with El, I'd like to take a couple techs and Loka and Eldon and go back to see what we can find. While we are gone I need you to see how Lord P is doing on the portable fort. We need it to push ahead."

"Okay, but take Tici too, he writes all the reports to Lord P on what we are doing," El said

"It is late afternoon, say 6AM in the morning good for everyone?" Lucy asked. No one said anything. "Fine, six it is and Loka, bring the counter, no surprises this time."

We actually managed some real sleep as I had dreams of fighting MKs and saving my lady fair.

At 6AM we were up, fed, and ready to go. As we entered through the Earth Gate Loka said radiation was low in the green. As we neared the E-2 area it started rising to the low yellows and Lucy backed us off. We went to the control room and it was again in the green so it wasn't radiation killed them either.

Lucy spent a few minutes at the power console, by the computer terminal. "Nice, I'm in. Hmmm, interesting. Not quite what I expected but logical. The four here died from a sleeping drug overdose, on purpose. I am recording it. Also I found an inventory list and several messages from the surface, the last was from the town. There is nothing here anywhere about the gate but a few classified files are in code and I don't have the key to break them yet.

"Seems they were responsible for the nuke on the city, I'll wait to show all of you. It is quite a bit." When she was done she said to us, "We need to reseal that E-2 area again. I'll program the work bots to do that and the last thing I want to do on the way out is reactivate the guards."

"Couldn't other parts of Earth be safe from radiation?" I asked her.

"Sure, probably are. It isn't that I'm worried about. The MKs have returned at least once, or are still there. We do not want our presence known. Maybe someday you can go back and check it out but not right now. Right now we still want to stay hidden from the enemy."

It took two days for them to repack the room, then she had them doing like before, moving things just for the sake of moving them. "They have maintenance bots, the whole system is self perpetuating until they run out of parts. They need to keep moving or they will rot in place and cease to function. We need the guards working, just in case."

As we retreated and she sent the robots on their merry way to nowhere, I felt a loss, to know billions of humans died.

Lucy has spent the next three weeks working on the data from Earth. She stood in the Lab staring at the computer terminals, hour after hour and day after day. She was fine, but we checked every once in a while as we continued to train. Lord P had gone into overdrive as he sent more and more equipment to El. The latest was Lucy's modified fort idea. Lord P modified her mods some as well. The ratchets were now two man winches that raised the wall in winds up to thirty-five miles an hour. Also, clipping onto the hooks up top were 20MM gun platforms with nasty spikes around the edges. If you had enough of them you could ring the whole fort in 20MMs. I had no clue how you would reload them, but impressive none-the-less. The reason 20MMs were chosen was because we found and removed tons of the shells from the supplies on Earth along with a few of the cannons that fired them.

We had a command meeting every Monday to plan the week's training. Lucy had not attended any since our return from Earth so it was a shock when she showed up and acted like nothing happened on the fourth week.

"El, may I speak?" she asked, after the meeting was called to order.

"Of course."

"Thanks. I have been very busy redoing all the videos so you can understand them; also it took a full week to decipher the code they used on the files. A very tough one with multiple floating algorithms that all floated at different speeds." She looked to us all and saw we had no clue what she was talking about.

"Earth destroyed itself on purpose. They tried to send some humans out through the gates but both Houston and M-7 were soon overrun with MKs, so they set their own reactors to critical and destroyed all the gates. Why not ours? I found a short passage in one of the classified documents that mentioned the original Honor experiments were at the NORAD defense center because both of the Honors worked there. Apparently the original idea was to use it as some space defense weapon, but it was felt the theory wasn't a weapon, but a means of travel—however NORAD was not seen as the best site. It was not really a function of space defense so it was moved to Houston to be part of space exploration, after both the original teams were lost. It was classified and tucked away and forgotten about."

"How? Well never-mind," El said.

"How can you forget? Simple, they had other gates that worked and drew all the attention. Like a deserted mine, people remember where it is for a few years then it slips from memory since it no longer has anything worth holding interest," Lucy said.

"Now, let me show you the last days of Earth, as seen from the people left behind to push a couple buttons. This is the first day they went underground and the speaker is Captain Danny Levington. A wounded war hero, recuperating at NORAD."

What she showed was a video of someone talking, but you could see that it was dubbed as the mouth didn't quite match the words.

"Hey, this is Captain Levington. Just got word they are taking all the able bodied people and rallying them at Area 51, the secret special operations testing facility north of Vegas. They will try and hold the bugs there. That leaves sixteen of us disabled troops to hold down the fort. It isn't as bad as it sounds. Everything is automated, the supplies come in and go out by robotic trucks. We just watch the skies. We no longer have any anti-missile sites left, just the big nukes. There were too many of them using captured aircraft." It ended there.

"Turns out he was in charge. This is him again a month later," Lucy said.

"Hi, me again, got word the bugs are winning. Col Samuals stopped by to hand deliver the new launch codes and programming co-ordinates. We have to monitor a special freq for an authorization signal. If it comes, it means it will pretty much be the end, God help us."

"Next is a private Denson. As best I can guess it is a month later, he didn't date it."

"The Captain grabbed some grenades and a pistol and took all but us four out front to meet them. We blew the doors after they left like he said to, and have E-2 blocked. He will call from there when he wants in."

"Several days later. Same guy," she said.

"Damn, Captain was never heard from and we just received the launch authorization from Washington. I don't know what to do—we have six hours to get the codes set in and wait for the countdown. I'm thinking they have the bugs cornered and finally going to finish them."

"Seven hours later," Lucy said.

"We launched on time and reported all away. That was when the bastards told us we were destroying cities, with people in them, overseas, and we would soon be destroyed as well. Mutual destruction was felt preferable to being eaten alive. Not sure I'd want either way. Impacts start in twenty minutes."

"This next is the last—I think it was almost a year later. The guy has a beard."

"Private Hamilton here, nothing has been heard anywhere since impact except the chittering of the damn bugs by the main gates. We lost the cameras, just have the mikes. We discussed it and set the bots to move things to keep them functional. I figure we got enough spare parts to last five or six thousand years. I doubt any bugs will ever get in but we can't get out either. The last missile was a near miss on us—it hit the city and rocked the mountain. We drew lots, I will be the last. I will make sure the others are dead before I dose myself up. I don't know why I'm recording it but the Captain said to make records of important things. I guess our deaths are important, at least to me. Goodnight cruel world."

"That's it. There are others from spots in-between but you get the picture," she said. "Oh, wait, the last camera images."

On screen we saw a car driving down the road away from the city then, just a brilliant flash and you actually saw the shock-wave approach, then nothing. For all purposes the world ended.

"The area we were in was not the NORAD center, it was located below it. The elevator that was blown went up to where the launch control and tracking screens were. The bugs made it in there through ventilation systems or something so the privates blew it too as they moved down to the warehouse. Also there are long tunnels between the outer doors and the blown ones we saw inside. No map was included."

"Damn, to know you pulled the trigger on your whole world, shit, I don't think I could do that," Tici said.

El said, "Nor I. I suspect that was why that Captain went out to fight with the rest. They knew they would die, but they also knew they couldn't push the buttons either. What a decision to have to make."

To say the mood was foul was being kind. We now had a clue about what we were really up against, and it was frightening, not exciting.

"I have a lot more, but that is the key information. They lost a major battle that lasted for weeks at the Area 51 site. From what I read, it was the final stand for the United States. There was simply nothing left but a few cities scattered around and from the presidential bunker under Washington, the last word was most of Europe was gone, a few places in the coldest parts were still alive, but the bugs were using cars and trucks with heaters to get to them as well. Seems the cold slows them, not stops them. Oh, they aren't radiation-proof, it just takes longer to kill one than it does humans. Questions?"

She fielded half a dozen then Tally asked one—she so seldom spoke you forgot she was around. "Did you find what they tried to use on them?"

"Yes, I did. Wish I had encouraging news but I don't. Killing them amounts to blowing them up, burning them down, shooting or stabbing them. Earth tried mutated viruses, bacteria, pesticides, even common things like vitamin extracts and sugar and various common chemicals. Some slowed them down, but none stopped them."

"Did they leave or eat each other?" El asked.

"Looks like they might have left; not enough carcasses around to know for sure. All the dead ones I saw were from shots or fights. The ones seen by the main door were from the Captain's group. We couldn't get a real look at Earth to determine much more."

"Weapons?" I asked.

"Chain-guns were effective until the ammo ran out. Same with about everything else. Rockets, missiles, rifles, all were fine until the ammo ran out then they were simply overrun. There were just far too many of them," Lucy said.

I had an idea or two of something that might not run out, but I wanted to mull on it awhile. I wasn't a scientist, just a climber.

Lord P was given the information and was quite vexed we had no known defense.

We were not idle, we continued to train and Lucy took different groups to check the doors when there was time. We had seventeen in all and had searched six, counting Earth.

She said the swamp was in fact inhabited by an early human, almost Neanderthal, very low IQ, aggressive, no signs of tampering by the Earth people. Stone and wood tools.

There was one planet: soft grass, trees, a few old buildings made of mud bricks, no sign of recent habitation nor technology. Lucy took off in a chopper and after following a stream to another small town she beat feet back to the gate and sealed it. She found MK and human bodies. "Fresh, as in days old."

"I saw humans run from the town as we flew over so they hadn't been swarmed, maybe just an advance party. Want to see if we can capture one?"

That sent up a buzz. We all knew it would be up to El. She sat silent for a long time. "Okay, but I think we need some changes to our basic plan. I assume time is critical, I don't want to go against millions, but I am willing to take on a few and see how they work."

We spent the rest of the day, all night and into the wee hours of the morning, getting ideas and plans finalized.

The choppers were ready, the fort was ready, the troops were ready. I wasn't really sure if I was.

We lined up and at the signal Tici ran through the gate with the skirmish troops. I was in the back with El and Loka. Lucy was helping push the chopper to the door. When word came back it was clear the chopper and the rest of the main troops went through. The second chopper was waiting at the gate.

Soon we were all though the door as support dollies hauled the fort sections in. The immediate area was clear so Tici held off and had the first chopper flying top cover. The area was clear as the second was readied. It flew off to the east and came back. It was clear to the objective area.

At that point Tici broke the line and had the troops advancing while the choppers hooked onto the fort panels neatly stacked up, and took off east. They were soon out of sight. Tici set a fast, but cautious pace as we moved east. El secured her link-pen and box and hid them in a rock pile. Lucy hid hers in a small grove of trees near the door after it turned back to ice. We pushed ten miles and Lucy had troops covering our tracks as we moved.

I don't think anyone put up a fort faster. The winches helped a lot and it all came together in a hurry. Once it was up Lucy had someone unload boxes from the one chopper. She opened them up revealing 20MM cannons. She showed us the nasty spiked platforms and then mounted the guns on them, only two per side, but 1200 rounds of HE each—a lot of firepower. People on the walls could fire them remotely without exposing themselves, and reloads were possible, though a bit hard.

During the day we saw clothed people running around. They saw us, but none came near. From what I saw they looked very much like us but had a yellowish skin tone and slanted eyes.

The choppers sat outside the fort with a hundred guards and Tici. Their pilots slept in their seats. Lord P had been steadily increasing our troop strength but El didn't want everyone wiped out so we brought two-hundred-fifty troops. One-hundred-fifty manned the walls and slept on the floors of the fort.

At daylight, after the troops were fed, Tici and El took choppers and went different directions. Lucy was in the one with El.

Two and a half hours went by and both were back. El called a conference and after we showed up she laid it out. "Twenty or twenty-five are located about forty miles northeast of here. I want to move the fort thirty miles closer and reset it. Lucy says the choppers are strong enough that they can hold the fort parts— fifteen troops inside and another twenty brave souls willing to ride on the fort platforms. That would give us seventy to assemble on the spot while the choppers haul more troops in."

We moved, assembled and again we waited. This town had no humans running around—it had humans screaming—but nothing running around. We saw the MKs moving about the buildings and I worried the rest of the troops would not arrive in time to help. It seems the MKs were quite methodical. They were searching every home, every nook and cranny as they moved toward us sitting in our portable fort now just a bit over a mile away from their line.

El said, "I don't know where they came from, but there are more than twenty in that town."

The fort was ready, the choppers had brought in the last of the troops and were ready, and I guess we were ready again, as the last groups moved to form a perimeter around the choppers. Like before about a hundred guarded them.

The screams were causing us all to be jittery but El said there was nothing to be gained by trying to attack the town, wait. Like her I was sure our time to scream would come, and a quick glance over the top said I was probably right.

Lucy and Tici took a chopper on recon to the other side of the town and we heard hell breaking loose. When they came back and landed Lucy called the command group together. "Forget it, they are pulling in thousands by trucks and planes and a few spaceships to the other side of that town. They know we are here and are getting ready for an assault. El, I suggest the choppers start hauling as many back as we can. The rest will have to hold out until we can evacuate them. I'm glad we have a few platform sections left at the old base, it will help."

I saw people scrambling to resupply the chopper and the second was airborne and out of sight as well, but the noise of the rockets or missiles and the chatter of that cannon was unmistakable. The other chopper was again airborne and flew off.

"They are trying to get as many of the transports coming in as they can, but we are on desperate grounds here," Lucy said.

"Okay," El said, "pull back as many as we can. Tici and Loka and Eldon, rear guard, keep the troops in the fort, remove as many of the others as you can. If the MKs get to the gate we go nowhere, we will not open it, we die here instead, clear?" She didn't need to ask.

When the choppers came we packed twenty inside and Lucy even let some sit on the landing skids. Desperate times, desperate measures. Both were gone in minutes. We moved the remainder of the ammo boxes inside the fort and packed it full with the remainder of the troops from outside.

"Here they come!" someone screamed from the wall platform. Tici told us to get everyone organized, as people died or were wounded on the walls we needed to move replacements in.

"Fix Bayonets!" Tici screamed at the top of his lungs. He was on the wall. "20MM short bursts only, weapons free, fire at will."

The chatter of the wall guns were sporadic. As soon as they fired the MKs moved back into town. "Damn," Tici said. After I got up by him, bayonet finally fixed to a needler rifle I was assigned, he said, "Was hopping they would keep coming in a mindless charge. No such luck, they are planning. Only good thing is the two ships I saw were small transports and we destroyed them both."

About that time a weird looking chopper rose from the other side of the village—not one of ours, and Tici said, "Shit!" He stood at the wall. "Get to your posts, no sense all of us being in the same spot."

"All 20s that can see that chopper wait for my command to fire," he said, as Loka and I each took a different wall. I hadn't noticed but Tally hadn't gone with El, she had the back wall, rifle in hand and a fear-filled smile on her face as she saw me. The enemy chopper started shooting bullets, everyone ducked but I heard a couple screams from someplace.

I saw a rocket trail shoot overhead and miss the area completely as Tici told the 20MMs to fire. The entire fort rocked as they chattered. The chopper sort of bounced as a couple explosive HE rounds hit it, then it disintegrated in a burst of fire and smoke and fell to the ground.

About that time I heard the deep whup, whup of more but it was our choppers returning with slung platforms. While all this was going on Tici told the gunners to reload the 20s.

That was the flaw in the system. To do it someone had to stand on the platform and lift the heavy drum top off, then hand load the shells into the firing bins. Fully exposed to anything the enemy had. Some were doing it and it looked like it was going well but one fell forward, off the platform and to the ground outside, dead. Another took his place and finished the job. Our first combat casualty had a nasty hole where his chest had been.

"Sniper, but from the look of it, very slow and only one," the Lieutenant next to me said.

"That is a good thing?" I asked.

"If you're not one of the ones it shoots."

Eighty more troops were hanging all over the two choppers as they hauled them back toward the gate. Tally was in one of them. Lucy was in another one, she assured us the first group was back through the gate. She'd be back as soon as possible.

The next hours were a blur as the MKs finally started making frontal assaults. They were packed twenty and thirty deep, no weapons that I saw, just ringing the fort. As they got close Tici finally told the 20s to fire. They were mowed down by the hundreds, and hundreds more came to replace them. I now knew what area 51 must have felt as their ammo depleted but the MKs just kept coming. All the 20s were empty and Tici had us all doing volley fire. So far it kept them at bay.

"Choose a target, steady your aim, fire! Reload, target, fire! Reload, aim, fire!" But they finally closed on us and Tici said, "Fire at will!" He raised his reloaded ten gauge shotgun and fired off seven shots in a row as the MKs finally hit my wall and we became so engaged I lost track of time and reality.

It was pull pin, throw the grenade, shoot the heads, reload, shoot the heads; when they got to the walls throw a grenade, but they kept coming. Wave after damn wave. I saw pincers coming over the wall, I saw people losing their heads, I heard screams, I saw bodies disappear as the pincers got them—it didn't register. I just kept shooting, reloading and throwing grenades then we heard the whup, whup of the choppers.

They came in and opened fire and hell enveloped the fort as pieces of MKs were raining from the skies. Lucy and Col Garth wreaked havoc on the MKs about the fort. As they cleared the area I went to help Loka—her wall was hardest hit and many of the troops were wounded or dead. She was still okay. Runners were restocking the ammo on the walls and we laid out fresh grenades as one chopper hovered over the fort and lowered a platform inside.

I jumped down and helped load wounded onto the platform. Most were the lucky ones, they had arms and legs or hands snipped off instead of heads. After it was full it landed outside long enough to fill up with troops while the other flew cover. Then we did it all again for the other one. During the lull Tici had all the working 20s reloaded. Again, one person was shot from a building in town but only wounded. She was evacuated as well. Lucy said one more trip, they'd be back soon.

As soon as the choppers were out of sight they attacked again, wave after wave. Again the 20s mowed them down, but again they filled in and kept coming.

People kept running up to Loka and I giving reports and we acknowledged them, but it was almost an auto response. I knew we were running out of ammo and grenades and we no longer had replacements for the walls. We needed to hold on until the choppers returned one more time.

With the reduction in firepower and numbers on the walls the MKs were all over us and we moved to using bayonets as MK heads presented themselves. Loka and I had been grabbing grenades from now empty firing points and between reloads were stabbing and cussing and yelling. I was so tired.

I heard Tici say, "North wall, help!"

I told Loka to stay and several of us ran to help. The MKs had a big tractor looking thing they were bringing up. "Shit," I think I said.

I grabbed a handful of 20 rounds, almost the last, a spill pack of ten. I jumped on the wall and threw off the lid. As I dumped them in I felt pain on my head, but I finished and jumped down. "Don't miss!" I told Tici.

He took the gun control, lined up the sight and squeezed off a short burst, about six rounds of the ten. The tractor thing disintegrated, as in big boom. It was packed with explosives.

Tici fired off the last of the 20mm rounds into a crowd of MKs that gathered to see what was going to happen. Soon they retreated to regroup and we redistributed our remaining people along the walls. I watched as the MKs spread out all the way around the fort, getting ready for another push. I knew in my soul we couldn't hold too many more pushes.

"Here they come!" Tici yelled from the north wall.

I had camped next to Loka—if it was the end, I wanted to be with her. "I love you dear," I heard me say.

"I know, now quit the mushy stuff and let's kick some ass." She smiled as I took the needler off safe.

They hit again and again. Several times we had to fire inside the fort to an opposite wall that was getting overrun. We were failing, we were losing, but they were paying a huge cost for the privilege of killing us.

"Duck!" I screamed, as the pincer snapped shut just above Loka's head, bringing me out of my dream state. I stabbed the bayonet into the under area as we were taught, just between the eyes, it screamed in their weird way as my wife fired at it point blank. We each grabbed another grenade and threw it over the wall; we heard the screams as they went off. Then silence—as they came, they were gone. I didn't think we could last another charge. I checked to ensure Loka was not injured. Runners came by and resupplied us with ammo and the last of the grenades. Finally we had gotten a break in the fighting.

We came looking to find our history, not make it. I stood at the battlements, needler rifle in hand, six grenades lined neatly up along the inside shelf and waited, slowly scanning the horizon for their next attack.

We lost 83 in the last couple attacks. Compiled reports said fourteen were eaten alive, pulled over the walls and pulled apart as we watched, the rest had body parts snipped off, usually the head, or at the waist. If Lucy didn't get back before dark, we would all be dead. As my mind and eyes unfocused I found I again was dead tired. We'd been at it for twenty-eight hours straight counting the planning and fort setup. We had less than two dozen of us left alive. I didn't see Tici anymore. I felt hollow, like I didn't care, as a young soldier said she was scared and asked what to do.

"Fight, we always fight. We make them pay for the honor of killing us. Look at them, they are eating their own wounded just like we thought. Maybe they will get full and go home to sleep." I snickered at her as I wished I could do that.

At first I thought I was imagining it then I knew I heard it. Loka was yelling, "They are coming, they're back!" It was the choppers, the blessed or damned choppers. As they got close Lucy said over the earpiece, "Sorry we are late, had a few dozen MKs we had to take out to get reloaded. They are closing in from all over. Have everyone get down on the floor and keep your heads down. I couldn't see her chopper, just barely heard it above us.

"Everyone down on the floor NOW!" I screamed, and we jumped down off the wall.

"Bomb away, bomb away, bomb away, and bomb away," Lucy said. I saw a series of flashes—even with my eyes closed tight it seemed like a bright light came on. Then we felt the fort rock to the blasts from all sides. My ears hurt.

"Okay, everyone outside that can move, bring the wounded, we ain't commin' back," Garth said.

As I looked up I could see four well-placed mushroom clouds, one on all four sides of the fort half a mile away. Lucy jumped down and carried a small box. She set it in the middle of the fort floor as the last of us left. "Little present for them."

We beat feet with the choppers as we went straight to the gate—it was surrounded with 20s and two-hundred troops. As we landed the wounded went first, then the choppers. The 20s were dismounted and the troops withdrew into the door. The last I saw was an ice-block and the darkness of the door as it closed.

I found out the pain I'd felt when I reloaded the 20 was a sniper bullet that caught my neck. I'd been bleeding inside my armor vest, it had been hidden by the collar and I hadn't realized it. Probably why I was so tired. I guess I passed out.

I opened my eyes and saw a little girl staring at me. She had yellow skin, black pools for eyes that were slanted, and long black hair. Maybe six or seven. I think I groaned as she took off yelling something. I soon saw Loka and eventually Lucy was there too.

"Bit of a scare, love," Loka said. "Should have told someone you were wounded instead of keeping it a dark secret."

I was handed a glass of water by Lucy. "Drink it all, has a bit of pain killer in it," Lucy said.

I sat up, I was on a bed. As I looked around there were others there as well. I focused as I remembered the fight, the wounded, the smell of death. As I finished the water I found I was bandaged around the neck and I told them, "I didn't know. With the body armor on I thought it was just sweat."

"Well, as coated as the floors were with blood I never would have seen it either," Loka said.

"That strange girl, who?" I asked.

"I call her Myla. We inherited several from the village by the gate when we took the first group back," Lucy said. "They call themselves the Hum-Li. I think it means peaceful ones."

El showed up, looked me over and decided I was alive. "You see what happened to Tici, Eldon?"

"No ma'am, he was fighting the desperate fight like we were, then I noticed he was gone. Sorry, I didn't see, we had our hands full."

"Maybe it's better no one saw it. For me anyway." She sighed. "I authorized the children. When our first group came back and we set up skirmish while we rearmed the choppers, a man and a woman showed up at the edge. They never said a word. Each held a hand-sickle but her pleading eyes left no doubt. They wanted us to take their two girls. I nodded and he smiled then hugged me and they kissed the girls and walked back to that first village. They knew death was coming."

Lucy said, "We soon had almost twenty—others did exactly the same thing, came, dropped them off and left, all without a word. Thirteen girls, three to twelve, and the rest boys around the same ages. What could we do?

"As we carried out the final withdrawal we left loaded rifles behind, with bayonets fixed. Wouldn't help them much, except in taking a bigger toll and easing the heart. They were getting them as we put up the gate-shield."

"How many we lose?" I finally asked.

Loka said, "Hundred-three from direct action at the fort and another twenty-six, from shock and trauma and blood-loss."

"But the mission, as to its original purpose, is a success. I have six captive MKs for study," Lucy said, almost a human smile now. "We already shipped four to Lord P for study and I have two here. I have surgically implanted bombs in them. If they get away from our transmitters, boom!"

"Some of Seacodent's old supporters are screaming doomsday all over. Lucky us, few pay any heed now that the boogie monster has been seen and they know it can be killed," El said.

"Damn, how long have I been out?"

"Just two days. We feel time is an enemy as MKs have now been positively identified on three of the seventeen planets we have links too.

I was up and about as I realized three weeks have slipped by. We lost three more from their wounds and I was almost back to normal. Lucy had been feeding the MKs rodents and lizards gathered by Lord P from below. He also sent up some chickens but I have to admit, the soup we made was wonderful.

Two of Lord P's MKs died. From what I read of the report they were basically doing autopsies while they were still alive. True, they are bugs, still...

I mentioned it to El and Loka, and both said the same thing in different ways. The best way to find out how to kill something is to see what kills it. Nothing new had been learned.

I saw the bugs up close. I am sure they appeared just as ugly to me as I did to them. They chittered almost non-stop. I noticed

Lucy had surgically removed their big pincer arms. She stood behind me as I watched them and I jumped through my skin when she said, "I have no idea how they talk. The chitters are never the same. I ran test after test, nothing matches."

Loka came up. "We tried all our viruses and bacteria, nothing works. These bastards are immune to almost everything."

"Well, they are from a different galaxy — either they would be susceptible to almost everything or almost nothing. I think we need to work on finding that 'almost that they aren't', and soon," I told them.

El looked at me a few seconds, then nodded. "I see why Lord P likes you two." She turned and walked off.

I glanced at Loka who shrugged. "I think she was in love with Tici, fearless, young, virile and now, dead. Just a feeling. But she means your curiosity. The way you look at things a bit different than others. Well, enough emotional garbage. I know they communicate somehow, it has to be those chitters."

Loka said we were going to get some food, be back soon. Lucy dismissed her with a wave of the hand as Myla ran over from a corner where she sat in a small chair. I hadn't even seen her. She took Loka's hand and said, "Food?"

We went to the mess hall and ate well. The girl had a big smile as she wolfed down her food. I guess, even on a good day they had little to eat where she was from, or it was different. She talked to Loka like she was an MK, almost non-stop chittering, yet we had no idea what she said, but Loka smiled at her.

Then the girl did something silly that caught my attention. She kept chattering and pointing to her head then to Loka's and laughing. Loka said, "Yes, wish we could speak that way too."

I got on the earpiece. "Lucy! Mental telepathy! I bet they use it to communicate."

"Hmmm, didn't test that, I will see. I can measure most frequencies. Thanks," she said.

"Thank Myla, not me."

Later El said they were going to send all the children down to the capital for proper adoption procedures. Lucy had recorded their language and worked through it enough to start to talk to them, and most, except Myla, were willing to go. She wanted to stay with aunties Lucy and Loka. Damn, it was going to be hard.

Three days, it was only three days before hell erupted in Castle Gods-Cut. Loka and I were carrying out equipment maintenance by the choppers when the call came from El. "All officers to the mess hall—now damn it!"

We beat feet to it along with the rest. It was full. "I won't pull bullshit on you. Lucy was going to tell you but I think it is my job. We now know exactly how they can zoom in on food. People, listen, we have an impossible task ahead. We must, absolutely must, evacuate our entire planet, and do it now, today. I haven't even told Lord P yet. How do we get seven-hundred eighty-three million people off a planet in the shortest time?"

It floored me, I assure you. The buzz started and wasn't immediately quieted by El as it sank in.

"What happened?" Col Garth asked.

"Fucking MKs happened, what do you think happened?" She was almost yelling.

"El, calm down please? We all know that, but why do we

have to evacuate our planet?" I asked.

She apologized and told Lucy to fill us in.

"I ran tests, I know how they communicate with each other. I found how they zero in on food so fast too. They are freaking telepathic, not only that, strong ones. Two or three can project a combined thought wave to...anywhere!"

"You saying they are telling others where we are at?" someone in the back asked.

"Already told. The second we took them to Lord P they were blasting away. Probably are trying from in here too, but they can't. I checked that, and with certainty they can't. The warpfield generator cuts them off totally. They don't know about Honor Gate Central, but they do know about Olgreender, I am afraid."

"How long we got then?" It was Col Garth again, asking the right questions.

"How fast is thought? However long it takes or took to get to the closest place they are and for them to find a way to transport to here is exactly how long we have. And that clock started ticking almost a month ago," El said.

"Damn," Loka said.

"Fits," I whispered to her.

"Plan in effect now — break up, check all the remaining doors, find a planet we can live on and be as far away from them as we can get. Lucy needs night star charts for the remaining ones. I want all the rest checked in not less than 24 hours. We meet again then. Time has started people. MOVE!" El left no doubt what was the priority.

Soon the place was empty but for us, and Tally, and El, with Lucy.

"Too cocky, we were too damn cocky. We should have waited until we knew more about them before we sent them to Lord P. It was my decision and I may have doomed our people to a horrible death." El was almost ready to cry. I saw her emotions were raw and on edge since Tici was lost—this was almost the breaking point. I felt I had to say something.

"No El, you did exactly what we would have done. All our decisions were sound and based on what we knew. Lucy will tell you, she does billions of calculations a second and it didn't cross her mind as being a danger either. The important thing is we know now what must be done, and we need to start this second to focus on saving what and who we can. People first, then anything else we have time for. I need to talk to Lord P. I will break the news to him if you want, but we can't wait a second, or even twenty-four hours to start working on it."

"I am in charge, I will fill in Lord P. Tell Garth to start hauling people up…anyone wants to come from anyplace. Lucy, how many can we feed off the dehydrated supplies stored here?" El asked.

"Why? The machines can make enough to support hundreds of thousands," Lucy said.

"No, we are moving to one of these damn doorways and we have nothing in place for at least a year. Please just answer."

"We have two-million one-hundred-fifty thousand meals, give or take a few hundred. They can be stretched and supplemented to near three-hundred thousand, but I see what you want. I'll get all the molecular compilers on it."

"Lucy, our existence depends on the answer. Are you positive they can't find this place through the generator thing?" El asked.

"Yes, positive, but I see what you're worried about. If we can get everyone moved in time I'll leave it to you and Lord P and Eldon and Loka to decide if we shut it down or not.

"If anyone should have thought of mental telepathy, it should have been me. I'm sorry. Oh, there are several hundred-million of those meals additionally stored in the Earth complex, it was designed to be a nuclear war survival shelter, if we have time. They really were made to last forever." Lucy had her head down when she finished.

"Thanks Lucy, it will all be about time then. Everyone clear out, I have some bad news to tell Lord P and our people below and I don't want anyone here but Lucy when I do it."

"Umm, if we are going to use the choppers to move people tell Lord P to make permanent boxes from fort slabs, and add chairs, lots of them, then they drop off the filled containers of people like freight and pick up the empty ones. They know the weight limits. Only need to touch down for crew change, maintenance, and fuel. Just an idea," I told her.

"Excellent idea," El said.

"It will still take forever," Loka said.

Lucy said, "No, only fifteen point five million trips at forty-five people per trip." Though she snickered it was a sad one.

It was several hours before I had my next brainstorm as I watched Myla. Two actually.

"Umm, Lucy, want to know something I find interesting?" I asked.

"We are busy, Eldon, Lord P is quite upset," El replied.

"Umm, Lucy, want to know something I find interesting?" I asked it again more for spite than dramatics.

"What is it, Eldon?" she finally said, like a busy worker being interrupted by a kid asking dumb questions.

"Myla is a telepath—not only that, it was she who gave me the idea about it, and she gave me the idea of the boxes, and she just gave me the idea of a ruse to try on the MKs. Just thought I'd pass on that I found it interesting."

I waited for the explosion I knew would come. Loka half-smiled.

"What the hell are you talking about?" El yelled.

"I am sitting here watching her now and she is smiling. She knows exactly what we are saying and doing. I think it was why they never talked when they dropped the children off. Though they are capable of speech."

I didn't know El could move that fast as she came crashing into our apartment on the run. We'd left the door open for them. I ran a couple tests on Myla to ensure I knew what I was saying before I pointed it all out.

Lucy was a step behind her.

"Please come in." I laughed.

Tell us what the hell you are talking about, please?" El asked.

"Simple, watch." I handed El a paper after I wrote 4+4 and 2x3 on.

"Myla, I wrote on that paper, hold up your fingers with the answers please?"

She held up eight fingers then closed her hands and held up six.

"Myla, can you read my mind?" I asked her.

She flipped a hand a bit and nodded.

"I think she means some," Loka said.

El said, "I am thinking of a number, what is it?"

Myla shook her head and pointed to me again.

"I am not sure, but she can read mine some, not yours. Myla anyone else?"

"Uncle Garth," she said. "No more."

"El, who did they physically turn the kids over too? You or Garth?" Lucy asked.

"Well, Garth was there. We were trying to get the choppers reloaded."

"I think it was why she was staring at me when I woke, she could sense I was about to wake up. I get her thoughts only when I am calm and pretty much unfocused."

"Well, what is this ruse you mentioned and how will it help?" El asked.

"She thinks they might not come if they think there are only a few of us and that we evacuated to very cold areas."

"Explain?"

"They haven't been anywhere but here and Lord P's estate/lab. Find a really cold spot with a town and pretend everyone is being evacuated to there. Let the MKs see that everything is being emptied and evacuated, then, haul them up in a cage almost as high as you can and let them freeze a bit while they report we all moved to the mountains. Then move them even higher and let the cage fall, with them in it," I told them.

"Let them just die?" Loka asked.

"Sure, their last thoughts will be freezing and falling and all the food is hiding in the cold. Might stop a flood of them all at once; maybe they will just send a scout group first to verify. The thing is it might get us a little more time." I looked to Myla and she nodded and smiled.

I think Loka and I slept a few hours that night, maybe not that long. We sat in the mess hall very early, drinking hot coffee. Somehow Myla found us and patted my hand, then left. "I think your thoughts are upsetting her," Loka said.

"How come she can read me and Garth but no one else?"

"I'm sure if she went below she would find a lot more. Lucy said all minds work at different frequencies and sensitivities. It would be natural that they overlap within the narrow range she says they each produce. Not sure I understand all she says sometimes, but she usually makes sense." Loka drank more coffee and stared off into the netherworld momentarily.

"Will we be able to get everyone that wants to come off the planet in time?" she asked.

"I did some math: let us pretend exactly five-hundred million want to leave. Lucy said about forty-five per trip. That is eleven million and some change worth of trips. Now, if we could land containers on both sides of the ledge at the same time and say average a total of ninety people per minute, not counting any delays, and we have the ability to land them every single minute of the day and night we can deliver seven thousand seven hundred and some change loads per day or about six-hundred ninety thousand people per day. That comes out to over seven-hundred and twenty days or..."

"Or more than two years in the perfect scenario world, and we don't have two years," El said, as she came in and grabbed some coffee.

"Lord P is with Council now, they have been at it all night. He can get the choppers going to us, but it is convincing the people that it is really necessary, that the bugs will really come.

He doubts more than a hundred million will actually opt to leave for an unknown world on the say of a strange robot," she said.

"But they have too!" Loka exclaimed.

"No, no law says anyone can force you to leave your home. So I think what will happen is the factories will all convert to making arms and ammunition for a fight and freely distribute them to the citizenry. It may wake some up and take the threat seriously, might not. By then he says it won't be his problem because he will be long gone." She almost grinned.

"On the good side of the coin, the life mate rules have, according to Lucy, kept our planets numbers small compared to those records she has. She estimated the average planet settled for two-thousand years would have four to six billion people where we have only eight-hundred million." El shrugged. "If that is a good thing.

"Oh, Lucy and you two and some guards are going back to Earth. She can explain how we want it, but that gate will be open indefinitely and I want to be sure it stays safe. She is going to program the 'bots to start moving the food and ammo she found to here until we pick a new home. It will get very tight for awhile." She finished her coffee and left.

I suddenly said, "Lysergic acid diethylamide."

"What?" Loka asked.

"Lysergic acid diethylamide," I said again.

"What is that?"

"I have no idea."

Lucy said over the earpiece, "I do. A Serotonin receptor agonist."

"A what?" I asked.

"It is a drug, a very old one, causes hallucinations," Lucy said. "Myla?"

"I guess, I never heard of it," I told her honestly.

"Hmm, okay, will check on it. Meet you at the gate. El has a security force alerted and ready."

All in all it took Lucy five hours to secure the warehouse again, reprogram the robots and, leaving the gate open, to have them start hauling tons of equipment and food into our small Honor Central.

While we finished that, El had reports and star charts coming in from the gate testing teams. Only three looked promising. Our swamp with primitive life, one with strange plants and animals but it was rejected as being close to other known planets the MKs had already destroyed, and the third was a cold place with a small area for food growth. Minimal known animal life, some birds, rabbit-like creatures, a few rodents, and snakes. No larger ones. Lucy felt there may have been, but they died off as the climate changed.

Lucy looked over the data. "Maybe two hundred-fifty thousand can go there. Wouldn't want more until you know if it is in a warming or cooling cycle.

"The rest would do okay on the planet you call swamp. It isn't, just the area near the door. If the indigenous life doesn't care about being invaded."

"Do you really care?" El asked.

"Not really, unless your people found it a concern. Many planets, including Earth and Olgreender, have been invaded one way or another. They would just be absorbed over time."

"Or destroyed," I said.

"Always a possibility, but those are your options unless the desert planet is where they would rather go to die."

Put that way, her logic was hard to counter. Do or die, simple as that.

"Dissents? Questions?" Lucy asked.

"Um, do we want to go to both and split our forces?" Col Garth asked.

"I'd say yes—if one or the other is destroyed by MKs, our people can still continue," El said.

"True, and for awhile we can actually swap and adjust as needed. We can have some core samples made to tell if it is getting colder or not. All our people will be in for a rude awakening—it will be hard work with almost none of the conveniences they have now until an entire culture is rebuilt." A rare input from Tally, but valid.

Over the next two months the battles over going or fighting raged as families moved through the Honor Central to build new homes on foreign planets. Almost all chose the swamp, warmer, easier to survive.

Many of the climber families and entire villages of the colder regions opted for the colder planet.

We had almost a hundred-thousand on the cold planet and were in the millions to the swamp. Every second of every day Lord P's people flew more and more choppers to haul people. We lost three from crashes in storms and one that simply quit and crashed into the rock wall, far below the ledge, but we kept flying.

Seems less than three-hundred million wanted to leave, the

rest wanted to stay and fight. The entire planet was in overdrive to produce anything to fight with, anything at all. Towns were barricaded and walls built and trenches filled with burnables—it would be a grand fight, we could see that, but it would also be a losing one. A few hundred million against the hordes of MKs that took out billions on Earth alone. Still, I think if I had a home and land, I'd want to stay and try as well.

The MKs that were with Lord P saw the planet being abandoned, and all moving to the intolerable cold. I am sure they sent word. I am not sure what they saw, or thought they did after being fed large quantities of LSD for days on end, or what their last thoughts were as the cage was released from fifteen thousand feet up to fall free where it wished, into the icy valleys below.

We had a little over a year from that day before the first ship was detected by Lucy's new satellite. When it landed near a town, it was destroyed after it was positive they were MKs.

Lord P and most of the other Council decided to stay and die with their people. When he notified Lucy there were MKs, Lucy wished them the best of luck, but as planned, she was closing the gate, possibly forever. It was a sad day as goodbyes were sent back and forth.

After the last of the in air choppers were hauled in, with many more MK ships arriving, Lucy hit the red button on the linkpen and went to the Lab to enter the code that stopped those from functioning at Olgreender's door. She then went to a computer that went to a panel that eventually went to the warpfield generator and programmed it that the door no-longer should be opened. The last thing we did was move a dozen Earth guardbots to the tunnel and they started blasting the ceiling, sealing the tunnel forever. Our last link to our home world no longer existed.

Many cried for a long time, many were sullen as news was passed to both new colonies that going back was no longer an option.

As robots packed the center full of food, ammo, and equipment, people from both groups removed them. Lucy was in overdrive with her two captives to find something, anything, to use against them. She had us all choose which colony we wished to be associated with.

I actually had visited both sites with Loka and Myla and several others. I wanted to go to the planet with the swamp. Loka left it to me so I started to tell Lucy when Myla kept saying no and pulling me away, toward the cold one. Turns out all the children but two wanted the cold one and since Loka has all but adopted Myla now, I told Lucy I wasn't sure but probably the cold one.

"Fine, just need everyone to choose.

"Eldon, I wish we had something to use against them but the bastards are near impossible."

"Well, I am just a dumb climber but might I ask a question?"

"Sure, what?" she asked.

"The needlers, the small slivers. They work well against the MKs until we run out. Don't you agree?"

"And?"

"Well, if what you said holds true couldn't we make a slightly bigger version of them and have them like the chain-guns? Maybe use metal slivers rather than those special needles? I was thinking it all could be done with electricity from the reactor thing."

"And when they run out you're just as dead, so why bother when standard ammo is as effective?" Her look was curious, like she felt I had an answer, and I did.

"I may be wrong but you said the molecular constructors made metal, they made your body parts, and they run from the same reactor, no?" I asked.

I think if she had gears they would have been whirring. "I'll be damned." It took me a second to realize she was gone.

Twenty minutes later Lucy said over the earpieces, "El, I need a dozen electrical and mechanical engineers at the Earth gate as soon as possible, please. Eldon, you or Loka too. Just need one."

It fell to me then. Loka was taking Myla to the cold planet to start building us a home there. Myla even selected the spot, near a river and just at the edge of the growing area. Loka said they'd just be gone a few weeks.

I met Garth at the Earth gate. El placed him in charge because of the mechanical background in chopper maintenance and weapon systems he knew. We went to the Earth complex.

Most of the crew I'd seen and met some time or other. Lucy came up to me and said, "Let us test this idea shall we?"

Two full weeks went by as we disassembled a standard 5.56mm mini gun and replaced the barrels with smaller ones, ones that were just big enough to allow five almost microscopically thin slivers of metal to pass through, then when I thought they were done Garth talked to Lucy and they wound up getting totally redone back to the original barrels. Lucy had Garth machine out rods of a solid ceramic material he'd found. When done she had lasers melt holes through them which took forever, then a resizing rod with abrasives glued to it was sent down them to give them a high polish. Finally they were pressed into the original barrels of the mini guns. Lucy said they were far harder than the steel and it would take years for them to show any wear at all. The goal was to be as close to indestructible as possible.

The next task was the conversion from electrically fired chemical rounds to high pressure air to push the slivers out the barrels. Sounds easy but maintaining a close tolerance for minimal air loss without anything actually rubbing was almost impossible. Lucy finally used some constructors to add molecules and lasers to remove them to get the tolerances we needed. The days slipped by as problems were solved one by one and we finally had a working test model. Two molecular constructors were set up in front of a high-speed belt affair and when ready everything was hooked to computers and the reactor power. There was a huge loading box mounted where the original ammo feed tray was. A huge spinning turbo compressor sat at the back and simply forced air into the firing chamber at an ungodly pressure.

We set it all up pointing at one of the collapsed door piles and Lucy said, "We are ready to test. All personnel move into the control center please?"

I found she had them wire it in through the switches, it was now the main door switch.

"Test in three, two, one, test..." She pushed the button and the lights went dim, then we heard a buzz and everything stopped and the lights went out.

A quick reset of the circuit breaker fixed that as we all went to see what the gun did.

The dust was thick but it had worked for a while. Two feet of the rock had simple disintegrated at the door. The designers and Lucy went over high-speed camera footage that barely kept up with what was happening but they all agreed it was too fast and jammed.

Motors were changed, systems adjusted and we tested again, and again, and slowly the bugs were wrung out and speeds further adjusted. We next had to adjust the constructors—they were making too many slivers and the box overflowed until one of the techs figured out a way to make a sensor that shut it off when full. Took two more weeks and the final design was agreed upon, changes made, and the solution tested. We soon had a design about half the original size, sealed against the dust, dirt, and weather, and was calculated to last for two years firing nonstop before the motors burned up or bearings jammed.

"Now the power supplies," Lucy said.

It boiled down to more of the small F/F reactors like Lucy had used to power her body. She searched all the Earth stores and only found four, but then Garth asked the logical question, "What powers the robots here?"

We went back to Honor Central with tons of equipment and a working design.

After two months of the constructors making parts, and Lucy making more constructors, we finally had two semi-portable needlers. We tried using a single F/F to power them both but it overloaded and shut down so each received one.

I saw Lucy by the old door to Olgreender and asked what was up.

"I have kept track through Lord P of the goings on below. I didn't want to tell anyone, the pain was bad enough when we sealed the door. At first the MKs showed in a few ships, all were destroyed but word got out. More started coming in, more and more.

"About a month ago I received the last communication from him. He said they were out of ammo and the MKs were climbing over his walls. I just came to listen and see if I heard anything. Like you I feel the tragedy. I wanted to see if we might have been in time to send two of the guns to them—we aren't."

"I guess that would be my fault then," I told her.

"How?"

"I thought of the idea when we were back there at Lord P's and I saw what they did to the guard and the other guy, but felt it wasn't the place of a climber to think silly ideas when he was surrounded by such brilliant people as Lord P and you and the rest," I told her honestly.

"Eldon, being smart doesn't, of itself, create ideas. It only helps after the idea has been formed and divulged. In your way you and Loka are as smart as anyone I have met. Your focus is different, you're geared to different paths, but all people are geared to their own paths."

"So it is my fault then? I should have spoken sooner?" I really felt bad now.

"I can't answer that. At the time I probably would have dismissed it. We hadn't run into the MKs yet, remember?"

"Guess we'll never know now," I told her, as I started back to the mess hall. She followed a bit behind.

As I entered the mess hall I was met by Loka and Myra. She gave me a kiss and Myra looked at me for a while as I sat drinking coffee, then she cried and shook her head and ran off.

I think she saw what I felt about the guns idea. I told Loka and she started at me a bit too. "No husband. I don't think it would have mattered at the time. We hadn't even known there was any rush until you figured out how they communicated. No dear, feel sad, but feel happy as well—look how many you saved, how many would have been food."

"But it was Myla telling me. I didn't figure out anything." At that I remembered something else. "Lucy, how do the MKs mate?"

"The female lays eggs and the male fertilizes them. Why?"

"Not really sure yet, but something tells me it might be important. They one on one or do you know something different?"

She looked at me and finally said, "Not sure. I think they don't much care who fertilizes what."

"Okay, thank you. If anything comes to me I'll let you know." There was something in that place I call a brain that wanted out but I still couldn't see it.

As I headed back to the mess hall I found Myla staring at the caged MKs. She was learning our language but she was only a little girl. I asked Lucy to come by. Myla smiled and went back to staring at the two MKs.

Lucy arrived a few minutes later and saw what I saw. "Hmmm. Very interesting. Isn't that what she does when she seems to be reading you?"

I nodded. Lucy called Tally and asked her to bring an earpiece. Soon Lucy had one clipped to Myla and she was talking to her in both English and I guess her own language.

"She is still too young to grasp any complicated ideas, I think, but she sees the one MK is agitated because he can't do something or other.

"She isn't sure what it is. Probably talking to the others. She says they think strange and are hungry," Lucy said.

Parts of it I picked up on my earpiece but she said the child's lack of enunciation skills caused the computer to lose a lot of it.

The next day at Officers' Call El announced that the people of the swamp planet had a small skirmish with some of the indigenous people, won, and set free those they captured after ensuring they were properly fed and that they saw some of our tech advances. Also a vote among them gave the planet the name, Olgreender II. Our cold planet was going to call themselves Niketu, which meant Ice Fields in our old tongue.

She ordered a week off for non-essential staff, which included Loka and me. Since I had not seen what they had done on our cold planet I decided we'd go there. El sent a crew with a chopper to each for transport but we had to be careful. In the end we had eighteen functional and three for parts from the crashes in our attempt to clear Olgreender, but we also had no spares, and other than Earth's warehouse equipment, little to make things with. The loss of Lord P's manufacturing plants and his highly organized supply line would be sorely missed.

The doorway to Niketu was in a cold valley less than a mile from where we had started building our town. It was summer so all the snow was melted in a wide band that averaged one-hundred miles wide at this planet's equator. Our Geologists' quick study indicated the place was coming out of an ice age so that was good news. Lucy confirmed some of her instruments showed large deposits of many minerals and there was no sign of it ever being inhabited by sentient beings.

I was led by Myla and Loka to a simple A-Frame home with a door in the front, two windows built into the roof/sides with strong shutters, and a small window in the back that looked over a garden growing well, but over-run with weeds. Loka admitted they planted it and had to return to Honor Central soon after.

Over the next week we met neighbors, collected some food, wild berries, and a fruit that was sweet and round and grew locally. It had been tested and was safe to eat. I put in a general call to Lucy on the third day and it was another before she heard of it back inside the gate.

"Yes Eldon?" she asked over the earpiece at about three in the morning.

"Lucy, we have an A-Frame house, meets survival needs and is designed to take the harsh winters we suspect they have. Loka did a wonderful job but I was wondering, since we both spend more time at Honor Central than here, and everyone that actually lives here are scrambling to try to survive and develop a viable planet, um, do you have a robot that can be programmed for domestic duties like cleaning and gardening, and canning? I have about two acres of food grown but no people to pick or can it," I said.

"Hmm, well, guard 'bots are out. Heavy ones won't work in the soft ground. Won't be anything soon but let me see what we can do. I suspect you aren't the only one and I should have already thought of it. Olgreender II needs some along that line too for land clearing and lumbering operations," she said. "Got to admit, the loss of Lord P's expertise hurts."

On our last day there a neighbor offered to take Myla in and care for her while we worked at Honor Central. I liked the idea but both Myla and Loka made it quite clear that was not an option. Loka had even slipped a few times and called her our daughter. I know Myla felt the same, at least about Loka.

I thanked them but declined and told them if they knew anyone needed the food they were welcome to pick and can it. He thanked us and said he'd handle it. Turns out he was one of the small group of amateur climbers that tried to get the job when we found Honor Central. He and several others were exploring and had established several mines already. Lucy promised them a powered smelter to allow quicker production, and six of Lord P's best manufacturing gurus had decided to come here—all told, two-hundred came.

"If we can help, relay a message to the gate guards, we'll get it," I told him.

Our week was up, it had been tiring and fun as we set up the basics needed for a home and headed back to Honor Central.

As soon as we were inside El contacted me—Officers call at 6AM for all available staff. Rumor was we were getting more recruits from the swamp and El thought she found a replacement for Tici.

The morning seemed to come earlier than I remembered, maybe it was just getting soft from the vacation.

"Listen up people. This young man here is Captain Korklile. He is my new Second as part of my HQ group. Also trained by Lord P in counter intelligence and assigned by him to us as his last official act before we sealed the gate. I think he will be a help to our efforts.

He was definitely young. If she had him for other reasons I think he'd do okay, but what I didn't like was he was pretty soft. Tici was hard as stone physically as well as mentally.

"Oh, Lord Lansill left Olgreender at the last second—he resides with the Olgreender II crowd and is trying to win election to their new Council. At this time he no longer holds any say over anything, though I am sure he'll try somehow. This brings up a point we need to address. With Lord P gone and Olgreender gone we no longer represent anyone. Olgreender II is still organizing, as is Niketu.

Hadn't dawned on me, but leave it to a general to realize we were basically rudderless. Leave it to Loka to have already thought of it months ago.

"El, permission?" Loka asked.

"Of course."

"Lord P gave me three sticks when it looked like Seacodent wanted to kill them. I gave them to Lucy for keeping. Lucy said she'd get them and be right back."

El said, "While she's gone, here are some figures. Three gates are now down for the duration as far as general movement is concerned. Myla's planet, Olgreender and Earth. Earth because it goes no place and still has a lot of dangerous items. The other two because of the MKs.

"As soon as Olgreender II gets a bit more stable I have been assured they will have a standing army ready of around a million men, many ordered there by Lord P who knew it was pretty hopeless to stand and fight," she said.

Lucy came in and gave El the three sticks. El read the attached notes and called us back to order.

"Well, the first is if he's assassinated, who gets his holdings. Doesn't apply here. The second says 'If the MKs over run Honor Central' what to do. Also doesn't apply. The third says E.E.O. Not sure but I think it means Emergency Evacuation Order. Lucy, play this one please?" El asked, and handed her a stick.

Lord P came on the holographic screen. "I am doing all this in a hurry since Eldon leaves in the morning. If you are seeing this, the unthinkable has happened or you're being nosy. I will assume the first. We are under attack and we have to evacuate.

"Item one is Edict #5 from Council. As most of you should remember from school an Edict suspends all of the individuals' rights during insurrections, riots, or invasions and puts everyone, even us Council, under a unified command designated by this Council until the crisis is over." He held up a paper, very clear, Edict #5, and signed by all the Council members.

"All these are scanned in as attachments by the way. Anyway, if Olgreender has come under attack by the MKs the E.E.O. goes into effect immediately but doesn't involve you really. Council has set up certain mandatory evacuations to Gods-Cut as we feel is necessary to allow our culture to continue. I already have a staff uploading everything we have in our Council library on our planet as fast as we can. Lucy is filing it for us."

At this Lucy nodded her head.

"The lists are at the end as well, but we have preplanned 150 of each of the finest minds in the fields listed. These people are aware and will be on standby, just in case.

"Again, not a major concern to you. What is, after talking to Council, Cullves, and all others involved, it has been decided that Lucy is now an officially recognized sentient being and is given full citizenship with full rights and privileges awarded there-to."

I saw Lucy jump and go strange. I think she would have cried if she could.

"This edict only applies from a time of disassociation with the mother planet, being us, and only until that association is re-established. If it is enforced then she is further designated as Head of Council in Exile until relieved by due process." That was a shock to everyone.

"Edict #5 further lists El, Eldon, Loka, and Tici, as Council members and another two as decided by you." He seemed to pause, thinking, as what he said started sinking in.

"Sub-Council shall still be elected as required to have one per fifty million citizens.

"For Lucy, this places her in charge, but still with no power. Like me, she can suggest and wrangle and threaten, but it is the Council and Sub-Council that make the rules all will abide by." He appeared to stare around the room.

"One more thing. All of Council has agreed we will stay here and fight for our homes, not evacuate, so if any do turn up after this is in force they have no powers at all and should be reminded of their cowardice. A copy of that document is also attached.

"People, I wish all my heartfelt best and know in my heart, regardless of the outcome, all have tried. I have to close now or I won't get it to them before they leave," he said to someone and I saw his wife come in view for a second as the vid shut down.

"Um, wow. Never figured that," El said.

"Told Eldon and will tell you all, Lord P was a very smart man, a lot smarter than many gave him credit for," Loka said.

Once again El took the lead. "Tici is dead so we need three

for Council to form, then have a meeting and install Lucy as official head. After that I suggest we have one sub from Niketu and the rest from Olgreender II elected as practicable. Might I start with suggesting Garth, and I honestly think Nebulis would make a great councilman as well."

Nebulis I agreed with, but another military bothered me a bit. I ran it by them and we argued. "My position is that only Loka and I marginally represent the people, and we have been absorbed into the military as well. At least one should be a true civilian to keep reminding us it isn't all about the MKs—people will live or die on two planets based on our decisions."

I actually won my first political battle. It was set up that a council member would be elected based on both planets' wishes.

Lucy said, "El reopened the desert for sand training for all the new recruits and Captain Korklile will train them for two week periods. Then to Niketu for cold training, then repeat. If we get enough they will start on both and alternate." I knew if it didn't kill him the Captain wouldn't stay skinny very long.

I was coming back from the mess hall after breakfast and again found Myla sitting and staring at the MKs. One was dying and El said both might soon—we had run out of live food to feed them. Fish from the swamp didn't seem to help much. She saw me and I had the distinct impression that once again I wanted to find out about egg fertilization. It had some fear, some dread, but Myla either couldn't understand it or she couldn't get me to.

I called on the earpiece, "El, can I get one or two of Myla's older people that have learned English to meet me in the mess hall in, say, two hours? It may be important."

"Sure Eldon, I'll have a couple rounded up in no time," she sent back.

Myla smiled and took my hand. She pulled me back to the mess hall and she had some toast and juice from the machine and waited. Meanwhile I told Lucy what I was doing—she wanted to be there as well.

Loka found us and as she picked up some coffee I filled her in. "The MK is afraid of something, something to do with the fertilization of the female eggs. I see what looks like a male MK pissing on the eggs, then screams and holds his tool as it turns to powder or something. That is all she shows me, over and over. I don't feel she understands what she is seeing."

It took less than two hours. El showed up with a young man and girl and Lucy was right behind her. El said, "This young man we now call Thomas and the girl Reta, they are brother and sister. He is the younger by a year, she is almost fifteen."

Lucy gave them earpieces and spoke to them in their language then the girl turned to me and said, "Yes, General Eldon, we speak English now. How may we help you?"

"I'm not a...oh, never mind, I am. Forgot. We are doing our best to find out what Myla is trying to tell us—she is trying to learn English but hasn't done well, but she can read the MKs minds, those are the bugs that killed your people. Anyway, can you two see if you can find out what the bugs are afraid of? It has something to do with their eggs, which is about all I get from her."

"Okay, we will if it will help," the boy said.

I had them sit and we gave them some juice as well. They

stared at Myla and she back at them for what seemed like hours.

The girl spoke first. "You are aware, of course, how we humans mate. When the boy releases in the girl the sperm find her egg if one is present."

"Yes," Loka said. "And?"

"The MK male has his orgasm the same way, when he sprays the sperm on the stack of eggs. A grand feeling of euphoria I guess, not being male I can't say. Well, that is what it fears, something that stops that feeling."

Her brother took over. "They ate something, something they now think was bad for them, at least the ones who attacked our planet, but Myla doesn't recognize what it is so I will guess it is not from our planet."

"Whatever it is they fear it," Reta said. "May I ask an honest question about this basic subject?"

Loka said, "Sure."

"I know you used to mate for life and it is now different but among our people we had several mothers for each father. Will this be permitted under your domination of us? It is our way and we have been afraid to ask. We mate starting at fifteen yet they said you wait until you're almost twenty—seems like a waste of a lot of productive years to us."

Hmm, this wasn't even thought of. I was going to say something but El asked the same idea I had, "So you don't have love, the guy just uses the women to make babies?"

Thomas looked at us funny, then Myla, then to Reta, and she said, "No, we love each other. Remember, we use mind speak, we know who we want almost at puberty. The male keeps us happy and provides for us and we in turn produce children for him, to help run the farm until they leave to mate. It has always been thus. I have found my mate, it is Herieum, or Henry to you, on the cold planet. Will we be able to continue our culture or are we doomed to follow yours?"

I finally got a word in, "The male is how old?"

"We must be able to provide and have land to sow. Most wait until they are at least sixteen. I have land already but no home built, so I will probably be late fifteen or early sixteen as well. I have located one mate, but the others didn't get out so I will need to find two more."

They looked at Myla and both laughed. Lucy asked what was funny.

"Myla volunteered to be his mate," Reta said.

"Oh, Myla, wait awhile. Mr. Right will be along in time," Loka said.

Lucy said, "Reta, I am more or less in charge. I am aware of your mating habits, having talked to most of you already. As a machine I more or less know what you mean, but I ask you to give us a little more time to get organized and figure out if we can even survive before we start having new children to have to try and raise. I don't think I would want to bring a child into the world at this time, knowing it might wind up being a snack to an MK, would you?"

All three looked toward each other a while, and the boy said, "We have ways to stop the birth of children among us, if that is your only concern. What we don't have is permission from our current Lords and Ladies to continue with our practices, or even our religious worships for that matter."

Lucy filled us in, "They believe in one God, a good and kind one who made them and told them to multiply and be happy. They also had a basic fiefdom type lifestyle. Kings parceled out the land among themselves and then taxed the normal citizens for the right to grow crops and raise families. It was to raise income to support themselves and provide security. Overall I saw no overt abuses, probably because they could read minds and identify any problems with the people early on."

El was next. "I think this caught us all off guard. We are deep in a destructive war and seriously hadn't contemplated such problems. We have established a Council and as soon as a couple more are elected I promise we will address it at the first official meeting. It is a big deviation from our norm but I think we all are willing to adjust even our own norms of late. I will ask you two and others to speak at that meeting so all will understand and a ruling be made. By the way, with us you have no lords or masters, at all, you are as free as we all are."

"You forget, we read some of your peoples' minds as well, but we will wait and see," Reta said. "Now, back to our enemies. Myla wants to study them some more, neither Thomas or I have seen them, maybe one of us can see something as well. Is this permissible or not?"

"Not only permissible but an excellent idea. Loka, why don't you take the children to the MK; the rest of us will start discussing ideas here. Don't want Eldon cluttering Myla's mind," Lucy told them.

After they left, Lucy said, "Young humans, hormones raging, you're not going to be able to tell them no, and I don't need to be a mind reader to know that. Your people, as a species, are mixed enough you don't have the drive they do, the desire. Oh it's there, just better able to be controlled. In the long run a good thing as it was billions less people to try and save. As to them, they had high infant mortality and they did in fact kill many evil ones as early as a year old. Problem is, will your people be able to accept such barbarity, even knowing it is the right thing to do?"

"How many went to the swamp?" El asked Lucy.

"Three, a boy and two girls, why?"

"Move them all to the cold planet, by force if needed. They can have their own little area and follow both their religion and customs with less trouble from us," she said.

"One problem, there aren't enough girls for that, nor enough of them to sustain a culture as they described," I pointed out.

"I know, if any of our people are willing to join them, fine, they will eventually be absorbed, as were the humans and all of us. Maybe their mind reading will be an inheritable trait to all of us down the line, who can say?" El said.

"Ha, the idea of three wives, jeez, one is enough to drive a man crazy," I said.

"Different cultures is all. On Earth there were several sects and religions who believed in multiple wives as well. If you have high mortality rates it even makes sense in order to maintain a survivable level of people," Lucy said.

I finished my coffee having daydreams I really shouldn't have. El and Lucy were going over our supplies and manufacturing abilities and a long list of things we wished we had but didn't. They were looking for ideas and items that we could use as replacements under the present circumstances.

"Lucy, how can we find out where those MKs came from before they attacked Myla's planet?"

"Not sure, why?"

"This sperm thing. Myla didn't know what they ate that they were afraid of so it was some other place before they got there. Also, whatever planet it was, they obviously identified the problem and left them alone so they will either have been exterminated or left to roam. I think we need to find out which and where," I told her.

"Agree, let the children work on the MKs a bit and let's see what happens. Meanwhile, I want to kick-start the Olgreender II industry. We still need a lot. They found some iron and other metals and most of the basic minerals, and with most of Lord P's experts there it should be a quick re-invent."

"Need help?" El asked her.

"No, keep the new recruits training and be ready to have them move out. I did get one shipment of the new fort parts before the shit hit so I want to adapt the one on Earth to it to give us a new platform. Oh, elections on both planets next week, be sure to vote."

She was gone as El sat there. "Interesting culture Myla's people had, small and agrarian, yet they were fully capable of industrialization. Makes you wonder."

"We industrialized, but we stayed small as well," I told her.

"True, I wonder if somewhere someone didn't see this all coming. Just curious. I also wonder, they were a lot more open with their sexual ideas. Multiple wives instead of the single wife we have. The funny part is most of our men cheated. I wonder if three wives would actually stop that."

"I wouldn't know, seems three would more than cover a man's needs but maybe not his wandering eye."

"Well, I think you know Lord P and Cullves were an item—his wife knew yet said nothing. I think you suspected Tici and me, and it was true. Did you know he was married too?"

"No."

"Yes, his wife flat told me as long as she had him when he was home. Anyway, I suspect most men wander. Have you?"

I remembered the innkeeper at the village but started to say no, then, for some reason nodded.

"I won't say anything. Maybe their way is better, who knows?" El finished her coffee. "Check the chopper maintenance crews for me? I want them ready to go in a moment's notice. Also see if anyone can adapt those heavy ass things you and Lucy made, those needler cannons, to the top of a fort piece without it falling and killing everyone inside." With that she stood and was gone.

I finished my coffee and went to find Garth. He assured me all was in order. I went looking for the new guy replacing Tici but he was in the desert, Lucy was on Olgreender II, so I drifted to the MKs. Myla was looking at them but glanced up at me for a minute. I got the clear impression of a rat-like thing as Reta saw me too and stood.

"Henry can read a little off the other, it is female. This male can't fertilize the eggs so she eats them after she lays them. You're right; it was a small rodent, not of our planet. If they were bitten or if they ate one the male became sterile and unable to perform. The female is seriously thinking of eating him for nourishment."

Henry added, "They are guarding their thoughts now—they sense we can read them; still, they aren't good at it."

"Can you all concentrate on finding out where, from your

planet, these rodents are? How far and how long to get there? Any information will help," I told him.

"We are trying, but our star names and theirs are different. Myra is trying to draw a star map and she will pinpoint it with time, if the female doesn't eat him first. I am trying to get her to think of it but she refuses. Also, she thought of something else, some mineral that burns their mind links, sometimes they use it to numb up sick or dying so the pain doesn't hurt them when they eat them. Really weird beings," Henry said.

"Yes, I expect we are just as weird to them. Keep at it."

I started to leave but Myla grabbed my leg and pulled me down. She kissed my cheek. "It will be okay," she said in perfect English.

Loka pulled me aside as I started to leave. "Henry said the female will most likely kill and eat the other tonight unless we separate them."

"I see no reason to care, other than the information they may have. When Lucy or El get back leave it to them. I need to go to the sand dunes and find El's new lover, dang, forgot the kid's name."

"Korkilite I think, call him Kork," Loka said. "And he's married, don't start rumors."

"Sorry...Um, Tici was too. Got to go, see you tonight." I gave her a peck and she nodded.

I found the kid just off the gate, they weren't doing it like Tici, too close to the gate, but what the hell, they'd get just as sore.

"Have you studied the fort and the mods El wants yet?" I asked him.

"Sure have."

"See if anyone can figure a way to mount the new needlers on them please? If you come up with anything pass it on to El or Lucy will you?" I asked.

"Sure will," he said. "Anything else?"

"Maybe move a little further from the gate is all, but up to you."

"Okay, General, I will, we have no idea what we are doing really."

"Ask the others who trained here already, they can tell you," I suggested.

He laughed. "No one wanted to come."

"Okay, then carry on. If you can move at the end of the day you're not pushing hard enough. I went through it."

"Thank you, sir," he said, and saluted. I returned it and headed back. He was already getting a tan anyway.

That night Myla wasn't there—Loka wanted some personal time so she sent Myla with Reta for the night.

El called a staff meeting for 6AM and it sure felt like it came early. Loka and I were at the mess hall eating when El came in with Lucy and Tally who just returned from a vacation on Olgreender II. There were eight new people I'd never met, though there was a couple I'd seen before at Lord P's compound. She introduced them all as the elected Council members and Sub-Council.

"After breakfast we will hold the first full meeting," Lucy said.

Most ate in silence and a few had small talk, nothing important enough that I remembered any of it.

After the center had finished eating El called the Council to order and had guards posted outside with do not disturb orders unless dire.

"Lucy, call the meeting to order please?" El asked.

"I am Lucy, Head of Council and I call this meeting to order. You represent the remnants of the planet Orgreender now split into Olgreender II and Niketu. We are one Council member short aren't we? The Tici replacement?" Lucy asked.

"Training, not yet ready. Continue," El said.

"Okay. First the new planets—any problems that require Council approval or advice? Call it old business."

A person raised her hand. "Elected Sub-Councilwoman Janice Freedmont. Can we beat these bugs for real or are we doomed like all the rest? Most of us were block moved by Lord P against our will. If he hadn't said it must be done we'd have been there fighting."

It was the first I'd heard of it but I saw no response from any of the rest except Loka. Lucy addressed it. "I am a computing machine, before a couple days ago I'd have said little chance, a chance but not much. Since then Eldon has come up with a weapon that may allow us far better results against them. The adopted child Myla, who Loka and Eldon take care of, has found a sign of a weakness unknown until the last few days as well. I'd say the odds are now better, say 50/50 at the moment, but if what I think may happen does, it could shoot to 80% in a hurry. At this time it is restricted to need to know, not because it is that sensitive but rather that it might give hope that isn't there yet."

"I am James F. Are we also denied that information?"

Lucy looked to El who answered, "All but one of you went to Olgreender II by Lord P's orders. For a while I didn't agree, but when I found out only the people of the Lord whose name no-longer exists in our records wanted to come here I agreed to leave them behind. Sorry to you all, but we needed fighters with spunk, not cowards and wimps so, to my knowledge, not one of his people left Olgreender." El looked around and I saw heads nod.

"That one exception is the rep from Niketu of course, she is welcome as well to comment. Malisa Pitviper Nancing Loganith, do you have anything to say?"

Lord Pitvipers daughter? Didn't know he had one old enough to be married.

"Thank you, not really. Like all of you he forced my younger sister and I off planet. I almost had to come alone—my mate wanted to stay and fight. We had to slip him some knockouts before our flight time." She smiled at that. "Anyway, I promised we'd try our best to revenge his death, my mother's, and all the rest somehow. So, how do we?"

El said it, "You are all sworn to secrecy and know I will kill you if you fail to keep it. We have identified a mating problem among the MK. We are looking into it now, it involves a single rodent from a single planet that seems to have disagreed with them, causing sterility of the males. We have much to do, including finding that planet and being able to find that rodent and see if we can isolate what causes it. Then see if we can manufacture it and spread it somehow, across two galaxies. That is what Lucy meant by changing the odds. Also there seems to be some mineral, as yet unknown, that affects their minds besides the LSD stuff we used—we are again looking into it. We have a problem there, only one MK is left, the other was eaten last night."

I almost smiled then got a shock when she continued, "The

male ate the female while she was laying eggs, and all the eggs as well. He will die soon, as there's nothing to feed it."

Someone raised his hand and Lucy recognized him. "We found some lizards, a lot of them in the woods a few miles north of the forest, out past the swamp. Still a lot to explore but they are a pest there. We are trying to build new factories in that area now. I think we killed a couple dozen and captured a few dozen more, and they seem to average about a pound to two pounds. You're welcome to them; even their hides are useless to us, too thin." He looked around, then said, "Oops, sorry, everyone calls me Tommy the tinkerer. Lord P told me to build the new factories as soon as I could find what was needed for either plastic or concrete walls. We now can make fired bricks and a type of light block from some volcanic cinders we found."

"Thank you, Tommy, we will collect them and see if he finds them to his liking," El replied with a smile. "Glad to hear things are getting done too."

He nodded and sat down.

"Any more old business?" Lucy asked. None. "New business?" All the hands went up.

The next several hours went by with this and that being done on both planets as production and life tried to move on. Most were routine until Lord P's daughter, representing us on the cold planet, asked a question.

"One of the new children, a Reta, has asked permission to marry. But not like we do, she wants to be one of three wives to a single husband. On top of that one of our women wants to be part of it. As if that wasn't bad enough several of our young men say they like the idea and wish to try it as well. I told her no of course, but she demanded I bring it to Council, so I have."

El laughed and said, "Lucy, why don't you call for discussion on that idea rather than dismiss it out of hand?"

"I open the floor to discussion and will allow El to comment first, then I will, then each of you as you feel is appropriate. El your thoughts if you will."

"I say approve it. They don't have the numbers to rebuild their culture or people but let them try. Let our people try too. Look, they read minds, they talk through the mind, I'd give anything to be able to do that. If they interbreed with us either it will spread among us or it will disappear from them but worth the chance."

Lord P's daughter said, "But our men, our home life would be destroyed."

"Look, most of you know me, or think you do," El said. "Let me tell you something delicate. I have polled many of the men. Many. Care to try to guess the percentage that have had an affair while married? So what is being proposed for the young is probably more honest than what it is now. I know us women can accept it from personal experience. I am unmarried but have had affairs with two married men, and I assure you both of their wives know of it, though they don't approve they claim to understand. Don't discount it out of hand, I'm done."

Lucy looked around as hands went up but she stopped them. "I have looked at all of Diboca Honor's tapes now. She was the human in the group who set this place up. Before they came you were a small tribal planet, like those on Olgreender II are now.

"She compiled a lot of data, among it was the fact you had strong males that had from five to ten females they claimed by force as mates. The male protected them and fed them and they gave him children. Once the females were of breeding age young males from other tribes challenged that male for the right to take one to himself, so a male would have to fight once for each female he added to his clan or family. Over time it settled down to around three or four per. Then the Earth people came and they introduced their ideas so you adapted and adjusted to one and one. Then you went extreme and went to life mates. Only recently realizing this was silly." She held up her hand and held silence as it sank in.

"I have studied Earth and all I found was like El said—men cheated all the time. It is not their nature to have one wife: that is forced on them. It is easily the nature of the females to have but one husband so I feel nature has been left out of the equation."

Soon we all had our opinions but the overall belief was to let the young ones experiment while us old fogies stodgily stuck to our current beliefs, wrong or right. Only thing was it was still a no divorce scenario.

On vote, two of the six females voted no, the rest passed it. "Motion carried and approved that anyone 16 or older may engage in this new idea with the understanding it is for life."

A few more problems were discussed over different needs between both planets including food distribution, planting seasons, housing needs and developments, and hospitals finished the meeting.

It was well after noon and most were hungry. As I ate I realized how far we had come from the little bickering pre-space technological planet we had been so short a time ago. How absolutely everything had been turned topsy-turvy by a simple act of saving a computer that thinks she should be a gorgeous human female. How we now battle to save a damn galaxy and still hadn't built a single space ship. I found I was smiling.

Loka saw it and whispered, "You thinking of getting more wives? Forget it!"

I laughed out loud and told her and the rest what I had been thinking.

"Yes, we damn sure have come a long way," El said, as she released the guards to allow people in to eat. "Next Council one month on Olgreender II unless we need an emergency session."

I had my mouth full of food when I remembered, as El was standing to leave. "Wait," I managed to gurgle as I washed it down. "Forgot one thing. They haven't got a single person who is trained in the desert with them out there and he said he had no idea what they were doing."

"Okay, got an itch anyway. I'll take Tally and a couple others and go whip them into shape. You know where I'll be if needed."

I smiled as she left and Loka punched me under the table.

Over the next two weeks we found Myla drew good star charts, the MK liked the Lizards, and El liked her new Intel Officer. Reta and Henry came by and both thanked us—they'd heard about the Council's decision. Reta even agreed they'd be absorbed, as there wasn't anything that could be done about it.

Myla and Reta kept working on the MK but nothing new. A few scientists stopped by every few days trying different minerals and compounds. It seemed the MK knew of it, just not what it was.

The third week we had a break—some bronze sulfate had a strange reaction, a few more experiments and some minerals found in blood were added and we soon had the MKs mind numbing drug. He appeared to almost go to sleep, he seemed to feel no pain, and Myla said his thoughts completely stopped. El was ecstatic over the news. Especially when she was told it was non-toxic to humans.

By the next Council meeting we had a plan, dangerous, but a plan. We took a chopper flight from the swamp exit to the cleared area north of the forest. They had already built several brick and cinder-block buildings. One was a large open room like a factory floor. Tables and chairs were set at one end and rows of chairs were set at the other.

As we went in Lucy took charge. She had been studying our procedures after being appointed to Council. She centered herself and ran the seating of Council in the rear then the Sub-Council by what were now called districts. She passed out an old fashion paper file folder to each of us. Inside were printed papers covering the agendas we were going to discuss and various items requested for rulings from the Council. I could tell by it alone that it was going to be a long day.

Once everyone was in place it was almost 9AM on Olgreender II. We'd been up, fed, and flown in before eight. Lucy called it all to order at exactly 9AM and the building was packed to standing room only.

"Quiet please, quiet," she said. "For all those so inclined a moment of silent prayer. While I say my feelings out loud."

"Oh supreme being, creator of our universe, if you exist, grant us the strength to complete the tasks required of us and let all who have died rest in peace. Amen." I heard a few 'amen's, mine included.

"This Council meeting is called to session. Will the secretary call the roll please? For those not in the know, Col. Tally is General El's Aid-de-Camp and has agreed to fill the roll until one is elected or hired."

Tally ran a quick name call for the record, all but one were present—that one was in the hospital with a bad flu bug the swamp planet had going around.

"Thank you. I will dispense with the last meetings minutes and we have no treasury or bills yet so we can dispense with those. Let us move on to old business please. Anyone having old business among the Council members or Sub-Council, a show of hands please?"

I saw three.

"As I point to you, identify yourself and your business. This is not Olgreender and we don't want or need long-winded, flowery speeches. State it and be done." That got some applause from the crowd.

Lucy pointed to one, who stood. "Councilwoman Delanor, the food supply, winter is upon us and food is tight, are we going to be able to feed everyone?"

El said she could address that so Lucy recognized her. "Ma'am, your people have done miracles, I mean that. This building attests to it. I understand quarters will be tight for the winter as well but accommodations have been made for most of you. I also received and compiled reports of the farming effort. Thousands of acres of land have been cleared, plowed and are ready for seed, another accomplishment of unparalleled proportions. We have in stock enough to make it almost to spring, not quite. However!" She had to raise her voice to be heard over the murmur rising from the audience.

"Please, allow her to finish," Lucy said.

"Thank you, Lucy...however, we have Lucy and her replicators working night and day to make additional supplements. Also I understand the other planet has a slight surplus, we might be hungry but we'll not starve, I promise. Eat what you need, not what you want, and we'll be fine." She sat as the crowd settled down.

"Answered your question, Councilwoman?" Lucy asked her.

"Yes, thank you. Guess we all go on a diet." She snickered and got some laughs.

"I tested them, those lizards you were complaining about can be made into a stew with a few vegetables. No idea what it tastes like—us androids don't eat food, but food is food and it is safe to eat."

After staring around a bit she said, "Closed. Next, you young man?"

"Weapons, we left most of those on Olgreender for the rest of them to use. Oh, I'm Sub-Council Troy."

"Weapons for other than choppers and our troops are pretty much non-existent as stated. Get these factories running and make them, meanwhile improvise with what you have. I also need a million more. I have artillery up the ass but few hand weapons. Does that answer your question?" Lucy asked him.

He stood, said, "Yes, thank you." Then sat down.

"And last, El, you had yours up as well?"

"Yes, I am General El, Commander of our fighting force. When can I expect more troops to arrive from here? Now that winter is coming I suspect it should allow for a large number of idle hands. We train in the desert and small ops to be ready in case. Also it lowers the amount of food required at planet side."

Lucy asked, "Have you ever had a draft?" She addressed it to El.

"Sorry, a what?"

"About what I thought. Open to suggestions but it would go like this—everyone born between the winter to, say, midsummer, goes for two months training in, say, two or three weeks. When they return the rest go for two months, then it repeats keeping all fit and combat ready as well as familiar with any new equipment."

Well, that took an hour to hash out as to age, marriage, exempts for construction or other critical jobs. It finally went to the floor for vote, was passed, then to the people in the hall—they were mixed in view, but it still passed.

"Okay, it shall start in three weeks; all Council will inform their constituents. Last call for old business. None? Okay, on to new business after lunch."

After a meal of soup and a sandwich we were back at it.

"New business?"

I saw a dozen hands. About half involved the idea of changing the marriage rules. Lucy did her spiel, El did one, Reta was called as a rep for her people and explained how they did it. Lucy then brought up the mental reading aspect, that it might be able to be passed to the mixed children. Finally a vote was taken and including all those present it split down the middle with a plus two lead to the yes group—motion passed with some murmurs.

"I will say it again, no one is required to do this, but it can be done if they want. Let me reiterate it is a for life deal, so tell all to choose their paths wisely," Lucy said.

She fielded questions on the MKs, anything new? Any progress in defeating them? Etc. etc. She told them there was hope now, something that was lacking just a few short months ago.

Council wound up appointing committees for building a transportation infrastructure, a farm co-op for sharing the limited machinery to ensure maximum planting and harvesting in the spring, various construction projects. The last item was a monetary system. That was tabled until next full Council meeting.

The sky was dark when we arrived and so it was when we finally left. I know I was tired. We would someday sleep in our real home, not an apartment on Honor Central. Myla was already asleep in her little bed and I think I was asleep thirty seconds after I touched the pillow.

I more felt than knew it wasn't yet 6AM but I was wide awake. It dawned on me Myla was pulling my arm, saying, "Come."

I finally followed her as she went to the MK. It was dead, you could tell. I notified Lucy who came from the lab where she was doing some studies on Earth's old weapons. She went in the cage and verified it was dead. I helped her get it to the lab as she said to Myla, "Thank you, I'll autopsy it and let you guys know at officers' call. Go back to sleep."

I looked at the clock, it was only 2:30AM. Didn't take me long to be assured I was still sleepy, but damn six came very freaking early.

"Headquarters Staff call, Mess Hall," El said.

Loka and I were eating already when it was called. Always six but it actually started after we had our food or coffee, informal and informative, El liked to say.

"As most know already, our last MK died. First it isn't a big deal, we had almost all the information we needed. Second it wasn't anything we did, looks like it had the equivalent of a heart failure. A valve ruptured," Lucy said.

El took it from there. "Using all the charts we have on the area, Myla and Henry felt these rodents are from one of two different planets in two systems that are close to each other. We need to find some way to get to those rodents. We are open to suggestions."

"Didn't Earth have ships?" Tally asked. I knew the answer to that one.

Lucy said, "Yes, they did, all those not destroyed in the war or from the nukes were taken by the MKs."

"Oh, okay," Tally said.

"Well, we can't use Lucy's—she blew it to space dust." Loka laughed.

"No choice, but that was a fine ship."

"How long do the MKs stay after they attack a planet?" I asked.

Once the food's gone I imagine they are too. Why? I know you always have something before you ask," Lucy said. El smiled.

"If so I never realized it. I was asking because we shot down a couple spaceships on Myla's planet when they came in to land, remember? If what you said is true they won't try to fix them. Might be enough of something left to use. You said we needed to get the rodents and they seem to have been at the planet those ships came from."

El said, "Sorry, we can't risk it yet. We haven't the troops or manufacturing capability to mount an offensive."

"Not what I meant. Lucy is a machine, so are the guard bots from Earth—use them, let her go in and see what is what. The terrain was flat and there was even a road near the gate, remember?"

"But Lucy can't battle them alone," Tally said.

"No, see if there is something recoverable and usable. See if the robots can drag it and see if the MKs follow them or not. More a scouting mission. If she is followed she can hide and send the 'bots on alone while she sneaks back through the gate. Just an idea," I told her.

El started to reply but Lucy cut her off. "Excellent idea really, not like I haven't had to rebuild myself before now is it? I'll take two of the guard 'bots but if their treads get stuck I'll disable them and leave them behind. Yes, Eldon, an excellent idea. We need to fly from there one way or other. I'll work a plan with El." She was thoughtful.

"Kork still in desert training, El?" Lucy asked.

"Yes, need him?" she asked.

"Yes please, I want a guard force on this side of the gate just in case."

"Okay, Tally dear, send word to him. Have him pull his entire force back for an immediate mission. Report to me in four hours."

"Yes ma'am, on my way." She was gone at a run.

El snickered. "That girl has too much energy—need to find her a man."

"Okay Lucy, if all goes to plan how long before we may need to see action? They modified the new fort and even found a way to mount four of Eldon's cannons on it, one in each corner. The heaviest weight was the power supply so they have it cabled and sitting in the corners now. We have about one million trained and ready but only weapons for 200,000 troops."

"I think we need a crew of four trained on each 20MM and we mount them on carriage assemblies, like the cannons of old. Some sort of armor shielding for the crews. I'd love a hundred of them lined up in two rows deep and forming a square. One row fires while one reloads. With chopper backup and reloads available we can take out 20 million of those bastards.

"Wait a minute, we only have two of the converted needlers," she said. Why four points?"

"Well, my turn to surprise the robot then. We actually have three now and the fourth sits on Earth, almost modified. I think they just need the ceramic inserts for the barrels and both need power supplies," EL said.

I think she said something like "Hot Damn!" Whatever that means.

By the end of that one single day we had a real plan and it was designed to start to stick it to them. As Lucy said.

Two Earth service 'bots gave up their chassis so we could power the two latest needlers.

Kork showed up, but not the same Kork as before; no, this guy was golden tanned and muscled as much, or more than even Tici had been. Funny what a few months working in the sands will do. I remember the aches. Nah, he could keep it. I saw El's eyes dancing though. She liked what she saw. Wonder if his wife would too?

The plan was simple, maybe too simple. Time would tell. Lucy would take two guard 'bots under her control and try to scout Myla's planet for the downed spaceships and see if we could get to them and recover enough to bother. Kork would have two needlers in the tunnel and ready to cover it if things went bad. Behind them, in the room would be the other two and as many 20MMs as we could fit. Lucy gave El some codes and two of the little cylinders she took from us so long ago. Just in case.

It was all set for two days from now.

Loka called and we went to Garth to find our weapons and ensure we were ready. We cleaned everything, making sure all was functional. I had a chance to look at the modified fort as well.

Each corner of it had been reinforced and had a large slot cut out of it. If we placed the barrel there it could traverse close to 160 degrees and there was a thick shield that hooked to the lower frame of the gun so almost all the slot was protected. Looked good, we'd see how it worked.

The meeting was set at 6AM as always. I had Loka take Myla to our friends' home on Niketu yesterday. She didn't like that at all.

As we sat, coffee in hand and chatting with Garth and Tally, El came in, picked up a cup of coffee and sat down.

Lucy showed at seven on the dot. "Well people, today we know where we stand. I went over all our videos and the placement of the nukes. No, I don't see radiation problems. Maybe a little hot spot where each went off, but they were airbursts. Also the ships we are looking for were far enough away from any of them to be safe. I went over it with El. Loka and Eldon know the procedure if I don't come back. I have an old robot carcass ready in the lab, the sticks are in the file."

"I will try to take two 'bots along but if they get stuck I'll leave them. My plan is to go first to the second village then see what is left of the ships. A quick scout of MK positions and situations, then back here, and we go from there. If I'm not back in two and a half days then energize a new me and we will send it to see what happened and adjust from there. Questions?"

None, a pretty straight forward plan.

At 9:30 she stood in the tunnel, linkpen in hand, two 'bots following her around. We had the guns in place all the way back to the main connector room. "Wish me luck," she said with a smile. A few of us mumbled something and she disappeared into that black wall. Now we sit back and bite our nails.

The day went by with the usual nervousness. Not so much because of Lucy but because it was fairly certain combat actions were going to happen in the near future.

Loka and I spent the day out on the desert planet, not only for some exercise, which we did almost daily, but some combat shooting as well. Kork had built a semi-permanent shooting range there. Paper MK targets were the choice and most had their heads shot off. We both used handguns, our weakest areas. For practice we used some modified 45 cal semi-auto pistols Lucy found on Earth and Lord P had been making. Fairly accurate, cheap to make, and there had been millions of rounds in storage. Officers now had them and swords. Normal troops had rifles of some type and swords were being issued as fast as they could be made. A normal human could thrust a sword or bayonet into either vital spot of an MK if they were close, but the object lesson being stressed was, 'don't let them get that close'.

After spending the afternoon at the range we came back and showered and were in the mess in time for evening meal. El and Tally and Kork had showed, a bit later Garth was there. The chit chat was about nothing being heard from Lucy, everyone being ready, and did Loka and I think Lucy was a bit unhinged, even as a sentient robot.

"Oh, she actually has some quirks and fetishes, but in reality most of us do too," I said.

Loka said, "She wants to feel like a woman, to feel she looks good and that people appreciate her for something besides her brains—exactly the opposite of the rest of us women, but still, it is her. She has never done a single thing that I felt jeopardized our goals."

"She allowed us to send the MKs to Olgreender, resulting in the total destruction of our homes and people," Kork said.

I had to respond. "Look, she had no power then, none. I was there, Lord P told her to send four, so his scientists could study them. Lucy actually suggested they stay here but was overruled by Council. Lord P admitted fault and blame—watch the damn tapes."

El told him to sit down, I was right. Kork apologized, he claimed he didn't know.

El said, "This group is not run of the mill yes sir, no sir people, Kork. You need to learn that. Lucy accepted Lord P as did the rest of us. He selected us to try and save Olgreender and perhaps humanity. We lost our first round, fine, we all are to blame. Now we ready for the second round, then the third. Until we win or lose. If I hear any person on my team ever question the motives of anyone again they will be cleaning shitters on the desert planet until they die of the stench or old age, we clear?" She was glaring at Kork. Apparently she was a real General, she could keep her private life totally separate from business, and she was right of course.

We all let it slide, except Kork. "I just meant it was her final call to release them and she let Lord P take the blame for her bad decision."

No one said a thing as I saw El twitch once. We ate in silence and the day ended with no word from Lucy.

Next morning El had a formal combat officer's call at the mess at 6AM. There was one conspicuous absence, Kork. After we had our food and coffee I found the number of officers had increased significantly. It was standing room only as El rose and called them to attention, and put them at ease.

She said a prayer for us all while we did one silently, then she said, "Ladies and gentleman, we wait for Lucy's return to see if we go to fight again. Fine, we wait. I called you all here to remind you of something. I am second under Lucy, that means what she or I say goes."

She glared around the room at them, then sipped her coffee. Finally I saw her twitch again. "An officer under my command disobeyed my order last night—what it involved and who it was doesn't matter. What matters is when the discussions are over, the plans set, it is far too late to voice your opinion of anything, especially when I said I did not want to hear another word. This is even more irksome when it involves talk of 'shoulda-woulda-coulda' crap. We make mistakes, we all do. The trouble is when we do, people die. All of you will make those types of mistakes and sometimes your troops will die as a result. If I ever hear another person criticize Lord P or his picks and decisions I will put them in the cage where the MKs were and they will starve to death. Anyone got any damn questions?"

Not surprisingly there weren't any.

"Good, there is a new private cleaning the latrines at the desert range, feel free to shit there to your heart's content. Now, get back to your men and be sure they are ready to go. Dismissed!" Guess Kork thought he was immune to her wrath.

After the mess hall cleared, she said, "I refuse to show favoritism to anyone. I mean what I say. Tally, go find me a young, unmarried private I can promote to Captain please? You know my requirements."

"Unmarried?" she asked.

"Yes, tired of having to play games. I originally did it so as to have no attachments. Tici would have been unmarried, his wife didn't leave Olgreender. Anyway, unmarried is fine."

"Yes ma'am, give me a few days."

"Not a problem," she said. "Okay, we still wait until tomorrow noon but I have a gut feeling we are going back to Reta's planet in force."

"I know, my gut has been twisting around all day," Loka said.

"That was that spiced food you ate for a snack last night," I said, laughing.

"Not funny, but I forgot about that. I miss Myla not being under foot."

I wouldn't admit it, but I did too.

We spent the day rechecking our equipment, then on El's orders, as many of the troops as we could handle. I found we were varied as to equipment. Some had shoes, some boots, some had green shirts, some brown. I found one young boy didn't have a uniform of any type. I sent him to Garth with a note. He reported back to me later in the day, a fresh uniform with new boots and even gloves. He was grinning ear to ear.

I had lost track of Loka, she was checking a lot of the others. I finally found her. She had gone to the desert planet, seemed her stomach was creating a lot of aromatic air and rather nasty runs, so she wished to pass them on to Mr. Kork. Women could be nasty, vile, vindictive creatures when riled. Guess it's why I love her.

The day passed and I could see all were nervous. The closer the deadline came the more the nervousness manifested.

After we ate the evening meal and retired Loka was too nervous to sleep so she wanted attention. As we lay there the clock said just short of 2AM when we got the call. "All officers to the mess hall at once. Not an emergency." It came over the earpieces as well as the intercom and I'm sure if we had the reader on it would have been on it too.

As I went in I saw Lucy, well, it wasn't the prim and proper robot we called Lucy but it was still her. Her uniform was in tatters, she was covered in dirt and weeds, and I saw an arm clearly broken. She had seen some rough times.

After El was sure most of the officers were present she asked for a report.

"Sorry I'm not presentable, I'll fix that later. Listen, we need to really try to take back Myla's Planet, for several reasons. The main one is there are only a few hundred there now and they have an operational ship. Additional reason—they have captives. I got banged up falling down a cliff, but I was able to get close enough to see what was going on. They are holding captives and raising animals. I will give my basic impressions but have no conclusive proof. I think they found they can communicate with some of Myla's people. Somehow they were convinced to try and raise food rather than destroy it all. I say that because we know they never did it anyplace else.

"People, I saw some of our uniforms in there too. Whether they were our people or just theirs wearing our clothes I couldn't tell. I saw a lot of hands, arms, and legs missing. We need to either rescue them or kill them. El, take over, you have the sticks with all I know. I'll get repaired. I should be ready in two or three hours." She didn't wait for a response and left.

El called the buzzing to order. Soon she had one of the sticks up. It showed a long range view of the second city. She had both robots in front of her. As they started to get close missiles attacked without warning. Both robots disappeared and she was blown off the side of the road and over a cliff.

She managed to skirt the town to the plains area on the other side. In the middle of the open field sat a large wall of wooden stakes surrounding an area. Like a fort but the points faced inward. A prison. From towers around it MKs fired at anything that moved. Animal or vegetable or machine, they didn't care in the least. She zoomed in the camera as far as it would go but, as she said, you could only make out animals and people, not detail. I estimated the distance from her to the first tower at a little over a mile. As she turned to leave a missile blew near her. I had the feeling the MKs were very jittery, not sure I saw anything that would indicate why.

"The other stick is just the two wrecked ships and the one good one," she said. "Get to your men and get ready to move out."

I finished my coffee and stood to leave and she said, "Wait one, you two." She sat there so we sat back down. "Garth, wait one also, please?"

After most of the rest left, El said, "Lucy said she erased some of it. They have some kids there as well, but they aren't raising them. One a day is eaten. She said they drug a little boy out into the field and several MKs snipped off parts of legs and arms to munch on. The kids' screams got to one who slapped the kid up the side of the head. Lucy thinks it killed him. They slowly tore him apart and distributed him among them. She felt the knowing, which we already do, and the seeing probably aren't compatible."

Loka was shaking and I saw tears. "Probably she was right," I told her.

"We are going to see if we can save anyone. Okay, get ready. I'll meet you at the gate," she said in a dismissive tone.

El was talking to Garth and others in her real battle staff. I heard Lucy talking over the earpiece several times, making clarifications. Seems we were not going to take the spaceship, just disable it. Took me a few minutes to realize why. It wouldn't fit through the gate and we weren't prepared to make a space flight yet.

"Two missions at the same time," El finally said. "Change of plans, officers call on the desert planet first. Sorry, I didn't realize what Lucy had in mind. We still move in about three hours from now. See you all there."

Loka and I arrived with a large mass of Captains and Lieutenants at the weapons range. Funny, Kork didn't seem the least bit pleased to see anyone.

El was already there and so was Lucy. Once everyone had gathered around, Lucy took a stick and was drawing in the sand. "Through the gate and to the northwest five miles is the spaceship, about here." She drew a circle. "We need to get to it. Garth knows what to look for and how to disable it. You people need to cover him for at least twenty minutes. He will remove some parts that will ensure they can't fly it for awhile, if ever. Once that main force is engaged—all on foot by the way—a second group will hit the storage area and free the hostages which are eight miles in and slightly north-east. There are about six miles between the two sites. We need enough time to move them back to safety. My idea is like the evac of Olgreender, the chairs. We can try to get ten choppers in the air and hauling them. Each chopper can cover the rescue until full, then they pull out. I want two of the new guns moved outside to cover the gate and four 20s as well, with crews. We need to secure the gate at all costs until all the teams are back and the hostages rescued." All the time she was drawing lines and circles pointing to the various areas.

Garth suggested we send two choppers with the attack group on the ship. It was all they ever saw before, and it might have them call for all the MK guards and the like. Lucy said fine, it was a six day space flight with a time/space fold to get to the possible rodent planet so if we could kill all of these MKs we'd have time to setup a space plan, but for now the focus was getting the ship disabled and the hostages rescued.

"How many troops for the spaceship?" Some Col. Asked.

"I think 100,000 armed and ready. I want two hundred with us on the rescue, any more and we'll be spotted long before we get in range. And the chopper crews of course. I don't have any idea how many MKs are physically on planet so I want a relief group of 100,000 to be ready to go either way as well," El said.

I raised my hand and waited until finally called on. "El, you realize if we move that many troops and choppers through our little gate that if the MKs are in overwhelming numbers again there is no physical way to get even a small portion of them back through in time and close the gate?"

"Yes General Eldon, that fact was noted and discussed. The planet was not heavily populated and the MKs have veracious appetites so we do not anticipate overly large numbers to be present now. It will be everyone's job to ensure we kill every damn bug we can find and secure the areas until an orderly retreat can be accomplished," El said.

"Just checking, thank you," I told her. She just nodded.

"Any other questions?" Lucy asked. There wasn't any so she turned it to El.

"Good, we start moving in one hour. Myself, Garth and the first through fourth divisions will go to the space ship. Eldon, Loka and Lucy with two hundred men from the fifth will secure the hostages and the remainder of the fifth and the sixth and seventh will guard the gate. I want a full division standing by here in Honor as a last resort. Tally, you will stay here and you already know what to do if they enter Honor Central. It is only a 60 second timer so don't be slow."

That was the nuke to blow the reactor and destroy not only the Center but a good portion of the mountain on Olgreender too. We still had millions of pounds of weapons ammo stored here.

"Good, let's get back inside and in thirty minutes the first troops move. Unless spotted, we will form outside the gate to the west, Lucy's group to the east. We will take a two-hour head start to engage them first, then call the two choppers to attack and start the ruckus. Let's go and good luck to all."

As we headed back through the gate I saw Kork pleading with El and Lucy. I knew in my heart he was not a coward, just a fool. I saw Lucy nod and knew Kork was now going.

How to describe 100,000 troops beating feet? Running from their staging areas on Olgreender II at port arms with full gear, through the gate, through Honor Central and out the gate to Myla's planet four abreast and in perfect unison. Perfection? Pride? Conviction? I don't know, but I sure hope we didn't lose too many. People yelling cadence, troops singing, it really was awe-inspiring.

After more than an hour of them running by it was our turn. To my surprise Reta was there and in uniform. Lucy said, "We need someone who can tell the prisoners we are coming and to be ready. Seems the range is less than a mile though. Still, we need her to explain to her people."

That many troops in a huge square was breathtaking. I could barely hear El screaming to them to 'fix bayonets'.

Lucy pulled our two hundred to the right of the gate, and said, "Listen, all you regulars, drop everything but your ammo and water, and grenades here. Nothing that makes noise—fix bayonets and wait. We will slip along a valley cliff as far as we can go and see what happens with the guards. If we are spotted I don't doubt the MKs will kill them all so we really need to try and get in range first."

Finally the various choppers were through and the blades locked in place. While that was happening El said she was moving out. The massed Army separated into four divisions that spread out a bit and moved out in eight abreast columns that were broken down to fast-march battalions. I noticed each had its own battle standard and El had our blue and gold at the front.

As they cleared the area and we sat waiting, out came the needlers which were set up along each side of the gate. Then protecting them came the 20s and more troops. We moved off a half-mile to give them room as Lucy went through what she wanted. Two wide, hug the base of the steep hill or cliff. Total silence.

Finally it was time to go. As we left, someone on a 20mm wished us luck. I was surprised, we actually were pretty quiet. If anyone was making noise it was Reta, not in shape nor skilled, she stumbled and knocked rocks loose at first but she adapted quickly. I locked and loaded my pistol. As I did, so did the other officers. Better to jack in the round back here than chance someone hearing it later.

We moved fairly quickly and I saw the remains of the second town come into view then slowly recede behind us.

Lucy stopped and said, "We wait to see how El is doing. It is a little over a mile of open terrain now. Who brought the periscope?"

"The what?" I asked.

A bit back behind us someone whispered, "I have it ma'am."

Soon it was up front and Lucy set up this thing with two tubes on it. Took a few seconds to realize how it worked as she set up its little tripod stand. I saw her looking through the eyepieces and making adjustments, and then she told Loka to look.

"I only see a few guards," she said.

"I saw that, but look to the left a little, see that square green thing?"

"Yes."

"That is the barracks. I think there are about twenty guards in it," Lucy said.

Loka finally let me look. A huge wooden fort thing like the video came into view. To the left, about one-hundred yards, a large green plastic-looking building sat with a single MK standing near its door. I saw four guards this side of the compound so there probably were another four on the rear side.

El came over the earpiece as I let Reta look through the scope. "Almost there, so far nothing. I would think as big as we are they'd have spotted us by now."

"Seems they are lulled. They appear lazy over here too," I said.

"Scouts said there are about a hundred around the ship area ahead, maybe another hundred in green buildings behind it. We are spreading abreast now. I will charge as soon as they all get in position. Going to use a U to encircle them. You ready?"

Lucy assured her we were in position. Just waiting to go.

Reta kept watching, and said, "I get a few collective feelings of despair, too far for anything else," she said. "Can't we get closer?"

"Not yet, wait a bit," Lucy said, and took over the scope.

I finally heard shots over the earpiece then the filters cut in and we were in silence but I knew El had started the engagement.

Lucy said, "They seemed to know almost instantly. They are agitated and all went to the green building, more are coming out. Yes, they are sending all but the eight guards to help, I think. They are moving that way. We will give them half an hour head start, and it will be too late to stop us. I want twenty snipers to set up along the crest and cover our retreat. Remember, head shots."

"The two choppers are attacking. Seems there are always a few more of these bastards," El said. I see hundreds more coming up from further behind. We are heavily engaged, Lucy."

"Roger El, I'll give them another five minutes then we move out," she said.

"Good luck, good hunting, out," El said.

Garth said, "All rescue choppers are warmed up and waiting. Estimated flight time of eight minutes."

"Roger," Lucy said. "Stand by."

I saw something different. Lucy took her left hand off and place it in her backpack and inserted a wicked looking half circle knife that I knew was razor sharp.

"Okay, Lieutenant, you in charge of the snipers?"

"Yes, ma'am," a young man said.

"Good, once we free the prisoners you move forward enough to cover our asses, you got me?"

"Yes, ma'am."

El said, "We are at the ship, Garth is now inside."

Lucy motioned us forward. At a half crouch we came over the rise. I think all the MK guards were facing toward the spaceship because we went close to a quarter mile before we were seen. When Lucy said to fire, all the visible guards went down in a hail of headshots. No one came out of the building. Took several minutes for the other guards on the back to get around our side, they dropped just as fast. Lucy then ran at a slow pace, like we'd practiced in the desert.

Reta said she contacted someone. "They are ready. There are still two very nervous guards by the door in the back." She said this while running. Lucky she was young.

"They say all the MKs here are spoiled," Reta said. She wasn't sure what they meant. We had fifty yards to go.

As our front line hit the fort-like structure the two gate guards tried to run. They died.

I couldn't believe the squalor, or the stench from in there.

"Get the Choppers airborne," Lucy said, as she used her hand to slash ropes and ties at both the door and the poles near it. By the time the first choppers arrived we had a good size hole with people near it. Reta told them to wait and few moved. It was eerie to see so many people, some clearly happy, yet not a word except a few of ours talking and yelling. One of them was Tici. He was too far back to see, but I recognized his voice.

As the choppers started arriving we had to help many out, like Lucy said, so many were maimed. We did save some children. Reta spent most of the time telling them we were all here to help, what to do, and crying. I could only imagine the pain she was feeling from them. She did extremely well.

Four choppers in, four loaded without a hitch, then as the fifth landed, one of our outer scouts said a large force was moving fast from the north. Maybe a thousand. I knew it was going far too easy.

As we set a skirmish line Garth took two choppers and engaged them beyond our vision. He reported that about 500 ceased to exist. He came back as another moved to engage while Garth landed and filled up. About that time I saw at least three-hundred MKs closing on us, then, for no reason, they stopped and went off to the west, toward El's group. I guess someone read our thoughts. Reta said, "They are spoiled so don't care."

"Spoiled?" Lucy asked.

"No ability to fertilize eggs."

"Oh, great then," Loka said.

"Some are sempoc also," Reta said.

"Crazy? Really? Interesting," Lucy said.

"Lucy, I have another idea," I said, as it hit me.

"What?"

"Have Reta's people broadcast that the sempoc is caused by a new gene we are adding to all new humans."

She caught on instantly of course and Reta received orders. "Tell them we are spreading it throughout the galaxy through our new gate system." She smiled, then she frowned. "Damn, so freaking simple, all these years and so simple. The billions upon billions that died, for what? Damn it!" She was mad...obviously.

Garth relayed a message; El had been shot in the leg with a 45, from behind. She'd be okay but there would be a new private soon. Only officers carried the 45s.

Although not funny, at the same time it was hilarious. I found I was laughing almost to tears. I think it may have been nervous tension releasing but it still cracked me up.

It slowly dawned on me what Lucy said. "What do you mean?" I asked her.

"Nothing, later, get these people back to the gate," she said, and left with the latest loaded chopper.

Loka gave me a questioning look and I shrugged.

For our group, the rest was anti-climatic. We finished loading all the choppers and withdrew to the gate. As the last of the captives were hustled into the gate El's army called for additional cover for their withdrawal. I told Garth to go ahead and use as many choppers as needed to allow a safe retreat—we were done, mission accomplished.

We returned to the gate and ensured all the people rescued were moved to Honor Central. Except Tici. He asked we say nothing to El for now. Once I finally saw him I noticed he looked terrible. The tips of his right fingers were missing, leaving nasty scars, and he was sickly looking, almost starving. He came up to Loka and I and asked some questions about El and what all happened after he was captured. I filled him in on the rough time line.

"I am not sure what happened myself. I know we were repelling another wave of attacks, and I remember seeing a pincer swinging and that is all. I woke up in a cage with the fingertips missing. They actually knew I was a leader somehow. So why the rescue? I know it wasn't for me, you didn't know I was alive."

"No, it was a twofold plan. We need a spaceship and we found you captives so we sent a main force to disable the ship and a small quick strike force to rescue. Now we need to eradicate as many of the MKs as we can and see if we can get space-borne. All a bit complicated."

"I need to get back into shape. They wouldn't let us do more than stand around, get all the women pregnant, and watch as they ate the damn kids. They used most of us for feeding and raising the cattle, some new plan they are trying. Still, they left at least a hundred-fifty thousand behind when they left. Sure our people can handle them?"

"Have a couple new tricks to try," Loka said with a smile.

"How's El?" he asked.

"Wounded, one of her officers shot her in the ass from behind." I couldn't help it, I cracked up again.

"They did not! She was hit in the leg," Loka told him. "They are retreating back here now. Garth is moving some chopper support to help cover the withdrawal but we will stand here and fight I guess. Not sure what is up with Lucy, she went off in a huff. The comlinks to El's group are down, I think to keep it tight with their elements. We should see them soon."

Almost on cue I could see choppers firing missiles in the distance then, like ants, a swarm of specks slowly were heading our way. As they closed the gap between us I saw they were quite orderly. We moved back out of the way as the leading edge filtered past the ring of 20s and needlers.

A Col. said, "We are to march straight to Olgreender II. General El and five thousand troops will hold the gate. I think we killed at least fifty thousand of those bastards!" He smiled.

Loka told him, "Good job, Col. Now follow orders and get your men safely inside."

"Yes ma'am." He saluted and hollered to his men to keep moving as they went back through the gate to safety.

We wound up moving back and even further to the right as litters started coming in with wounded. It wasn't a sterile fight. Lucy had told us of the perfect fight, which meant it was a totally one-sided fight. You killed the enemy while you lost no one at all. I'd give a very rough guess and say three thousand wounded came by, then several hundred walking wounded, most with gashes and missing hands or the like. Then it was back to regular, orderly troops.

You don't appreciate how many a hundred thousand of anything is until you see them. Battalion after battalion, their individual flags flying, marching by in good order.

The choppers were almost overhead, some shooting, some firing missiles as the tail end of the troops came into view. They were slowly walking backwards, firing into the packs of MKs now also in view, but not the masses like at the fort, more cautious. Near the rear, hobbling along, was El. She had her 45 in one hand and using a rifle as a crutch in the other as she retreated.

As this last group came in toward us, Loka said, "Why not go help her, Tici?" He smiled and took off at a fast pace, he wasn't strong enough to run.

I could see El, then Tici came up behind her to offer support and El shook it off, never turning to see. He tried again and finally El turned, obviously to chew him out then saw who it was and stumbled. Her 45 dropped in the dirt then she recovered as Tici handed her the 45 back and smiled. We were too far away to hear anything but the shooting.

I had Loka position herself next to one of the 20s and I stood near another as the remainder of the troops fell behind the line of cannons.

"Fire!" I yelled, as all hell broke loose. Those 20MMs started exploding among the MKs, the new needlers finally went into action and the MKs actually formed a wall out to the front, a wall of dead getting higher and higher. As the 20s finally ran low on ammo they were pulled back through the gate and it left the two needlers firing nonstop along with, I would guess, 5000 troops as rear guard, we stood and held the gate for what seemed hours. As the 20s came back with fresh ammo loads, the choppers were taken down and moved back through the gate and runners brought more ammo for us. Tally came through the gate and found us about the same time as El and Tici showed. I saw Tally almost pass out when she saw Tici, and smiled.

"El, Lucy said to slowly withdraw everyone and everything and leave the gate open for the last few MKs please."

"What?" I think we all said it about the same time.

Tally wasn't sure either, but she repeated, "She said to slowly withdraw and leave the gate open for the MKs, honest. She wants to try something. The inside is covered with 20s and the other two needlers as well as fresh troops, but honest, it's what she said. She'll meet us just inside."

"No," EL said. "I won't allow those damn bugs inside, I'll die first! I override her now. They still have thousands of them."

"I'll go tell her then." Tally took off at a run back through the gate.

Almost a minute went by and Lucy came out and up to us. "Hi Tici, heard you're back from the dead, congratulations."

"Thanks."

"El, it was so simple, stared everyone in the face daring us to see it for two-thousand years. It was so simple that almost no one needed to have died. The Warpfield Generator, it was all right there and so simple! Trust me, not a single MK will set foot in Honor Central. Pull back and see," Lucy said.

I wasn't sure what she meant, the warp core generator was what kept the gates open, actually created the permanent fold in the space continuum. I was trying hard to catch up on the thousands of years of science we were behind. Still, how could that help?

"Are you sure? No surprises? No bugs popping up and marching through?" El asked.

Lucy looked at us all. "If I am wrong I will sit on top of the damn nuke that blows up Honor Central, with no backups. I am positive! We can even reopen the gate to Olgreender. It was all so simple that no one saw it."

"I don't know—Tici?" El was back to having him around for advice.

"She's been on the up with us, I believe her. Unless something changed while I was gone?"

"No, no changes. Okay." El looked around and talked to her earpiece as I saw officers talking to their men.

"Garth, get the last two choppers back through now."

As they landed the maintenance crews went into action, collapsing the rotor masts and folding the blades over the rear, then placing the little dollies under the skids, and lastly hauling them back through the gate. They were a lot faster than the first time in the desert. Training actually did make a huge difference in time.

All but the two needle guns were moved back, then there was one gun as the MKs came close enough to see the gate. They knew what it was and that it was open so they pushed even harder. Loka and I helped push the last needler though the gate and I turned and watched with El and Tici, Lucy, and Garth. We all waited to see this miracle.

They were on the run, right at the gate. I saw them getting closer and just as they were to burst in upon us they simply vanished. Lucy said, "YES!! I knew it!"

I stood and watched as hundreds and hundreds ran at the gate and vanished. I couldn't believe it. What's more was they kept coming.

"They aren't coming in, where are they going?" I asked.

"Honestly not sure yet, just not here," Lucy said. "Let's get all the wounded treated and get ready to move to the ship. It is an eight man light cruiser so I want Garth, Eldon, Loka, Reta and any other three El wants to send. Leave both needlers here and a guard force but don't close the gate unless something goes wrong."

With that we all withdrew to the Lab. Lucy took El and Tici—she soon had him hooked on the medical machine.

Lucy looked at all the telltales. "He'll be fine other than the fingers. Weak and low on vitamins.

"Tici, what happened?" Lucy asked.

"Still not sure, we were being rushed. I shot a couple then stabbed one, then was knocked out and woke up in that damn cage with a massive headache and short a few fingers. Took me a while to realize these people were telepathic, but two could tell me things after awhile. They thanked us for saving a few of the children, which I didn't know about. They helped keep my hand clean and they told me things about the MK as time went on. We all tried to stop them from eating the children, but it wasn't to be.

"Turns out one of them gave the MKs the idea to raise the cows and such for food. We were just kept alive for slave labor. We cleaned pens, fed the livestock, harvested the crops, so it went. They made us keep the women pregnant and when they birthed the MKs let the babies live until the mother's milk stopped, then the children became snack food. Meanwhile, many MKs left, but the ones who stayed appeared to all be sterile or something. Not sure what it all was about, but apparently something affects them."

"Yes, we know about it. Some rodent they ate on the planet before Myla's. We raided to capture a ship to go find the rodent, see if we can isolate what it is, synthesize it and eventually spread it to all the MK planets," El told him.

"Well good. Glad to hear all the deaths weren't in vain.

"They know of Lucy. I was told about the walking robot that killed. There is supposed to be some special reward for those who capture or kill her."

"Well good luck on that," I said.

Lucy smiled. "We now have two weapons in less than three years to use against them. More than all humanity had for two thousand."

"Two?" Tici asked.

"Yes, I didn't have time to explain to anyone. Not sure if it just popped in or one of Myla's people put it there. The Honor Gates are all programmed. Once I saw it, it was so simple!" Lucy was beaming. "Why don't poison gases or deadly viruses come through the gates from all the planets we visited?" She only glanced around a second, sure we had no clue.

"Because the gates are programmed through the Warpfield Generators to only allow certain biological life and non-bio materials through. It is all based on their chains of DNA and chemical compounds. It stops anti-matter, known deadly viruses, poisons, all things dangerous to the inventors at the time of invention, which was the pre-MK period.

"All I did was tell the warp generator that the MKs' DNA strands were dangerous and needed to go to very cold places where they belonged. By that I mean the middle of space. Since they aren't cold proof it means instant annihilation where ever they went because the generator doesn't care."

"If it was that simple why didn't others think of it?" Loka asked.

"The group that made this gate center here did. Remember they had a virus they were worried about spreading to Earth, but they couldn't identify it. A virus is a non-living thing that hides inside a cell and replicates, eventually killing the cell. Honor and her group were stranded here until they could isolate and block it, then they had the reactor trouble, it piled on and effectively prevented their return to Earth. She knew how, but she died here, her Center isolated from the rest of the galaxy.

"When the MKs showed up through the other gates everyone panicked, blowing the gates in fear. If they would have just shut off the warpfield generators and thought on it awhile, someone would have realized it, I'm sure. Still, all it would have done is slowed them down, forcing them to use regular ships."

"So what do we do?" El asked finally, coming back to join reality as a medic cleaned and bandaged her wound. The bullet passed through her leg and did little serious damage.

Lucy thought a second, doing her billion or so functions. "We find that rodent, identify what it is that sterilizes the MKs and see if it is safe for you humanoids. If it is, we start plans to seed our galaxy, then theirs, and hope they find no cure before they become extinct. That is the basic plan."

"Hm, no way," I said. I think they all looked at me so I explained. "We were barely into space before Lucy came. We have come a long way, but we no longer have Lord P's factories, we have no ability to replace them yet, and we are one small group of humans. You want us to take on two galaxies with one small ship?"

Lucy said, "You're right, but we aren't alone out there. Before we crashed I received a flash of various groups on other planets from the records. I know they exist, but I didn't have time or room to upload it all. I barely had time to get me uploaded. No, we need to find what it is that hurts them and try to get the word out. We can also open more gates now. I just need a few scientists versed in the theories of the Honor search procedures and a smidgen in Warpfield Dynamics would help.

"First we need to go find that rat. That is a major key to getting our galaxy back.

"Have the MKs quit attacking the gate?" she asked.

El was on her earpiece talking. "Looks like it. They think the last ran through it about ten minutes ago."

"Good, have Garth take a couple choppers out to make sure. I don't know how far away any planets the MK own are, so we need to press the advantage. I am pretty sure the MKs, realizing fresh meat waited, did not hesitate to send all of them through the gate. I am also sure they blasted the message to the rest of the universe as well so we need to try and get the rodent. If any are alive we need to capture them and beat the MKs back here to the gate," Lucy said. Clearly she now had a full plan developed.

"Hmm, that warp thing you did, it works on all the gates or just the one to Hum-Li?"

"All of them. Why?" Lucy asked.

"I want to open the rest we haven't finished exploring yet. But needed to ensure we wouldn't get invaded."

"No, should be safe, the warpfield applies it to all gates, which brings up another subject. You need to have solid plans in place to evacuate all your people from either planet if the MKs should attack from space. For now I'd limit how far away from the gate they can settle," she said.

"Good idea. Olgreender II would be the problem," I said.

"Not really. Like Olgreender, they have to find it, identify it as having life, then call their forces. Should have enough time now that we know how they communicate and have people that can identify that communication when close," El said.

"Correct," was Lucy's comment. "Just make sure everyone knows if the whistle blows it is time to run. No heroic stands."

"Find Reta, then you guys take off. I'll handle the evacuation setups and I will get the choppers to explore the rest of the worlds this center is linked to. Garth, just add a crew of Lord P's scientists to fill the ship," El said.

With that we broke up and headed to our various duties.

Lucy reworked the earpiece links so the ship's crew was separate. "Loka, bring a reader, spare sticks, two spectral analyzers, the high band and low. Umm, see what Lord P's guys need for equipment and get everyone to the gate in, say, three hours?"

"Be a bit tight," I said.

"Okay four then, but I want to be off that planet before more MK reinforcements show up. We may need an interdiction crew when we return."

Three of Lord P's scientists volunteered. One was a biologist, one was a chemist, and the last was studying microbiology. I felt we might be able to use all three.

It took a little under four hours and we were all at the gate, two choppers loaded with gear and us.

Loka asked Garth, "Got the part?"

"Yes, Ma'am," he said, patting a small box.

We saw no MKs on the way, but we found a lot of cleaned out exoskeletons as we neared the ship. No doubt, they ate their dead.

We landed near the ship—it was nothing like the one we found Lucy in. The outer skin was a dull brownish color, with weird black and green symbols on its side. The hatch and several panels along its hull stood open.

Garth took the parts box and jumped down, and with his co-pilot and the crew from the other chopper they started putting the ship back together. Lucy had us all grabbing rags and buckets and gear and bags, and hauling them into the ship. I almost gagged at the stench, not unlike the cages that had been at the center, but stronger.

Lucy spent time figuring out different functions and marking them as I, Loka, and the others used the water cans off the choppers to clean the shit and slime off the deck of the ship. Lucy said not to splash a lot of water around doing it. Finally we transferred food and water. After thirty minutes another chopper showed with additional supplies along with cleaning people to help the ship get a full sanitization. Next I knew Garth was inside, all the extra people were gone, and I watched the choppers leave.

The smell was still there faintly, but the stronger smell of soaps and sanitizers prevailed. "Damn they are pigs!" I said.

"Maybe or maybe it was because the toilets were all broken? I have two working, but the external dumps had been locked closed and I don't think the MKs knew how to open them, so they tried to break them open—they just broke them instead," Garth said, as he crawled out from under a console.

"Lucy, ready here," he told her.

"Okay people, we are ready to start. I will run the checklist with Garth. Secure hatches and find a seat to strap into," Lucy said.

The ship was small and tight. It had two benches down the sides and four chairs around the nose. Pilot, co-pilot, communications, and last was a navigation station. In the middle was a single seat with a small console, the captain's seat. They were all designed for someone a little taller than we were, but not a lot.

"Garth Pilot, Loka Co-pilot, I'll sit Captain, Eldon take the nav station, anyone can have communications—we won't do anything but monitoring. The rest of you grab a bench and strap in please?"

I guess Reta was fastest; she got the com chair and smiled.

"Garth and Loka, I found the manuals on this, it is early spaceflight. Just past where time/space jumps developed. Give me a few minutes, I am figuring out the rest of the language structure. It has no common base that I recognize.

I watched her take a couple of markers and her hands flew over the various consoles, writing names and notes on the parts not already marked. The com console she left alone. The nav took the longest. When I asked she said all their measurement systems were different and not as linear as ours; also the conversions were going to be tricky for some of it.

"Okay, I think we are ready. While we work to get airborne I need Eldon to work on finding where we are and where we want to go. Seems their name for their home planet was Dinhja. It is as close as I can get. I wrote it on the pad there. I need to know a three dimensional direction as soon as you can find one for me.

"Garth, and Loka, follow my thoughts here. For them yellow was our green and red was our red, they had no green as we use it. If it is yellow say green.

"Let's go. Forward converters on."

Garth flipped a switch. "On, umm, green."

"In order, battery banks one through four," Lucy said.

"One green, two, three, four, all green," Loka said.

"This is weird the way they wrote it, oh well. Aux one and two on."

"Green," Garth said.

"Stabilization comps one and three on."

"Green," Garth said again.

"Stabilization comps two and four on."

"Green," Loka said.

"Rear converters on."

Garth flipped, and said, "Green."

"Main Comp on."

"On and green," Garth said.

"Says wait one minute for warm-up," Lucy said. "Then looks like we start the reactor."

The minute took forever. "Reactor main cooling valves open, shield check active, pumps active, start sequencer to one, fuel rods to auto, dampers to auto, check all status. If green then close the activate switch and wait for final power green." Lucy was reading from her memory as Garth or Loka activated each and acknowledged a green.

"Final power is green," Garth said.

"Excellent. Forward thrust to zero, rear thrust to zero, both lateral thrusts to zero, vertical thrust two clicks."

I heard a light buzz then a rumble. Looking out the forward view ports I saw flames of red/yellow as the ship started to shake a bit then I sensed we were rising. Oh shit, I was supposed to get a heading. I heard Lucy say, "Vertical to four."

I looked at the console and found a map could be brought up on a screen and expanded or contracted with my fingers. I kept comparing the name she gave to what I was seeing labeled on the screen.

It took a bit of work and Lucy came over to help. "Dang, I thought the Honor Central crap was old—this is old school. Okay, here is our destination. Use the two little sticks to maneuver the vertical and horizontal hairs over top, then hit the side view, this button here." When she hit it everything changed, like a side view. "Turn the knob up or down until the dot is exactly on-top of the cross then flip back to front." She did. "And here is all the information, which of course you can't read, but I can." She grinned.

"Pilot and co-pilot, both set these as I read them. When done and set hit the orange buttons next to each to lock them, then each read them back to verify. Clear?"

Garth and Loka both said it was clear.

"Line A: 25361.23, next is Line B: 44912.22, Line C: 72134.17, set those, lock and read back, both of you."

They each did as instructed, then Lucy said, "Pilot, thrust is 16 more clicks from where it is now then, at 80,000 feet stop vertical and neutralize it with negative clicks. When vertical rate is zero switch forward to 100% and the computer will handle the rest."

I couldn't see the altitude meter, but knew Lucy had marked it. Garth finally said, "We are at 80,000 feet and holding, switching to forward now."

"Okay, both of you hit the auto pilot, and when it turns green we are officially space-borne."

Loka was the last to say, "Green," as out of the corner of my eye I saw lights blink to yellow.

"People, you are free to move about. Loka, that round green screen to your left is the radar and laser detection scope, keep an eye on it for other vessels. Let me know if you see any. There is an alarm for it, but they miss things sometimes. This ship is barely reliable.

"Garth, you or Loka keep an eye on the yellow dot, which is us—make sure it stays in the center of all three of your screens; holler if it moves," she said. "Reta, let you mind flow as far as it will. Relax and report anything strange or different you feel. I also want a full bandwidth sweep of all radio, microwave, and laser frequencies at least once an hour."

"I thought they use mental waves?" I asked.

"I am looking for human signals from anyplace."

"Oh, I see."

As the reality of being in space set in we all looked to a window and watched Myla's planet as it slowly shrunk. To be among the gods, to be in space. Damn, what a rush!

Lucy sat in the Captains chair and it took a few seconds for me to realize she really didn't need any of us. All of our telltales were on her panels as well.

Time passed in what became boring routine, nothing changing, nothing spotted, nothing heard for several days.

The detection gear went red, as in warning, one day. I will call it morning for the sake of argument. Loka spotted it first. It was a long thin wavy red line on the scope.

Lucy smiled as she analyzed it. "A space fold. Good. We will be in range in another day. For those that don't know, it can shorten our travel time from years to days, depending on the fold's size."

She showed us the how and why of fold jumping, the earliest version that eventually led to the development of the warpfield generators. Lucy studied it and calculated where to enter and leave to present ourselves as close as safety permitted to our target area.

"Okay, I think I can get us about two days out from the planet. Full scans as we go through. Eldon, you're on weapons. I'll show them to you in a minute. The rest of you secure all loose items—sometimes it gets bumpy."

People were putting up water cups, writing instruments, papers and books, as Lucy stood beside me. "I can do this of course."

"Of course, but you have to make us feel needed."

"Something like that," she laughed. "Not really, I want to focus on the scans of space and ground and see if we can find that rodent. Also we will need crews as time goes on. All humanoid ships are similar, just a matter of finding the correct sequences. You are our training base.

"If we find these rodents we'll need to land. If any MKs show up here is what you need to do, it is all a straight forward system." With that she went to the top right hand corner of my nav screen and I saw her push the corner with a short jab. The whole panel pivoted around and a new panel locked in place.

"This uses 32MM projectiles. It fires four at a time. We found eight reloads. Only eight, Eldon. They are HE. Pretty simple, your center stick now controls the aim. When it flashes red you're on target, computer does ranging. Now this one here," she pushed a button and a different screen came up, "this one shoots the fairytale."

She was baiting me and I knew it. "What's a fairytale?"

She smiled. "It is what many people on many planets always hoped would be the cheap ultimate weapon, the pulsed laser. Good idea, but a fairytale."

Okay, we'd had this discussion before. The pulsed laser was okay on stationary targets where you had time to let it penetrate metal or stone. It was what they used to cut the rooms in rock like Honor Central. Efficient but slow.

"This is actually one of the better designs. A 1.6kV pulsed Nd: yttrium-aluminum-garnet beam. It uses a 12.5 cm transmissive focusing lens but I won't bore you with the details. It can work on thin metal and soft rocks if they are sitting still or you are very accurate with repeated shots. I think the people who made this used it for the mining of asteroids, not sure. Anyway, that's it, just those two. We didn't have time to rearm it with weapons we actually have ammo for so if needed make it all count. You just need to keep us flying if we are jumped until I can help.

"Okay, here is the targeting system. For the 32MM just point, lock and shoot. But the laser uses focus as well, that is why it is on your station. The second is the depth of field or focus. Bring up the second screen and line it up so the dot is just past the line that makes the target. In other words the depth of penetration. Once in place hit this and it will adjust the depth from then on. You'd think the computer would do it and it would be automatic, but no, which is why I think it was used for mining. Different rocks and minerals required different depths rather than metal ship skins. Oh, this button gives the forward view and is guided by the left hand stick. You'll need to practice a bit, but it isn't hard.

"Everybody strap in please, we jump in forty-five seconds." She sat in her chair and we were ready.

How do I describe feeling like my body was being disassembled and then put back together? I could actually see other me's staring at me or ahead, lines of them on both sides. I did notice as they went further away there were more and more differences, but I may have been seeing things. All felt weird, a bit like the gates, but different and slower.

As the room refocused there was some bumping around, not a lot, then things settled down.

"Scans, please," Lucy said, as we all were looking for anything.

The planet was a greenish blue orb that hung in space, we came out pretty damn close. It had a single moon and from what I saw, the planet had several land masses and vast oceans. Very pretty. I scanned the screen in front of me and zoomed in and out, but a laser sight wasn't a telescope. Lucy brought it up on her main screen and zoomed in—it worked and we could see woods and fields. After a bit she zoomed in on a large city, not unlike ours had been, but bigger, much bigger. As she went to max the view blurred but one thing was eerily clear, the place was empty. Some buildings had been destroyed. Around the perimeters of it was major damage, shells of buildings, ghosts of what once was. From what Lucy had said and I knew, they had put up a fierce fight in their last desperate gasps to live, like Earth and Olgreender; they also failed. After a bit I saw Reta was crying silently. Tears flowing freely as what she saw registered. Loka was sad, others were as well—it was clear we all had memories of what was and is no more.

"I register nothing," Reta said. "A lot of static, a few bursts in the light region I'm recording. I don't feel anything alive either."

All of our scans were negative until Reta yelped.

"What?" Lucy asked.

"Pain burst. Someone or something is alive."

"I thought you could only receive at close range," Garth said.

"We can only transmit at close range," Reta said.

"Oh, sorry."

"From the planet?" Lucy asked.

"Not sure, it was fairly strong."

Lucy took over some scans and finally said, "They have eighteen satellites, they had global communications networks. Three of them are large enough to hold life. Check them first, look for signs of heat and electrical energies."

The scientists came into play as we were crowded out of our chairs. They knew what to look for. Lucy spent time showing them how to use the instruments and soon Loka and I were on the benches in back. Actually a comforting change. I stretched out and Loka put my head in her lap as she watched the happenings in the ship. I think I was instantly asleep.

When I woke up Loka was asleep, she swapped her lap for a pillow and stretched out as well. What woke me was Lucy talking in my ear. "Sorry Eldon, I am sure you are all very tired but I need you for a bit. Let her sleep."

I slowly rubbed circulation into my one numb arm as I stood up.

"We found something alive, actually two somethings. I think they are humanoids. Too soon to tell. The Station ahead. Reta says one is hurt or dying. She isn't sure, not a normal reading. She says it is cluttered or jumbled.

"I need you to navigate the ship. I am the only one who can go outside without a suit, but only for a few minutes—my core processor isn't heated. I also need to go out through the rear engine room, this ship has no pressure hatches."

"No what?" I asked.

"Never mind. I will go into the engine room and void it then go out the cargo hatch to the station. It seems big enough for a crew of ten or twelve. I need you to keep the tail of this ship as close as you can to it until I return. Just like setting the nav point, just keep all three dots where I set them, okay?"

"Sure," I told her. She smiled one of her weird smiles and I felt she hadn't told me all. She patted me on the back and stepped through the rear door with one of our portable med units and locked it.

"Eldon, see the station in the view screen?" she asked through the earpiece.

"Yes," I told her, as I saw the outside tail of our ship and the hatch of the other very close to it.

"Good, mark the points on the three screens and keep this ship exactly where it is."

"Okay, I will," I told her.

I saw her go to the hatch and tap on the door—nothing. Then she was at a window and looked in, then to a lower window. This seemed to have a full ring of windows. Lucy tapped on it several times and kept pointing to the hatch.

"They are humanoid and very afraid. One is female and pregnant from the looks of it," Lucy said over the com. "I think they will cycle the hatch. If not I have to get back inside and warm up again."

I found out why she had smiled as I realized the ship was drifting. I carefully realigned the dots and guess I said "shit" as Lucy laughed. I spent the next few minutes learning to try and move the ship gently, in the smallest of microbursts, all as I watched Lucy finally go into the satellite hatch and close the outer door.

"I'm in, the male has a weapon on me but he's not sure what to do with it. Though I know how to read their language from the ship's manuals I find the verbal is quite different."

I could hear her chattering away and his responses. Lucy kept changing how she talked and soon she was speaking to him. "He wants me to help her, she is in pain. He says he is sorry, they weren't supposed to be able to conceive. All the rest are dead, most committed suicide once they saw what happened to their planet; she refused so he stayed as well. They don't know how the MKs missed them, they had found the other satellite and ate them. Only thing I can think of is he said they pushed all the dead out into space around the station." She chatted some more with him. "He says the woman has been in pain, almost all the food is gone, and there is little water. Systems are breaking down, it wasn't designed to last so long without resupplies.

"Eldon, they have suits but none to fit her condition. Anyone have any ideas?"

Those awake shook their heads. "Nothing this second, Lucy."

Loka came awake at all the commotion. I explained it to her.

"Ship her over," she said.

"Excuse me?" Lucy asked.

"They transport supplies like Honor Central. I am sure some were pressurized crates." So simple a blind man could see it, but I wasn't blind.

I could hear Lucy chatting in the background. "Going to be very tight but it will work, good idea, Loka."

I think I heard moans and grunts. Her moans, his grunts. As I maneuvered the ship back to position I saw Lucy come out the hatch and it closed then opened and a box just barely fitting emerged as Lucy guided it into the engine room. Soon a space suit followed. After they were in and our hatch closed Lucy told one of the scientists to do something and soon the door unlocked as Lucy carried the box into the small cabin.

She laid it on a bench and immediately opened it. A woman started gasping for air. She was very like us, a rusty gold hair color, a pinkish skin, even about Loka's size, a little shorter. She had longer, more slender fingers. When she glanced my way, surveying the ship, I could see brown eyes. Not pretty, but not ugly, I guess normal would fit.

The man was very similar. He had stripped off his suit. His eyes drifted to green and he was taller than me, darker brown hair. He also held what clearly was a pistol.

Lucy said, "Everyone meet Hamel something or other. I told him he could keep the weapon until he felt safe."

I nodded, so did Garth, and most of the others. Lucy helped the woman out of the box, who was in discomfort and was clearly far along. As she moaned I saw Reta wince.

"She is called Fawnelia Flemdon, they are not married or anything. She feels she will deliver in a few days at the latest." Lucy was talking to her for a while as she sat on the bench.

Reta said, "It isn't her I am sensing."

"Not her?" I asked.

"No. No organized thoughts, it is her baby, and it is in pain," Reta said.

Lucy hooked her to the med kit and started running tests, the guy was concerned but wary as Lucy kept asking him questions. I saw Lucy run her tests, give the woman a shot of something, then she and Loka carried her into the engine room and closed the door.

I would guess it was less than thirty minutes later Loka came out smiling. "It is a wonderful baby boy. Alive and well."

Reta said yes, birth seemed to hurt quite a bit. I hadn't noticed she was biting her lip and sweating.

Loka went near the guy who held up his weapon and said, "Suta pela. Suta pela."

"Pela?" he asked.

"Yes, it's a boy." He relaxed.

Finally Lucy opened the door and said something and he went inside. I could hear a baby crying.

Loka smiled. "They are so precious when born," she said. Talk about a subtle hint.

Lucy came out and closed the door. She handed the pistol the man had been carrying to Garth. "I'll be back. He said they recorded a lot of the final battles, I'll get them off their station."

It took forty-five minutes and she was back, arms full of gear. "Okay, from initial viewing, when the MKs arrived the station was saved because the heat was broken. Everyone alive was in thermal protective gear wrapped around their space suits while they tried to fix it. Some had already died and were put out the hatch. They never showed on the MK heat sensors. Unfortunately the other station did show. When they saw what happened below and realized they were never to be rescued all but these two committed suicide. If they hadn't the supplies would have run out long ago.

"I'm guessing here, but it looks like there was a huge main force that attacked. I suspect this planet just happened to be in the way because soon after the planet's armies were defeated the majority of the MK force loaded up with food, which was them of course, and moved on in a hurry. They left about 100,000 MKs behind.

"We know they caught and ate rodents, nothing I can see in the vids. They finished off the people and moved on to Reta's planet.

"I am afraid we have two more refugees. Three if you count the baby. She was not supposed to be able to get pregnant. He said it was rather a shock to them both as they waited to die."

"You asked about the rodents?" one of the scientists asked.

"Not yet, been rather busy. I will wait until he relaxes. They have been under terrible strain. Everyone dead, no transportation, no supplies, station falling apart, and her having a baby. Let them be for a few hours."

Lucy dropped the gear on the worktable behind the commander's chair and was studying it as we watched a planet die on the videos. This MK group had huge ships that they herded people into like cattle, then took off. With luck maybe these rodents got aboard too. From the vids everything took place in a few weeks and a once pretty planet was a deserted orb, floating in space.

"Darn, nothing new in technological ideas here. They were quite a bit farther along the discovery trail than Olgreender, but not as far as you are now on Olgreender II. Still, a few ideas here for factory improvements," Lucy said.

"Pilots, take us to the planet please? I want to be near, but not in, a big city."

"Yes, ma'am," Garth said, and started talking and working some checklist with Loka. As we started to move the man came out, eyes clearly bloodshot but a bit more relaxed.

He and Lucy exchanged words. I had the impression Lucy was still learning their language. He watched the various goings on in the ship and stared out the port at his now extinct planet and he cried, quietly and alone. Finally he talked a bit more to Lucy and went back inside the engine room with the woman and child.

"He said he has no idea what rodent we are looking for. All are pests and none are poisonous that he is aware of. If the MKs identified it early then only it would be alive, if it found enough food to continue to survive. Since most ate vegetable matter when needed, I feel that a good probability."

We spent several hours working entry calculations with Lucy. This ship wasn't strong enough to go straight in to planet; we had to shed heat along the way. Overall the trip was uneventful, thermal scans all came up empty, and we touched down a mile from a partially damaged city. A few thousand MK skeletal shells were scattered around, all picked clean, also a lot of human bones picked clean as well.

From the vids the MKs didn't land outside and attack—they literately landed on rooftops, in parks, on streets, almost everywhere in every city. I'd estimated billions of them. In, munch, roundup, and gone in a few weeks. It was graphic and tragic. It also left the possibility that some life might have hid and survived. For whatever reason, these MK moved on faster than what Lucy felt was normal for them.

Once on the ground several things came together as a plan. Lucy reiterated that time was of the essence. Not for here, but to get back to Honor Central before the MKs returned.

The scientists would camp near the city with Loka and me as guards. I thought the man would join us as a guide but Lucy said no. They would spend the time scanning for any survivors on the planet. What was known was the ocean life remained intact. Lucy said she had been informed of several arctic projects as well as several ocean farming sites that had been touted as being viable when the man and woman had went to space.

We were there less than a week. The scientists found three distinct types of vermin. Two were rats and the third was like a roach with hard outer body armor, but with a skeleton. Five sites had been found where the people of the planet survived and our three were added to an ocean farming site. Lucy spent time filling them in on what we knew and what we suspected. Unfortunately, the MKs were the first space visitors they knew of. Lucy did the calculations for them. If they all kept in contact physically, there were enough to continue their population safely. She told me there were fifteen thousand left alive. Many felt there were others in caves or mines.

"When we get back we will once again need MKs to study and experiment with," the biologist said.

All in all several weeks had passed and we finally were back to Myla's planet. The MKs had not arrived yet. We landed just outside the gate and soon were swarmed with people. Lucy guided the efforts as we unloaded. To my surprise, she had them partially dismantle the ship. The tail-fins and motors were removed and Lucy used the mining lasers to carefully cut the ship in half front to rear, then she halved those again and with careful maneuvering they fit through the gate. Lucky for us Lucy had insisted we move all four needlers out the gate, as well as twenty of the 20MM cannons...as the MKs arrived before we were done. Only a few hundred thousand in a few ships. Two tried to land next to the gate and were destroyed, three more landed off in the distance. I'd guess sixty-five thousand attacked. Lucy, Garth, El and ten thousand troops surprised them from the side as they charged us at the gate. We hit them hard, El had secured several dozen MKs and cut off all their pincers. They were moved by the gate and secured.

These MKs had more small arms than before and we lost

several hundred people in the battle. We finally slipped the last of the ship through the gate.

"Meeting now, inside the gate please," El said.

Leaving fresh troops on the various guns we popped back inside. El made it short. "I want those extra ships. Garth! Tici still isn't fully functional, take twenty thousand out to the right and try to circle behind. I know you can't hide, fight your way through, disable those ships and hit the MKs from behind. Questions?" She only paused a few seconds. "Good, let's do this."

I was on a 20MM, reloading for what felt like hours. Others were as well. We hauled box after box of shells to try to keep them reloaded. The needlers were working flawlessly. Garth managed to take his troops and bust out through the ring of MKs. I think they sensed what he was trying to do—a lot tried retreating toward the ships and became the primary targets of those deadly 20MM bursts. Two days and nights later we had victory and secured three large ships along with twenty MKs. They lost one-hundred thousand, we lost eight-hundred dead and wounded. Now that we understood their tactics and how to kill them, we were far better than the first time.

As all the wounded were moved back to Central and the 20MMs on their new electric trucks were again moved back inside, Lucy and Garth set plans for the three captured ships. El called for a full Commanders meeting in the mess hall in Central in the morning. Lucy reprogrammed the warpfield generator to get the MKs in, then again to keep any others out.

Next morning Loka and I and all the rest were there, including reps from both our new planets. We all knew it was a meeting for war.

El coughed once and most of the noise ceased. The mess was full, as well as the halls and additional rooms. Rank had its privileges—Captains and below were not present and the lower ranks were stuck in the fringes of the meeting area. Lucy and El had set up remote viewers, of course.

"Ladies and gentleman, attention please," she said. The already hushed became totally silent. "Thank you. Short and sweet, we are going on the offensive. I want to start kicking these MKs' asses. Thanks to the efforts of many, including Lucy, Myla, Reta, Loka, Eldon and my staff, all the scientists from both planets, and every single one of you that has done something to help against these bastards. We finally have enough knowledge to do some serious damage to them." A cheer went up but she called it off.

"We have tons of work to do so let me outline it as quickly as I can—all will get written instructions in time. We secured three large ships on Reta's world. Garth will take as many as necessary to crew them and he will fly them back to here. Here as in Olgreender. I hope when he gets back it will once again be in our hands!"

Damn, I thought I could yell? The walls were rocking.

"Lucy has studied the charts and said it will take them four to five months to fly from where they are to here. I want to own our planet by then."

I saw the looks around our head table. I think dreams were fine in their place.

She saw the expressions and someone from Olgreender II said, "We have our new homes and planet, why go back to the terrors and the memories?"

"You are correct, we have done well on both planets—what we don't have are the factories. The old industrial complex is still sitting there, waiting for us and we need it. I want tens of thousands of those new nail guns, I want ships built, I want to be ready to kick some damn ass." Again the cheers went up as she shushed them.

"My basic plan is minimum manning for several reasons. We are physically located too high above Olgreender to have any kind of effective escape route, as all of you found out. I want to move and reprogram as many of the earth 'bots as we can to run the factories. The scientific people are already well versed in Lord P's operations so we need to replace the human worker with robots.

"Priority is smaller and lighter versions of the nail guns. Until we can make the MKs roll over and play dead for real we need them as our primary defense. I'll work that out with staff.

"All but battle staff may leave," El said. "Get the word out, I'd like an emergency meeting of Council in, say, two days, here please?"

Lucy and several scientists spent all the time with the rodents, then the idea on how to identify the right ones was found to be quite easy. She offered them to the MKs. The brownish rat was clearly not the one being devoured by them, so the hunt for the cause was on.

Reta and Myla and several others were spending most of the days studying the MKs, trying to piece them together as an entity. A big thing was Myla's constant star chart drawings. She was becoming very good at it and Loka or Lucy or one of the scientists would place them on the book of stars from Earth. Slowly the MK expansion into our galaxy was being plotted, just from their memories.

Time was flying. Myla spoke perfect English now. I was eating the morning of the Council meeting when Reta, now married, came in and asked to speak to Loka and me. I told her sure.

"We found why they just blasted through our planet and the others in this area," she said. "They just needed food to continue on. Here, look. She handed us another of Myla's drawings. "This whole section here? It is the center of this galaxy. Every one of these blue dots are unconquered planets found to contain life. Many of them humanoid types. They are trying to get most of their ships to these three clusters for an assault on them. They feel they can control the entire galaxy from there in just a few hundred years. All MKs in this galaxy are supposed to meet there in four years from now. Apparently it was a plan devised hundreds of years ago. From what I read and Myla and the rest sense, we are talking hundreds of millions of MKs. Maybe even billions."

"Okay Reta, thank you. Can you stand by? We have a Council meeting at 9AM and I want you to report it to them."

She nodded and grabbed some food and sat in a corner eating.

Myla came from nowhere and bombed Loka's lap, laughing. "We are good, yes?"

"Yes, Myla dear, you did very good!" Loka said, and kissed her.

Myla sat in Loka's lap and was helping herself to toast and eggs and a glass of milk. Quite a content scene that I had been thinking more and more about. Hard to believe years had passed since we topped the ledge and found the ice cube.

A while back I had talked to Lucy privately, and El. First I verified that Lucy could fix Loka's problem of sterility, then that El and the rest of us could, in-fact, do without her if needed. Both were answered in the affirmative. I kept getting the feeling from Myla—I was sure that she wanted a baby brother or sister and a full time mother. I just hadn't broached it with Loka yet. Seeing her joy with Myla, I think it might soon be time.

"A beautiful scene, Loka," I said.

She smiled at me as she helped Myla steady her glass of milk because they both had been giggling about something.

"Dear, I talked to Lucy again. She is ready when you are." I observed her; she had no idea.

"About what?" Loka asked.

"Letting you become pregnant. She said it is a minor operation. Myla keeps hinting she needs a brother or sister before she is too old. Someone to play with." I was a bit surprised when she actually dropped the glass on the floor. Glad it was plastic.

"But the war, the MKs, everything."

"Lucy said we can eventually win the war, you said you wanted to have Myla as family, and Myla said she wants a playmate. I see no reason to wait until we are too old. Besides, you wanted to spend time at the new house. Remember?"

"Eldon, can we wait and discuss it later please?" She was caught off guard.

"Nothing to discuss, dear, it is all up to you of course. If yes tell Lucy and El. If no, tell Myla and me." I smiled my littlest smile. I felt it would eventually be yes.

Myla climbed down from her lap and squeezed my hand then ran to sit by Reta.

Loka leaned over and stared deep into my eyes and gave me a kiss. "I said we'd talk about it later, okay?"

"Okay."

After cleaning up the mess and finishing breakfast we sat and talked to others until the time for the meeting came.

Lucy talked to us and El before the meeting. "Need your inputs. I'm a machine and not sure what you actually think. I want to try something dangerous to everyone here and all planets connected to it. I looked over everything I can find on the gate system, and I think I can open a new gate. We still have several slots available."

"To where?" I asked.

She brought up a holographic image. "One of these three systems."

I recognized them immediately from Myla's drawing. The ones in the center of the galaxy, the MKs' targets. "Why?" I asked.

"We have an item they can use if they have any tech skills. The nail guns! If the MKs haven't attacked them yet it could make a huge dent in them. Also I need a planetary platform to try the new aerosol we developed. The mixed sterility and mind-numbing one.

"We don't have time to fly there. Only a gate might help," she said.

"The danger is they could already be there and come back at us through the gate?" El asked.

"No, like here, they can't come back through the gates anymore. However, bombs and unknown viruses can. Something the warp field is not specifically programmed to keep out," Lucy said.

"The aerosol?" El asked.

"We isolated the compounds that caused the sterilization. We can mass produce it on Olgreender and fill the air on those planets and any other they may be attacking. We can't make a lot of the mind-numbing compounds but maybe enough to cause a little confusion. Every bit helps.

"Not only that, I want to try a second gate into their galaxy again, for the same reasons. Needlers to stop them cold, and we start a sterilization campaign against them."

"Umm, this doesn't sound like a year or two campaign," Loka said.

"It isn't. It will be more like lifetimes, perhaps many lifetimes, but it must start someplace."

"As a militarist I fully understand the need for aggressive action, but I also think that losing millions of our people on Olgreender will dampen enthusiasm for your plan," El said.

"I know, we made mistakes, but we didn't understand the enemy then. We do now. We can win, we must win or humanity in this galaxy is doomed."

The Council meeting started on time. Anyone who was anyone, or thought they were, was there from both planets.

A roll was taken of elected officials. All were present. Old business covered reports on food and housing as well as planting schedules. What new manufacturing had started. The normal items in any town-hall type meeting.

Under new business Lucy let her new assistants give various reports including the one about having the ability to make an airborne spray.

El brought up the idea of opening Olgreender back up for manufacturing. At first there was great opposition. Many of those that left the planet in the first place were the most afraid, having new families and children to worry about.

Lucy explained that the MKs no longer had access to the gates. She had stopped them. We needed Olgreender back for its factories. She went into detail of how she would use the Earth robots to run everything with minimal people involved. She also mentioned three brave crews were even now in space heading there and needed a way to get back here.

A vote to reopen the gate was taken and passed by six votes.

El took up the battle—how we could, after two thousand years, take back planets and destroy the MKs. We could finally go on the offensive. She listed all the developments already made and who to thank. Even Myla and Reta from another planet had been part of the great help needed to develop a plan. She caught me off guard—she didn't specifically ask for permission to open a gate. Rather, she asked permission to finally be allowed to take the war to the MKs instead of living in fear of them. To pursue them and destroy them as means became available. A vote had her resolution pass by almost forty votes. If they only knew how she was using them. We said nothing and most of us voted yes.

I t took five days to open the tunnel to Olgreender and another to get it large enough to get a chopper back through.

Loka and I finally had our private chat. If I promised to not go to the ends of the galaxy to fight the MKs she would take Myla to our new home and try the motherhood thing. Lucy fixed her and I was working to fulfill my part.

I helped Lucy move robots and parts from Earth to Olgreender. Lord P's people were a big help in getting factories up and running again, but we held mass funerals for piles of bones, some stacked six to eight feet high. None identifiable. The MKs ate our people and then threw the bones in big piles. We found no MKs on the planet, but also none of our people alive. That was the hardest part.

Months ticked by as Lucy made ready to open a gate and I found out Loka was pregnant. The factories started producing a hundred nail guns a week, then it was per day. Lucy set up the very special manufacturing processes needed to make the dangerous power supplies, using all robots but a few volunteers for control and maintenance. She was as afraid of the radiation as we were. We soon had all the helicopters in round-the-clock deliveries from below to the gate. Inside they were moved to storage areas on all the planets that could hold them. We fortified Olgreender II and our home first. If MKs found them they were in for a real shock.

Our three spaceships under Garth finally arrived to rounds of cheers and a series of parties. One ship went to a special factory where Lucy and robots and a select few scientists tore it apart and put it back together several times. In a few months they had what they were after. The ship was now separated into four quarters that just fit through the gate. Special dollies were built and it took two choppers to lift a section and set it on the ledge outside. A series of factories now dedicated their efforts to make copies of that ship.

We used people and robots to manhandle the sections onto the dollies and get them through the gate. Meantime I was told Lucy had activated the gate search program with the preferred area of search being the three blue dots in the center of the galaxy. She said it was putting the warpfield generator to the ultimate test as to distance, as it was way beyond recommended specifications. As she explained it, the gate on that end will search to find viable life sustaining planets. We had to wait until it locked onto one. After two months it was still searching and Lucy was getting worried it may either be too far or we were too late to help.

Almost a year from when Myla turned in the star-chart with their intentions Lucy announced she had a lock. She asked for me and El and Garth and a few other representatives from both planets to meet in the mess hall in Honor Central. Loka was due to deliver any day, but I went at her insistence.

"Okay, thanks for coming. I received a valid lock from a viable planet. If I do it, it is permanent and unless I do it we don't have any way of telling what is at the other end. It is on one of the blue dot systems—not sure of the planet until we lock it and go there. Anyone have qualms; now is the time to express them," she said.

"I'm curious of the overall plan. If the MKs are not there and there is intelligent life, then what?" Garth asked.

"It is what we actually want. Some place with at least a rudimentary industrial complex to make what is needed to defeat the MKs."

"If there is no advanced life? Then what?" he asked.

"Then we build one, or we find another planet if there is one near. We need to clobber them. We need to go on the offensive and clobber them!" El said with venom in her voice.

I told them, "I vote to open it, let's see what waits on the other side."

"Fine for you to say, you're an explorer type and you are partly to blame for this mess," a guy in a green suit said.

El took up my defense. "Yes, without him we'd still be sucking down our drinks and having arguments about our origins while the MKs came closer and closer, waiting to have us for snacks. Thank the gods he is responsible, as we may survive as a result."

That seemed to shut him up.

Lucy said, "Vote. All in favor for the opening raise your hands." All but three did.

"Opposed?" Two of those raised their hands.

"Passed and I will initiate final lock today. We will need an expeditionary force ready to move in twenty hours. Fort, choppers, nail guns, the works. If there are no more questions let's get to it."

As most left I drifted by El and Lucy.

El asked, "You coming with us?"

"I don't know. Loka made it clear she really didn't want me to leave until after the baby is born and she can go. We are a team you know."

"Oh, we know. Still, your help would be a boon," Lucy said. It was now so hard to think of her as a computer.

Garth said, "Loka isn't dumb, she knows the score, lay it out and ask her."

"I will, I'll let Lucy know."

I left them sitting there and went toward the gate to get home, going over all the arguments I could think of on why I really needed to go. I mentally rehearsed my pitch, over and over until I walked in the door and Myla said out loud to Loka, "Dad's home." Those two words floored me as she stood there with her smile and Loka came from the kitchen wiping her hands. Her belly was so far out she could rest a plate and eat off it. "He wants to go with them to the new gate."

"Myla, enough, let him speak. I told you it isn't polite to read minds without their permission," Loka chastised her, and gave me a wan smile. "Children, what can you do? Go out and play, Myla."

After Myla left Loka kissed me. "She is becoming a handful now that she understands us. She is also a very big help." She was trying to make conversation but knew it wouldn't work. "Hungry? Got a meatloaf in the oven, done in half an hour."

"Yes, had nothing but coffee at the meeting."

"Let me guess, they are going to open the gate and El, Lucy, and Garth want you to go with them." It wasn't a question.

"They'd prefer both of us, but yes."

"Dear, I'm selfish, I love you, I want our baby to know its father." She was absently rubbing her belly. "I want Myla to think she has a stable family. She started calling me mother a few days ago on her own. She is adapting well. Is it wrong to want you to stay here with me?" She had tears in her eyes.

"Do I really need to answer that? You know I love you and I have always bent to your wishes. Well, most of them. Still, as a guy at the meeting said, we, you and I and Duranu, and Cullves,

244

and Lord P opened this can of worms looking for our roots. You and I are the only two left alive to see what is at the bottom of it and I feel you can't go look right now, so shouldn't I?"

She smiled through her tears. "That really is a lousy analogy you know."

"Well, I had it all figured out until Myla called me dad, then my mind totally blanked."

"Then you answered my question. You feel you want and need to go." She placed her hands to each side of my face and kissed me. "My heart and mind are in conflict. We women tend to lead with our hearts but I will force my mind to control it. Go, if you die I will at least have a family to console me."

"I won't die; we're just going to have a look-see."

"Yes, you've been in front for more than one look-see dear. I was with you, remember? Call Myla, supper is done."

I mentally hollered and Myla walked in and sat at the table. "I'm hungry," she said, then, "I'm going to miss you."

"At most a few days. Just a quick peek."

"Did I tell you my name? It's Rock. I'd be dumb as a rock to believe that." Myla grinned and I did too.

"How long before you leave?" Loka asked.

"About fifteen hours," I told her.

"Damn, not wasting time are they?"

"Nope."

"My cue. I have a dissertation on the evils of socialistic behavior in modern human cultures for school tomorrow. Funny, ours was pure socialism," Myla said.

"But when they can read minds the truth of who can do what is known. Without that it is more a, 'why should I work if they will do it for me?' mentality."

"I know, and they are right, of course. Still, doesn't hurt for humanity to wish."

"Your school gets pretty deep for your age."

"AP, or Accelerated Placement, is performance based not age based. I should be into my first year college by next year at my current progression rate." She smiled. Somehow I felt she was getting her childhood ripped away from her.

"Take time to try to have fun," I told her.

She disappeared and Loka and I sat on the couch and snuggled. We dared do nothing else. I got to feel the baby kick and could hear its heartbeat. I fell asleep with her sitting there, resting her head on my shoulder and us both watching the fire dance. So peaceful and so short a time.

"**C**ommander Gnoth, I hate to disturb you Sir, but the General said to recall everyone."

"Thank you, tell her I'm on my way."

Loka woke, and asked, "Commander?"

"El gave us all some type of new ranks. I forgot, you're one too." I smiled and kissed her.

"Eldon, please come back to us."

I stood, showered, and was in uniform standing by the door when the car came to transport me to the Honor Gate. So much had changed in so little time. She handed me a bag with clean underwear and socks for my backpack at the base. "Try to come back to us Eldon, please?" she said again.

I kissed her. "I will. If I miss the baby being born, tell it I apologize, but I am trying to secure its future."

She kissed me and started crying but pushed me out the door and closed it.

Back at Central all was a madhouse, well, a coordinated one. Troops armed and ready stood by all over. The second connection room where the new gate was linked was packed with troops and nail guns on dollies. The helicopters and fort pieces were up various hallways. I had a sense of what it took to even try a mass invasion, all through a little gate.

Lucy and El were near the gate when I found them. El looked at her watch and hollered, "Ten Minutes. Pass the word."

Seems not everyone had earpieces yet, or they had different groups on different freqs. I slipped on my backpack as El said. "Lucy did air analysis: Oxygen 21%, air temperature at 41 degrees, no unknown pathogens in the sample taken. She did not enter, just a quick hand."

"Other data?" I asked.

"She sent a small rover through—it should have returned about five minutes ago. It hasn't."

"Might I suggest we wait a bit then? We seriously need to know the terrain we are entering. Like Olgreender, it could be on the edge of a ledge."

El Looked at her watch. "Four Minutes, pass it on." Then to me, she said, "Honest Eldon, we know what we are doing, well mostly. Us ten are first through—if we don't come back in a few minutes then the rest will come in with guns blazing." She smiled. Lucy had actually made a book of old Earth sayings and it was funny how so many referred to war. Well, maybe not so funny, but we all used them.

Tici said, "Lucy will step through and back first, then we all go in and ensure we don't drop dead. Then we see from there."

"Nice to see you fit and back in action, Tici," I said.

"Thanks. Lucy is working on a microglove to replace the fingers and I asked El to marry me. No answer yet."

"Thirty seconds," El said, as Lucy stood there, ready. "Won't get one either, not until this shit is over. Go."

Lucy disappeared, then was back. "Grassy tundra, sparse, cold, maybe winter. The rover is stuck a few feet away—fell off a rock. Let's go."

We moved through and spread in a quick defense, but for as far as we could see it was open, rocky and had turfs of grass clinging to life here and there.

Lucy did a quick scan. "Well, someone is here someplace. I'm getting various frequencies that are outside nature."

"MKs?" El asked.

"Doubt it. Not their frequencies."

"Garth, send someone back and go ahead and bring a small defense force in. Until we see who or what is here let's not assume they are hostile yet. Put the rest on standby alert for now," El said. "Oh, bring a chopper in. I don't feel like walking."

Within four hours we had a portable fort up, an array of both 20MMs and needler cannons, and Tici and Garth were putting the finish on the chopper. Lucy added two new items to our arsenal as well. RPVs. or Remote Piloted Vehicles. Fast, agile, minimally armed, with several hundred-mile range capability and good snoop gear.

I saw two techs with small computers to control them and soon they were airborne. One went west and another to the north.

Several hours passed as they scanned the areas and finally one tech called El, said, "Contact."

We crowded around the screen as he zoomed in. Looked like normal humanoids but they had bald heads except a long single tuft out the center-back of the head. Ears were more perpendicular to the head—they stuck almost straight out the sides. Other than that, the rest that was visible was about the same.

They had roads and what appeared to be three-wheeled cars. Their homes tended to be more like half cylinders laid on their sides. As the drone went further toward the center of the large town or city I clearly saw multistory buildings, but they were normal squares and rectangles with large glass fronts. The lack of people there was conspicuous.

"Well, they are not MKs, that is for sure," Reta said.

El asked if we saw their faces. Yes, hard to miss, they appeared to be similar to the drawings of what we called the in-between. The ones we thought were between what we were today and what we thought we were when living in the trees.

Lucy wasn't too familiar with those as we'd pretty much abandoned those beliefs long ago. She said, "They look very much like the early Mongols from Earth. A mix of tough short steppes people and Chinese."

"Does not matter what they look like as humans, they look like all of us, and capable of helping," Tici said.

"Staff conference, mess-tent," El said.

We all sat around, every month seemed to add more people, well, we were expanding. El asked, "Best approach?"

"Calm, easy, quiet I'd say. We don't want to spook them and

get them afraid of us as invaders," Garth said.

"True, but we need to show ability to use force as well," Tici said.

"Eldon?" El asked me.

"What?" I had been thinking of the past—so wrong for so long.

"What do you think?" El asked.

"Sorry, thoughts went elsewhere. I think maybe Lucy and I or some other representative, and possibly Reta, should try to make contact. Lucy for language analysis, Reta to see if she can read anything, and me as a male Olgreender for diversity and to try to cover Reta."

"Why not Garth or Tici?" El asked.

"You want someone close to them in stature. Sorry, Tici and Garth are so muscle-bound they could scare them, make them feel intimidated. No, someone more normal. Doesn't have to be me. Reta represents both our female cultures well, but their males are few and too tall to be representative of the majority of us. Just thoughts."

"Good ones, too," Lucy said.

They listened to other ideas and soon El called it quits as we were rehashing the same ideas. "Thank you all. Now clear out and let me have Command Staff only," El said.

Well, it had grown slightly now that Garth and Tici and others were part of it, but my wife's absence was felt—by me anyway.

They hashed around a bit more then El made her decision and we were done.

Two nail guns and two 20MMs would stay along with the

chopper and fort, everything else would be withdrawn. We'd do it quietly.

Two days later we found we had not been unobserved but not approached. A recon RPV was heading back and just before landing the screen showed two men on foot near a ridge a couple miles away. What looked like a large scope mounted on a tripod was there and back a few yards into the valley behind them sat a little four-wheeled machine towing a small two-wheeled cart.

Lucy said they appeared unarmed and would clearly have seen us withdrawing most of our equipment.

El made a snap decision. "Eldon, take Reta and Lucy and let's see what happens."

I put on a tight zip-suit, clearly showing I hid no weapons. Reta did the same. Lucy wore her silver suit with bright red sneakers, as she called them.

It took us a while to traverse the rough terrain as we headed for them. As we neared Lucy decided to stay back. She looked a lot better than the old clunking one-armed machine, but she still clearly was not human. I saw one head peeking down at us so I held up my hands and slowly turned, showing I had no weapons. Reta did too. We slowly moved forward and soon we stood twenty feet from them. Two males, what looked like light cotton or wool jackets in a camo hunting design. No weapons. They seemed to be sniffing the air—heightened smell?

Reta sub'd that she received nothing from either of them.

"Friends," I said.

I heard something that sounded like a couple words from one as the other looked at him, and then they shook their heads, turned, and went to the machine. I noticed they'd already packed up the scope in dull brown boxes. Soon they were riding to the west and disappeared from sight.

Lucy said, "Well, could have been better, but wasn't bad."

We turned and headed back to camp.

"Was that a language he spoke?" Reta asked.

Lucy said, "Not enough data. Could have been grunts or just a 'let's go'. I am not getting any form of radio or video that I yet recognize. Still analyzing it all but so far it seems to be just data, numerical data at that. I've seen octal and even some binary and hexadecimal base systems going by, but nothing I can link without a base rule to apply."

Once back, El was filled in and she thought it went well. No hostile actions noted. We'd wait a few days and see what happens before we pressed our presence.

By the next morning it was just a few guards and the chopper and defense rigs left, along with the command staff.

We sat at a table in the mess tent, the sides rolled up, as the morning was cool but nice.

Garth said, "Company coming from the west folks."

I saw a bit of dust and the same type of cart heading down the hill toward the camp. El had the 20MMs manned but it was made clear not to fire unless ordered. It was decided Reta and I'd wait for them outside. We walked to the west about twenty yards and stood waiting.

It was occupied by two men, but different from whom we saw earlier. They looked older—one had a white tuft and the other was streaked.

As they came close, Reta said, "Fear."

"Us?"

"No, but the old one is very afraid of something." She appeared to be concentrating on them, then shook her head. "Some type of strong mental block, yet I feel they aren't aware of it."

"Okay, let us see what they do," El sub'd back to us.

They pulled up and stopped ten feet away. The older man led the way toward us, hands in the air a bit, he was also unarmed. I raised mine as well, more to hope they understood we meant no harm.

When we were four feet apart he sniffed the air as the other sat on the ground. I had the impression they were submitting to us, like surrender. I sat and had Reta sit next to me. They looked to her, and me, then each other.

I can't describe what I heard— clicks, clacks, and pitched noises. I held up my hand to stop. They did. I said, "I'm sorry, we don't understand. Let me bring my translator forward." I turned and pointed to Lucy who slowly came forward and sat on the other side. I heard her pop a few clacks back then she was holding her hand up and clearly indicating numbers, one to ten. They made noises and soon she was catching on to some of it.

El sent Tally with a tray of water glasses and sugar cookies until we had an idea of their systems. As Reta and I both ate one and sipped the water, the younger man tried both. He smiled at the cookie.

Though we sat there almost an hour I was diligently trying to appear interested as Reta laughed. "Hard isn't it?" she sub'd.

Lucy looked to us both a second. "Sorry, as complicated a language as I've ever seen. Oh, so you know, I think they know of the MKs." She immediately went back to clicks and clacks.

After another thirty minutes they stood and left. We stood and watched them drive off into the desert tundra.

"They have a small village outside the city. This is not their home planet—all I could tell is that it no longer exists. I think maybe the MKs already hit it. Anyway, they will meet us in the town tomorrow. I think he said it was okay to bring the machine." She pointed to the chopper.

El asked, "What did they say?"

"Numbers, one to a hundred. Food, water, female, male, and they know I'm a computer. About all at this time."

I had MK nightmares once again that night. Been a while. I sat up with a start and Lucy was sitting there with Reta.

"I think I have nightmares too. I know I dream at least—of course I don't sleep, just rest my circuits," Lucy said. "Reta was awakened by yours and we were debating if to wake you or not."

"We were in the fort and losing bad. I was about to shoot my wife to stop them from getting her," I explained.

"Ah, let us hope it is just a dream then," Lucy said, and smiled her metal smile.

"Time?" I asked.

"Hour to sunrise," Reta said.

"Reta, I forgot, where is your husband? Guard force?" I asked.

"No, he stayed home with the other wives. Julia was due to deliver any day."

"Oh, okay. I wonder if mine delivered yet." I smiled remembering how close she was.

She patted my leg and smiled. "I just hope we didn't do wrong bringing them into this messed up world."

We went to the mess tent, finding the cooks hard at it. Some eggs and toast and biscuits and gravy waited for those with the desire to eat. Coffee and tea were hot and ready as well. It was still early, but a few people were there. Tici and El among them.

I had some biscuits and gravy and toast and coffee and sat at El's table after she indicated she wished my presence. Reta had eggs and joined us, as did Lucy. A few minutes went by and we were joined by Tally and Garth.

El said, "Lucy thinks they know of the MKs. I want to start bringing all the defense forces back in today. If they are already here we need protection. Lucy, Garth, Eldon, Reta and I will go to their town on the chopper. If we are detained or killed Tici will initiate responses as necessary." She looked to him. She saw concern in his eyes but he just nodded.

"Lucy, I want info and fast. Where are the MKs? How many people are on this planet and what are their defense capabilities? Learning their flowers smell sweet is fine but I want hard data before you even find out their word for sex, we clear?"

"Yes, ma'am. Their language is based on sound and its many nuances, as complicated as I could even imagine, but I will do it as fast as I can. I'm taking a reader along with the MK battles and other videos to see their responses. Reta gets some weak readings but says they have a natural block. Still, she does get some readings."

"When the MKs come they will be in force, that is my concern. How much time?"

"Yes, El, I know, we all have the same concerns," Lucy said, and Tici smiled.

"She is wound up tight as a lizard about to attack a scorpion, knowing it has no chance," he said, and we all grinned.

"I...Never mind. Garth, warm the chopper, thirty minutes we go," she said.

Reta said, "No Tici, I think she wants to fight, to avenge. I don't read it; I feel it, because it is what I also want."

"If they are willing to help we may be at just the right spot to start just that, Reta. Let us hope Honor is watching and gives us her blessing," El said, moving to a more whimsical time in the not too distant past.

We chatted about data and supplies as Tici passed the word, "Set a tight camp, full defense and bring in the troops."

The little town of huts was over an hour flight time away. Those people must have driven a long time to get to us. We landed a mile away, far enough that none would think we were hostile. They didn't. Soon five of the car things pulled up. Each had room for two people in the back behind the driver. None spoke except for a type of greeting from Lucy—all knew it was useless.

The huts were exactly what they looked like from the air—homes. Windows had curtains, there were painted doors. I also noticed they were all exactly the same size and made of what I suspected was steel. Some type of mass-produced shelters. Maybe portable.

We were taken to an area that clearly was a meeting or communal center. Benches and tables sat around a fire pit and two of the huts had large sections of their sides opened forming some type of serving lines. Some people were there but all males and no children. We were tolerated at the moment, clearly not trusted.

The old man was sitting at a table drinking from a twisted glass container with ice and a bluish red liquid in it. Lucy brought the portable lab as well as the reader. He stood and indicated we should sit as we also wished.

El and Lucy and Reta sat with the old man. I sat the table to the right and Garth sat to the left. Reta sub'd, "Strong mental shields yet no one reads minds. Most strange. Still, without attacking their shields I get strong fear."

They didn't do much. Offered some drinks like the old man had and Lucy said they tested okay, indigenous fruits, very slight alcohol content. They also had a type of cookie, not as sweet, different and flavorful. Lucy and the old man and a young one clicked and clacked away for about a half hour when the old man burst into laughter and Lucy said, "Dear me. I think I just called him a whore. This is so different, the way you say it is as important as what you say." I think we all smiled a bit.

"Ouch!" Reta yelped.

"What?" Lucy subbed.

"I was just scanned and it hurt," she sub'ed.

"By who? Thought you said they couldn't," El sub'ed.

"Not sure, wild, uncontrolled."

"Can you block it?" I asked.

"Sure, now that I know about it."

After another two hours, Lucy said, "I think I have enough of the basics, let's see." She set up the reader and it started playing Diboca Honor in her usual opening greeting. Some of the new people showed a slight touch of fear, others curiosity.

Lucy finally said, "Sorry, been concentrating on them. These people call themselves the Klag. They say this is not their original home planet. I am checking that now."

If the noises they were making were talking it fooled me, sounded like the chickens in the yard on Reta's old planet.

I saw the reader switch to our various battles with the MKs and those we had in captivity. The clucks and clacks increased.

I saw Reta get up and walk toward the open field by the town. I figured I'd better stay with her. We still didn't know our status yet. As she walked out into the field she again said, "Ow!" and held her head, then looked around, up, and pointed. "There, those cause it, the mental pain." She was pointing toward some big birds that looked like our Lateias. I think Lucy called them eagles, birds of prey.

"I see what's going on now," she said out loud. "Those birds send mental blasts to stun their prey then they swoop down. I bet as children the Klag automatically build the mental shields to stop it. Interesting, very interesting. Explains why there are no actual thoughts."

She drifted back to the conference, and as it began Lucy stood, raised both hands, bowed to the old one and sub'd, "We can leave now." As she finished the old man did the same to her. "El, we have a lot to do and, as now seems the norm, little time. We need to deploy our entire forces south a few thousand miles, quickly. All these people will leave tonight."

We boarded the chopper and were again heading back to the Honor Gate as Lucy filled us in. "They have been here mining this planet for several hundred years. They were building that city we saw—it isn't complete yet.

"The Klag home system is the next planet out and one and a half light-years away is another system they sort of talk to through Tachyon links. That system told them the MKs were coming as they died. The Klag started mass defense building and from what the chief said they have been putting up a heck of a fight. Still they are losing.

"Same story, not enough bullets or energy in the world, they just keep coming and coming. Anyway, they funneled a few million extra people to the south to put up a final stand from the mines. This group were born and raised here, their ancestors were colonists that were to start building cities for expansion of population from their home-world. It will never happen now.

"El, we need to get 20s and needler cannons to those mines, set up as strong a defense as possible, and see how we stack. We also need to get some satellites up that can saturate the air with the sterilization and confusion formulas as well. We need the forts here and a defense force to see how we stand against them once more at the gate."

"Time?" El asked.

"Not sure—the old man said they are still receiving information from the home world—last transmission said they felt they were still good for a month but they were definitely dying. Also said they feel the MKs know where the refugees went. He is called either a Chief or Mayor, still not sure. Did I say their language is really hard?" She knew she did but got the chuckle anyway.

We spent several weeks moving equipment and personnel from the gate to the huge mine complex with the remaining Klag, a little over two million. Lucy was working on the language problems as we started planning defenses.

At Officer's Call El told us, "Defense will be needler cannons on the buildings out there, covering all approaches. Backed with 20MMs. As we come toward the entrances I want trenches to fight from, but I want them set to create a huge firewall too when we pull back. Two or three trench systems, all with needler cannons and 20s layered. I want every damn gun system booby-trapped. When we fall back we destroy them all and set the trenches afire.

"We fall back to the forts with solid double rows of needler cannons and 20s as the last line. People, if we're pushed behind that then we fight at each tunnel entrance—we don't run, we do or die!"

"Garth, make a run to the gate. I want them to be ready to stand there if needed. We absolutely must win this battle, regardless of how long it takes." El made it clear, it was humanity's revenge time.

As soon as Garth landed back by us he had his crews carry out maintenance. El told Tici to get one of the spaceships together here and loaded with satellites and bombs as soon as possible. That got me to thinking. "Lucy, can we get real bombs like RPVs to target MK ships or vehicles before they get to our defensive positions?"

"Already ahead of you. Olgreender factories were working on just such a thing. Why don't you check on those and your wife for a few days? This is all just co-ordination stuff until the MKs arrive anyway. If they come I'll get word to you, promise."

Well, I was put out to pasture, that is for sure. I bid the others farewell when Reta caught up. "Gave me my walking papers too." She grinned.

As we parted inside Honor Central I told Reta, "Thanks, you were a big help keeping me sane without Loka."

"Ah, nothing to it. Shall we see what our wives had for kids?" She knew it sounded strange as she smiled. "Later, Eldon. I hope you had a boy—Myla wanted a brother."

Before the time I finally walked through the door Myla knew I was home and I knew she had a brother. Loka didn't know I was there, so I got to surprise her as she held our son.

"He have a name?" I asked, as I kissed her and Myla, then looked at his face.

"I did like what Lucy said the humans did. Just called him Eldon Jr."

"Poor kid." I smiled.

I spent a pleasant two whole weeks relaxing when, at 3AM, I was wakened with someone at my door. "Commander, El said to tell you 'they come'. I'll wait here with the car."

Loka cried a bit as she once more shoved me out the door. I felt I was getting too old for this, as she said, "Come back to us."

We were all in the Center's mess hall. Lucy and El came in and El said, "Everyone listen up. I received reports that thousands of ships are landing on the planet, as in a black sky full. I suspect they know we are waiting. Remember, layered defense, no unnecessary deaths, if we can't hold slowly pull into the caves. I don't care how many they have but we hold at the entrances, we clear?" We'd all been over it a million times already.

Since there were no questions Lucy called us to attention. "Move out. Choppers wait for us outside the gate—good luck to all."

Five hours later I was in the forward trench lining up

grenades and waiting once more. I suddenly felt old as I looked at the sixteen and seventeen year old kids surrounding me. A mix of us, Reta's people and Klag's. Forward needler cannons and 20s on the rooftops had been active, dropping many of the incoming ships, maybe hundreds. Sounds impressive until you find out it is against tens of thousands of ships. A few of those defenders made it back to us, but not many.

"Commander Gnoth, may I ask a question, sir?"

I looked, it was a young Lieutenant. "Certainly, Lieutenant."

"Your first battle against the MKs, were you scared, sir?"

"Still am, Lieutenant. If a fool tells you they aren't, get away, he'll get you killed. Being brave has nothing to do with not being afraid; it has to do with overcoming it to do your duty."

"Well, what they say sounds nice. Still, I'm scared."

I patted his shoulder, "So am I son, go be with your men, you'll do fine."

Wasn't long and a wave of black formed to our front. "All systems hot. Here they come!" I realized it was me yelling it. I waited until the MKs hit our ranged markers. "Fix Bayonets, selective fire, make it count people, steady, steady, FIRE!"

Up and down the line I heard the commands being echoed. All hell broke loose as my fourteen hundred men opened up and a big pile of dead and wounded MKs started forming to our front, but I knew. The pile grew higher and moved closer, and closer. "Grenades loose!" I screamed, as I tossed all six I had to my front and left and right. The needler cannons buzzed and the twenties slammed their thump, thump, thump and the MKs kept coming.

"Destroy weapons, fall back to line two!"

We maintained our lines as we walked backwards out of the

trenches, never stopping firing. Left and right the 20s and needler cannons exploded.

When we were twenty yards behind the trenches, I told Lucy, "Fire the trench!"

I heard her say, "Roger."

A huge wall of flames erupted along where we had been. I prayed for the wounded souls that didn't make it out in time but it was a game of numbers and timing and inches as we backed into another trench. Of my fourteen hundred I doubt more than two-hundred-fifty made it to the second trench alive. Lucy had already sent reinforcements.

"Line secure, all systems fire!" I screamed, as this series of needler cannons and twenties came alive. The MKs were visibly slowed by the fire wall.

El said, "All sides at stage two now, keep sticking it to them, only a few billion to go." She snickered. She was on the command link so only us in the know heard her. To our front the scene repeated, MKs piled higher and higher and inched closer and closer.

"Air dispersion systems have fully deployed the spray. Our ships are airborne and hitting them from behind. Damn, people, even I didn't foresee this many."

"We'll manage, if nothing else they will have one big ass bloody nose," said Tici from the right flank.

They were affected by the spray. Some seemed confused, others just stood for long periods but we found the spray's effects were temporary and we had no more. At least a few hundred million of them would be sterile.

All day and into the night we held at the second stage but a sudden surge by them forced us to the forts, the last line before the cave entrances.

We abandoned the second trench and pulled behind the final wall—it was a solid ring of needler cannons and a second ring of twenties firing over them. Forts providing key points along it, men and women running their asses off with carts or flat trucks hauling tons of 20 ammo out and wounded back. Organized chaos at its finest.

I don't know when—I was punch drunk—I think it was the next day when the first fort fell in spite of our massed efforts to save it. I think two thousand of us were slaughtered there. I vaguely remember the screams as we were in hand to pincer combat. Stab, shoot, stab, slash, I just couldn't see straight.

El said, "Final stand, destroy equipment and fall to the caves."

I lined up the last ten or twelve people we had and we slowly backed toward the caves—somehow a group of MKs had slipped behind us from one of the flanks. I remember turning to shoot them when I saw a pincer. I reflexively threw my hand and rifle up and it was lights out.

I had visions of lights swinging above me, movement but not mine, hurting. I was being dragged across the ground. I vaguely remember someone saying, "Shit!" and others saying, "We're holding, they won't get through."

I felt time had passed, how much I couldn't say, but I was in Honor Central. I was on a metal table and someone said, "You'll be fine, sir."

I kept falling in and out of consciousness. Four men and a woman stood over me, no, it was Lucy. "No choice," someone said.

"Do it then," Lucy said.

She saw me awake, and said, "Sorry Eldon, the arm has got to go." I saw a needle and that was all.

The ceiling was the first thing to be seen clearly. Flat white and bright neon lighting. I heard beeping then I saw a face, a young woman in green. "Ah, Commander Eldon. Welcome back to the living. How do you feel, sir?"

"Like shit. Massive headache. Where am I and what happened?"

"Wait a few minutes. Loka and Tici are on the way."

When I saw Loka it was clear she had been crying. She came up and gave me a kiss, tears running down her face. I saw Tici limping in with a crutch.

"Children?" I asked.

"Fine, Eldon. They want to meet their father."

"Damn, what happened? We were ambushed from behind."

Tici came forward. "We held at the entrance. You were caught near it. Sorry Eldon, you lost your right arm. A young Lieutenant hauled you back into the cave. He lost most of a leg but refused to let anyone touch you until he pulled you inside. Made some comment about conquering fear."

I lifted my right arm—it felt odd but was there. "It feels funny but its fine," I said.

"No Eldon, it is a Lucy special. Feel it, it's metal like her," Loka said, and started crying again.

I placed it against my face. Okay, cold and no sense of touching me from it.

"Loka, it's okay. How is the battle going?"

Tici said, "Thanks to Garth we won."

"Garth?"

"He and his choppers were flying run after run from the gate and the two supply dumps we had set up. The same MKs came in behind you got control of a 20 and needler cannon before they were destroyed. How that Lieutenant got you through all that fire alone is a mystery to everyone. The forts and line collapsed suddenly. El was killed with her staff. I was trying to get to her. She was using her ceremonial sword to stab them, and a pistol to shoot them—then she was dead, no head." He clearly was in pain at the thought.

"We all pulled into the caves but the MKs opened up on an entrance with the 20 and needler cannon. It was a slug-fest for a while. From what I was told Garth saw it but was out of ammo. He crashed his chopper into them and probably saved the complex from being breached."

Loka took over, "They kept you alive for four days in the cave—they had to burn your arm off to stop the bleeding. You almost didn't come back to me, Eldon."

Tici said, "We beat them back, they soon abandoned the planet. Still a few million strong but we slaughtered hundreds of millions of them. Did Lucy tell you about the spray?"

"Sure, it would saturate the atmosphere and sterilize all of them on the ground."

"Millions left. She didn't tell anyone, to ensure the MKs couldn't find out by chance. Eldon, any other MKs, any of them that they come in contact with, will slowly become sterile too. It is a virus, any kids they have will be sterile. Depending on how long before they realize it is happening we could effectively eliminate half of all they have in our galaxy."

"I didn't know that."

"None of us did. Like she said, she couldn't take a chance," Loka said.

"The planet, it is safe now?"

"Maybe, they are worried about plagues. So many dead MK bodies. We've been burning them non-stop but it may take months to get them all. Lucy is designing bio filters for the caves and issuing suits. They may have to stay underground a few months but they will survive.

"Us?"

Tici said, "As expected, 62% died and 20% are some kind of walking wounded. Like you and I."

"I'm mad at you for that, Eldon, you said El expected light causalities."

"You had a baby to worry about."

"My heart is big enough to worry about you too!"

I sat up slowly, head pounding. "Damn, how long have I been out?"

"Five weeks heavily sedated," Lucy said, as she walked in. "I needed minimum movement as your nerves knitted to your new synaptic devices and muscles blended with metal. How does it feel?"

"Strange but functional."

"Good, your fingertips will take a few days more to develop tactility and feelings. Until then don't hold Eldon Junior in that arm."

Loka held my real hand, and said, "Reta lost both her

husband and one wife after they came to fight at the gate entrance."

Tici said, "We lost all the choppers and both ships but we gained a few thousand they left behind. As soon as we recover we can take it to them."

"No Tici, afraid not, not yet. I want to monitor the spread of the virus for a few years and modify all the ships to include needler cannon systems and integrated fire control systems. We'll make other stands down the road, but you will not be part of it. I need you and Eldon and Loka and the others to start rebuilding worlds, having children, training next generation fighters. I guess they call it being retired."

"I want to kill MKs!" Tici said.

"You can't bring El back. Go find a young lady or two and make babies, Tici, you may find that almost as much fun as killing MKs," Lucy said.

"Reta will be looking for a virile man once her mourning is over. She will add another wife or two," Loka said, and smiled.

"I...you, dang women!" He turned and limped out as Lucy and Loka smiled.

"He loved El very much," I said.

"Yes, but she was too old for children. He isn't and it is what we need now," Lucy said. "Eldon, this war will go on for a few hundred years. We can get the upper hand now. I'm training a crew, we will start linking in new Honor Centrals and expanding the grid once more. The Klag are smart enough, I'll set up a full center there and they can start expanding as well. We will destroy the MKs were we find them and we will bring more people into the system as we locate them. Think about it, we have mixed many cultures and different planets, all with the same desire: to kill MKs. We can and will win eventually."